By Rhys Ford

I0675931

Clockwork Tangerine
With Poppy Dennison: Creature Feature 2
Dim Sum Asylum
Grand Adventures (Dreamspinner Anthology)
Murder and Mayhem
There's This Guy

COLE MCGINNIS MYSTERIES
Dirty Kiss
Dirty Secret
Dirty Laundry
Dirty Deeds
Down and Dirty
Dirty Heart
Dirty Bites

HALF MOON BAY
Fish Stick Fridays
Hanging the Stars

HELLSINGER
Fish and Ghosts
Duck Duck Ghost

SINNERS SERIES
Sinner's Gin
Whiskey and Wry
The Devil's Brew
Tequila Mockingbird
Sloe Ride
Absinthe of Malice

Published by DREAMSPINNER PRESS
www.dreamspinnerpress.com

DUCK DUCK GHOST

RHYS FORD

REAMSPINNER
PRESS

Published by

DREAMSPINNER PRESS

5032 Capital Circle SW, Suite 2, PMB# 279, Tallahassee, FL 32305-7886 USA
www.dreamspinnerpress.com

Duck Duck Ghost
© 2014 Rhys Ford.

Cover Art
© 2017 Anne Cain.
annecain.art@gmail.com
Cover content is for illustrative purposes only and any person depicted on the cover is a model.

ISBN: 978-1-63216-218-2
Digital ISBN: 978-1-63216-219-9
Library of Congress Number: 2014944012
Published September 2014
v. 1.1

Printed in the United States of America
∞
This paper meets the requirements of
ANSI/NISO Z39.48-1992 (Permanence of Paper).

This book is dedicated to the most wonderful Amy Lane, fabulous Poppy Dennison, and the effervescent Jacob Flores.

And to Yoshiko who spends the night hunting my toes because she's certain they are deadly ghosts coming to get her from under the bed linens.

Acknowledgments

TO THE FIVE who are my beloved sisters of writing: Penn, Lea, Tamm, and Jenn. And to my darling siblings in love and coffee: Lisa, Ren and Ree.

So many thanks and wow, love outpourings to Elizabeth North and the rest of the Dreamspinner Press staff who make me stand up, pull up my socks and brush my hair so I look decent in public. A special shout out and heartfelt hugs to Grace and everyone she throws into my editing pool, because each and every one of them rocks so hardcore you can feel the bass in your teeth.

A rocking thank you covered in chocolate and caramel to my beta readers and the Dirty Ford Guinea Pigs. Oh, only the Gods in Heaven, Hell, and Starbucks Temples everywhere know how much you all endure my word spew and jerking you around with my plotting. Love you all. So damned much.

Chapter 1

THE SMELL of rot permeated the air.

It was a foul smell. A blackness to it Wolf would never get used to. With the proximity of the Florida swamp and Atlantic, there was a faint hint of stagnancy as well, with an overlay of brackish algae just for good measure. He couldn't imagine living in its stink every day. Like cigarette smoke, it would flavor everything he touched, breathed, or ate.

He'd expected some dampness, especially in the lower jut of an ill-advised half basement below the church turned hostel, but when his sneaker sloshed through an actual puddle in the kitchen, Wolf wondered if the owners had less of a ghost problem and were more in need of a home demolition.

The basement seemed to be where most of the noises were coming from. At least from what Wolf could figure out. Creaky, eerie sounds wafted through the sprawling hostel, carried through the antique ductwork set into heavily built walls, and they certainly appeared to be originating from underneath the first floor. Tapping at the plaster, Wolf frowned, wondering what the builders had been thinking when they'd put in so many tight hallways and corners. The maze made it difficult to find the source of the hostel's supposed haunting, but it apparently helped keep the place cool when it got too hot.

"It's like they got paid by the fucking corner," he grumbled. "Every single damned old house has a million stupid little corners."

An undulating groan drifted through the hostel, and a screeching wail followed close on its heels. A startled yelp nearly broke Wolf's eardrum, and he stopped for a moment with his foot on the second step down to the basement.

"Jesus, you trying to get me killed?" Wolf muttered, flipping the light switch at the top of the stairs one more time. "I could have fallen down this death trap and broken my neck."

Much like the other five times he'd clicked it, the light stayed off, and he glanced up, fumbling in his pocket for his flashlight. After finding it, Wolf turned the torch on and splashed the beam up along the ceiling, not surprised to find a pair of dangling capped-off wires where a light fixture should have been.

A woman's voice tickled Wolf's ear as he crept down along a tight spiral staircase. "I'm not exactly sure what I'm supposed to be doing here, Dr. Kincaid."

Wolf sighed and leaned his head against the cramped interior stairwell. Cupping his mouth over the wireless headset he wore to keep in contact with his intern, he counted to three, then said, "You're supposed to keep up with me."

"I'm trying to, Dr. Kincaid." The young woman sounded exasperated. "But your legs are too long. I can't keep up. I lost you back in the hallway. The lights aren't working in this end of the house. Everything went black."

"Where are you, Trixie?" he growled into his mic. "And more importantly, how soon can you get to the basement stairs?"

"Shit, you're going to go down there? Why? Can't we just use something to see underneath the house? Like they do for dinosaurs. What is that? Sonar? Can't we use that?"

Biting back a sarcastic reply, Wolf reminded himself that soon-to-be-Doctor Trixie Huff was his only staff on the hostel job, so snarling at her probably wouldn't necessarily endear him to her.

Initially, he'd agreed to use the headsets because he wanted to keep his communication to a whisper so as not to telegraph where they were in the building's labyrinth of cellar space and servants' quarters. Now Wolf was partially glad he had it on because he kept losing his damned intern.

It wasn't Trixie's fault.

Wolf was just too used to working with his team, and the intern, while highly intelligent and sharp, hadn't planned on spending her summer vacation hunting ghosts in tourist-infested St. Augustine, Florida. Instead of lounging about the pool—or beach—being brought drinks by hot cabana boys in tight, skimpy shorts, she was tromping behind a grumpy parapsychologist in cobweb-cluttered mazes while rats and spiders dropped down on her like turtle shells in a game of Mario Kart.

When Hellsinger Investigations agreed to take on a pair of summer interns from Berkeley, it sounded like a perfect solution to his staffing woes. His techs, Matt and Gidget, longed to explore the Welsh countryside with its rambling hills and ghostly apparitions, while his office manager,

Nahryn, planned on having a three-week visit with her grandparents in Los Angeles.

Trixie'd been a godsend. Especially since she was enthusiastic and, more importantly, a bit of a skeptic about paranormal activity.

If there was one thing Wolf needed in his life at the moment—it was a skeptic.

No, he wouldn't think about Tristan. Not while he stood halfway down a flight of stairs with one wet foot waiting for an intern he was probably abusing by dragging her off to Florida so she could record his progress through a haunted hostel.

Something dropped onto him from above and skittered across his neck. Wolf resisted the urge to slap at it. He'd done that piece of stupid when he was younger and bore a half-moon scar on his shoulder from the very pissed-off centipede he'd slammed his hand over.

A strong beam of light cut over him, and Wolf grinned, glancing up at Trixie as she aimed the shoulder camera down the stairs. At some point, she'd dragged her glossy brown hair back and pulled a ponytail through a Hellsinger Investigations ball cap. Having abandoned her contacts for a sturdy pair of glasses to protect her eyes against the hostel's dirt and cobwebs, Trixie's eyes glittered with excitement behind her clear lenses.

"You ready, Huff?" Wolf grinned in the bright light.

"Sneakers on, boss," she retorted saucily.

"Good, because we're going in."

They went down the stairs together, Trixie's camera beam lighting up Wolf's shoulders. It actually wasn't a bad thing, because in the dank darkness, any light was welcome. Aiming his own smaller flashlight up, Wolf trudged through the tiny rooms built into the hill under the hostel, noticing the damp air thickened into an almost mist as they drew closer to the outer wall.

"Isn't a basement in Florida kind of stupid?" Trixie asked above their squeaky footsteps.

"Yeah, not exactly the smartest thing. Whoever built this place made the hill first. It's called a berm. It's a smart thing to do to get your property above the flood line, but instead the asshole dug in and put half of the house into it. I'm surprised this place hasn't come tumbling down on their—" A hissing noise made Wolf pause, and he turned, holding up his hand to stop Trixie from going any farther into the dark.

"What was that?" She kept her voice as steady as she could. Wolf gave her that. Even with the tremble in her throat, she held the camera steady, trained just beyond Wolf's shoulder as he'd instructed her. "Oh God, something's over there."

Wolf's beam was too weak to do anything but catch a sliver of movement beyond a turn in the hall. He took a few steps forward, but the camera's light didn't follow him, so he turned around, staring into the beam at the silhouette behind it.

"Come on, almost-Doctor Huff. Time to chase our ghosts," he urged her on. The light bobbed once, and Trixie moved in step behind him, but he could still hear her mutter under her breath at his back.

"You are certifiable. No college credit is worth this."

The thick rough walls under the old church must have been the only thing shoring up the foundation, but Wolf had to acknowledge the builder might have had something going. Lifted up off the ground, the airspace below would keep the building's lower level cooler during the hot summer months, but he'd have been more scared of wood rot than a high air-conditioning bill.

Especially when his foot went through one of the floorboards, and his leg dropped out from under him, slamming his crotch into the rotted wooden planks.

Wolf grunted from the pain of getting his balls shoved up into his rib cage, but he stopped himself from whimpering out loud. Huffing to maintain his composure, he shouted back, "Trix, stay back there. The floor's gone here."

"Oh God, are you okay?" The large light bobbled and then dropped low when Trixie set the camera on the floor next to her. "Do you want me to go get someone?"

"Let me see if I can get out of this hole." Wolf hissed when he leaned back. Massive splinters from the rough floorboards drove into his palms, and for once he was glad Nahryn insisted they all were current on their tetanus shots. "Okay, I'm going to rock back and pull my leg out. Be careful in case the boards go down behind me. I don't know how big this hole in the ground is."

"Why would someone dig a hole in the basement, then cover it with boards?" Trixie scooted forward a bit. "Do you want me to grab you and help?"

"No," Wolf said with a shake of his head. "Our weight might bring the whole thing down. Stay back where we know it's solid."

Wolf gritted past the pain and pushed himself up, leveraging his weight back until he got his knee clear of the hole. His jeans were shot, torn along his thigh and flecked with blood where broken wood scratched into his skin. Another heave, and he cleared the hole up to his calf. Then the deep shadows beyond the camera's powerful beam moved, and a low hiss echoed through the confined space.

The movement was slow, nearly graceful, and Wolf froze, trying to see into the darkness.

Then he realized what he was looking at, and his stomach crawled up to lodge itself into his throat.

"Trixie, I need you to move slowly back and go up the stairs. Now."

"And leave you here?" she scoffed. "That makes—"

"Leave the camera and get the hell out of here. Use the flashlight I gave you." Wolf kept his voice low, not wanting to spook the young woman. "Like right—"

The gator lunged out of the shadows, its teeth flashing a sickly yellow in the light beam. The reptile was nearly as wide across as Wolf's hips, its quick legs whipping its long body back and forth as it moved across the floor. Its long tail slapped into one of the walls, making a wet sound on the hard surface.

Trixie screamed and fled, her cries for help seemingly coming from all directions as she ran out of the space. Wolf jerked himself free of the hole, rolling to the side as he tried to scramble to his feet. The alligator made another lunge, throwing its body up a few inches, and his sneaker sole caught in its teeth, ripping from the bottom of his shoe as the gator twisted its head.

"Fuck!" Wolf dodged the camera, catching his nearly bare foot in its harness.

The gator went after him again, the floors creaking under the reptile's enormous weight. The boards bounced, and Wolf heard them cracking under him as he ran toward the room's entrance. Trixie's anxious screaming continued to bounce about the basement, a high-pitched wail loud enough to drown out the gator's aggressive hissing.

His own flashlight flickered woefully when Wolf tried to aim it down the hallway outside the room. A fragmented beam warned him he'd probably broken the lens, but it still gave off enough light for him to see his way out. Something heavy slammed into his side, and Wolf's heart jerked in fear until he realized it was Trixie running out from another room.

"I can't find my way out!" she wailed, grabbing at his arm. "Oh God, it's right there!"

Wolf chanced a glance back, and the gator grumbled with a menacing roar. Nudging the discarded equipment, the gator made the camera's light flash and tilt against its hide, illuminating its variegated skin. Wolf grabbed Trixie's arm and dragged her with him, urging her to run. A loud cracking sound came from the room behind them, and some small part of Wolf's brain wondered if the gator would be trapped in the hole he'd almost fallen into.

The larger part of his brain shoved that thought down, intent on escaping the seemingly pissed-off reptile rather than pondering if the rot would give before the gator could catch up with them or if gators could climb stairs. They hit the steps at a run, and Wolf pushed Trixie up ahead of him. Her sneakers pounded up the staircase, and he followed close behind, his hands pressed on the small of her back.

All around them, they heard the hissing and screaming wails of the gator thrashing its way through the basement. Its vocalizations echoed through the ductwork, and somewhere in the hostel, someone else started screaming, matching Trixie and the gator in volume.

Voices called out from various rooms, but Wolf didn't have the breath to answer. He shoved the intern through the open door at the top of the stairs, flung himself through, and kicked the door closed behind him with a mighty thump.

He lay on the floor, panting as people poured into the kitchen. Trixie lay on her stomach next to him, her body heaving from the sprint up the tight staircase. Someone sounded alarmed at the sight of his leg, but Wolf didn't care about the pain. From what he could tell, he was still intact, if just a little bit winded.

The owner, a long-haired older woman, leaned over him, her bright blue eyes blinking in surprise at his bloodied and mud-caked body. Patting him on the shoulder, she asked someone to call 911 before Wolf could stop her.

"Oh my, Doctor Kincaid. Are you all right?" she murmured in her soft butterfly voice. "What happened?"

"Found your ghost," Wolf gasped, fighting to push words out as he sucked in clean air. "And it's big enough to make a whole set of luggage."

"THEY ARE never going to give you another intern," Nahryn, his girl Friday, complained loudly as Wolf came through the front door of Hellsinger Investigations. "You keep breaking them!"

"Hey, I returned that last one in perfect working order!" he shot back, dropping a bag of donuts on her desk as he hobbled by. They were damned good donuts, hot and yeasty malasadas from a nearby Portuguese bakery. Good enough to ward off a scolding from a girl ten years his junior, but Nahryn wasn't having any of it, judging by the look on her face. "I'm the one who got fucked up."

"Yeah, well, death by gator isn't something a lot of people want to put on their résumé." She sniffed at him and opened the bag. The pretty Armenian girl eyed him, as if searching for sugar around his mouth. "Did you already eat one?"

"Yeah, on the way in." He winced at the steady ache along his thigh. Eight dissolvable stitches and a few shots later, his leg was patched up, but he was reminded constantly of his refusal to take any of the painkillers the doctors shoved at him. A few ibuprofens would do the trick, he promised his leg, along with a very nice hot cup of coffee.

"Well, take one in with you. Meegan's here." His office manager stepped in behind him before Wolf could turn around and drag himself out of the office. "Oh no you don't, Kincaid. She's your mother, and she's here to ask you something."

"I'd rather be eaten alive by the gator," Wolf muttered darkly. "Go get me coffee, and if I buzz you in ten minutes, I expect you to come rescue me."

"You'll be lucky if I even answer," Nahryn shot back with a Cheshire cat smile. "But I'll bring you some coffee, you big baby."

His mother was standing at the wraparound glass window of his office, her hands cradling a large cup of fragrant jasmine tea and her eyes dreamy as she stared out at San Francisco's bay. Ferries jetted from shore to shore, carrying tourists and locals alike. The morning fog kept a light grip on the shoreline, but it was a weak one, with a lemony sun pushing its way through the watery mist.

The faint sunlight shone around the older woman, outlining her long, curly bright auburn hair and crazy-quilt peasant dress. Large chandelier earrings made of tiny bells and beads tinkled when she cocked her head, her eyes following the activity on the pier below. She'd lost her sandals somewhere in the office, her bare toes spread over the office's wooden floors, and she shifted slightly, adjusting her black cobweb lace shawl over her pale arms.

His coffee arrived with a filthy look, both courtesy of Nahryn, and Wolf nodded pleasantly at her, then shooed the young Armenian woman out. Meegan Ocean-Kincaid turned and caught her son's eye, but instead of the beatific, motherly smile she normally gave him, her mouth was set into a neutral straight line.

From his hippie-gypsy mother, this was tantamount to a scowl.

"Hello, Mom." Wolf leaned in to give his mother a kiss, but she tilted her head back to stare up at him. Sighing, he rolled his eyes and said, "What?"

"What now, you mean?" Meegan sniffed.

It was a mighty sniff. Possibly one of the greatest she'd ever given him. It rivaled the one she'd aimed at him and Bach when they'd shaved Ophelia Sunday's head with their Uncle Stavros's clippers, but he still thought the time he'd dumped an entire load of horse manure on their living room floor because he was looking for gold coins held the top spot.

Another sniff, and the Horse Manure Incident sadly dropped to second place.

"I take it this is about Tristan?" He wondered if he could bribe Nahryn to go to the corner store and grab him whiskey so he could doctor his coffee or if it was still too early to start some serious drinking. "Have you talked to him?"

Her arched eyebrow lift was pointed enough he could hang a Christmas ornament on it, and Wolf took a gulp of his coffee, wincing at its sugary taste.

"Great, now even my office manager is trying to poison me," he muttered, setting the mug down. "Okay, get it out of your system, Mom. Go on and scream at my head."

"I don't scream, Wolfgang," Meegan informed him smoothly. "What I am going to do is tell you how disappointed I am in you. You have a chance at so much happiness, and you're letting your pigheaded stubbornness get in the way."

So yes, his mother had spoken to Tristan, and knowing his reclusive lover, he'd probably been nudged, bothered, and poked at until he spilled every last detail of their argument.

He didn't need his mother to tell him he'd fucked up. He screwed up by starting up a fight with Tristan Pryce, owner and proprietor of Hoxne Grange, a spiritual hub for ghosts passing on to the afterlife, then walking out on Tris. The gorgeous blond man was reserved, quirky, and more importantly, willing to shove back at Wolf's strong personality—and damn it, if Wolf didn't miss the hell out of him.

Tristan ended up under Wolf's skin, and part of the argument—most of the argument, if Wolf was really honest—was that he was scared. He was frightened by how quickly Tristan hooked his soul and pulled in Wolf's heart. He hadn't been looking for love when he went to debunk Tristan's ghost-hosting inn, but that's what he found—and he didn't want to ever let him go.

And that scared Wolf most of all….

"We had a fight, Mom," Wolf protested. "Things like that happen—"

"You accused him of hallucinating everything the two of you went through!" She turned on him, setting her cup down. Jasmine tea sloshed over the cup's rim, leaving a small amber puddle on his desk. "What happened at the Grange was—"

"Mom, the iced tea you gave us to drink had euphoric honey in it, and then you left a quart of it in his kitchen cabinet!"

"How was I supposed to know he'd make baklava with it?" She waved off his disgusted look. "Really? Does he look like he's the type to bake homemade anything? Does one even bake baklava?"

"He could have poisoned us with it! Honey's a major ingredient in that."

"No, really, how do you make baklava? Does it really go into the oven?" Meegan's attention had obviously wandered off into the intricacies of Greek pastries.

"Jesus, Mom. That stuff was potent. Hell, no wonder we ate ten pizzas after that damned séance. We had the raging munchies. What were you thinking?"

"Just to calm everyone down after the haunting!" Meegan protested. "I'll even bet you the baklava was good. It was premium honey. So what if it was a bit hallucinogenic? Some of my best memories were when I was a bit baked. Hell, you're here because of a bit of that honey."

"That's not the point." He rubbed at his face, then dropped his hands to his hips. "And I didn't say what happened that day wasn't real. I just—"

"You accused him of drugging you and said the whole experience was a mass hallucination!"

"I did not say that." Wolf kept his voice as even as he could. "When I was done tripping along the Timothy Leary Highway—"

"Something that wasn't his fault—"

"Mom, will you let me finish one sentence?" Wolf gritted his teeth and took a long breath to steady himself. "Please?"

"Fine, go ahead." Meegan threw her hands up. "Talk, but nothing you say to me is going to fix what you messed up. So you got a little bit stoned. It's just a relaxer—"

"It wasn't the five minutes of fun-house-mirror world, it was the hour and a half of me living in the bathroom, wondering if I was going to have to reel my guts back in, after the two hours of trying to talk to Tristan's monster illustrations," he insisted. "I might have said a few things I wasn't proud of, but I never accused him of drugging us that day. You did that."

"Afterwards!"

"I told him I loved him and I'd call him in a bit. Did he tell you that?"

"I didn't actually talk to him about afterwards. He's very close-lipped," his mother hedged. "But I definitely got the feeling things went a bit haywire. Then you hied off to God knows where."

"Florida. I had a job in St. Augustine, and I couldn't cancel. I was going to call him this morning." Suddenly tired, he sat on the edge of his desk, wincing when his leg reminded him of his stitches and bruises. "I just needed to think of what I was going to say."

"I'm sorry is a good place to start," Meegan replied tartly. "Then I'm sorry again. Maybe even I love you? You do love him, don't you?"

"It's complicated." The weariness of dealing with his mother set in, and he rubbed at his leg. "But yeah, I love him. It's crazy because I've known him for what? A month? And it's not like he's totally normal. We're going to have to come to some kind of middle ground."

"Well, it's time to uncomplicate it," his mother ordered. "And I have just the thing for that. Something you both can do together."

"Why does that scare the shit out of me?" Wolf picked up his coffee and took another sip. The sugar in it hadn't magically evaporated. "God,

I'm going to kill Nahryn. This is like hummingbird food. I did text him while I was in Florida."

"And what did you say? That you were sorry?"

"That we needed to talk." Admittedly, his messages had gotten more and more insistent with each unanswered text. He hated being ignored, and Tristan could ostrich with the best of them. "And I was an asshole. He didn't text me back."

"You should have called. It's been over a week, Wolf," Meegan huffed. "Okay, we can fix this. I have just the thing."

"I'm already going to go up there, Mom. I don't think I need—" He intercepted her simmering glare. "Fine, what is it?"

"Do you remember Sey? Your second cousin from your Great-Aunt Natty?" Meegan frowned at Wolf's clueless look. "The one in San Luis Obispo."

"Sey with the toys? Yeah, I love her. We've kept in touch." A slender, brash woman known for her boisterous laugh and nearly endless energy, Sey was one of the few relatives he positively adored. He'd spent more than a couple of summers as his older cousin's satellite, a tall lanky girl with sharp elbows and freckles. She'd been the one who'd taught him how to shoot a crossbow… and more importantly, how to run away from a charging bull when he'd accidentally fallen into the temperamental bovine's corral. "Why? What's up with Sey?"

"Funny you should ask that," Meegan practically cackled as she rubbed her hands together. "Because she's got a problem, and it's one that is totally up your alley."

Chapter 2

THE PRETTY older woman wore her years mostly on her shoulders, even though they were straight and pushed back with an innate graceful pride. Her coppery hair was penny bright, curled up into a chignon, and a cameo hung from a shiny black ribbon around her neck. She carried a rosary, her fingers traveling soundlessly over the beads while she stood at the Grange's threshold. A wind somewhere else caught at her clothes, and Tristan could almost hear the crinolines rustling beneath her full skirt. She smoothed the frock, erasing imagined wrinkles. In life, her fitted dress might have been a vivid color, perhaps a pink or a green to go with her vibrant hair.

In death, it was a bleached white with a turquoise glow about it, shimmering in a trail behind her as she stepped into Hoxne Grange's main hall.

She hesitated at the threshold, casting one final look behind her. Tristan smiled in what he hoped she would perceive as a welcoming gesture, and when she glanced at him, her shoulders relaxed. The woman crossed over to the Grange's vintage reception desk, her pale sensible pumps oddly silent on the foyer's gleaming floors. Reaching forward, she flattened her hand and struck the old-fashioned bell sitting on the counter, its bright jangling startling the young woman standing next to Tristan.

"Do you see her, Ophelia Sunday?" Tristan asked the woman next to him, keeping his voice down to a soft whisper.

"Yes, a little bit. Mostly red hair and her hands." Her bright eyes, so much like her brother, Wolf's, studied the hazy image standing at the desk. "But definitely there. Oh, this is so cool. I always sensed them, but this—Gods, thank you, Tristan."

"It's—" he started to say.

The bell jingled again, and Ophelia Sunday winced at its shrill ring. "Of course, there's no missing *that*."

"I'm here about a room," the ghostly woman announced imperiously in a lush Irish accent. She was shorter than the slender woman behind the desk, but she still managed to look down her freckled nose. "And I want one of the best, ye hear? None of the back stairs mousetraps ye hear about in these fine places. If it's going to be me last, then I want something fine. Something posh."

Tristan smiled and pulled up the Grange's register. "Of course, I have just the suite for you. If you'd like to sign in?"

"Or I can if you like," Ophelia Sunday offered. Her nod reassured Tristan of being able to hear the woman, and he grinned, relaxing at her wink.

"I can write me name. Or I'd been able to when I was alive. It's harder to grab at things now." The woman struggled to pick up the pen. Like many specters, she had little control over physical objects, but after a few seconds, she gripped the instrument and left her name on the ledger, a scrawling cluster of letters in blue ink. "Ah, it's much easier here than in Galway. I had a devil of a time moving a scrap of paper off a desk back home."

"Missus Lisa McInroe," Tristan read off. "Welcome to Hoxne Grange."

Then he stepped back and let Ophelia Sunday finish checking Mrs. McInroe in.

There'd been a sense of—relief—when Meegan showed up the week before with her daughter in tow, especially when Ophelia Sunday *saw* Cook arrive, and the dead cockney woman spoke with Wolf's younger sister. It was like Tristan was suddenly a bit more... *normal*.

He had to stop himself from hugging Ophelia Sunday, but it was close. She'd hugged him instead and whispered in his ear, "You look like you need one."

So Tristan told himself he wasn't going to cry either.

Unlike her brother, Ophelia Sunday was enchanted by the prospect of ghostly interaction, and Tristan immediately asked if she would like to stay for a few days or years—just to see if he'd been broken somehow by the encounter with Matt's poltergeist great-grandmother. Things were off at the Grange, and he'd begun to worry if it was him or the mansion itself. Ophelia Sunday was like a gift from some God who'd finally taken pity on him.

"Ah, I have the crystal shop, but oh—" she'd started to say, but Meegan hushed her daughter.

"I can take care of the shop. It's not like we don't have help and managers," Wolf's mother said, clasping Ophelia Sunday's hands in glee. "You can *see* Tristan's guests. Do you have any idea how fantastic that is?"

"They're hazy, but I can certainly see them. It has to do with the desk, I think. For me, anyway. Maybe because so much activity is there?"

Her eyes lit up, and Tristan was struck by how similar her smile was to her brother's.

"I'd love to stay. Actual metaphysical contact is so rare. This is just so… incredible! I'd only gotten impressions before—and some mists, but *this*!"

Unfortunately for the Grange of late, its ghostly contact was now extremely rare. Mrs. Lisa McInroe made only the fourth spirit to walk through the mansion's double doors following the exorcism of Winifred Culpepper, and that was if Tristan counted the weekly reappearance of Heather Cook, the repeater who'd attached herself to the Grange's kitchen.

The exorcism of Winifred Culpepper.

Tristan couldn't stop thinking of that time as a turning point for the Grange—and himself. Summoned by a fierce argument between Wolf's technicians, Matt and Gidget, the haunting brought with it some serious damage to Hoxne Grange's interior, and Tristan's heart suffered probably as much if not more.

"Fucking Kincaid," he muttered, then gave Ophelia Sunday an apologetic look when she glanced up from explaining about the Grange's setup to the visiting ghost. "Sorry, different Kincaid. Your brother."

Ophelia Sunday nodded knowingly. At least he had an ally in Wolf's sister. It was odd—allies and family seemed to cross over lines Tristan had no experience negotiating, but the women were clearly on his side. If only he understood what his side *was* and why was it important he even take one?

Thinking about Wolf pissed him off, and Tristan longed for another cup of coffee, possibly even a walk out in the mist-coated gardens in the back. He needed to take a breather, but Tristan didn't want to leave Ophelia Sunday alone. As if knowing what he was thinking, she waved him off, flashing him a thumbs-up as she listened to something the ghost was saying.

"Okay, a walk it is." Tristan slapped his leg to get his wolfhound's attention. "Come on, Boris. Let's go."

Boris opened his eyes—well, one eye—and gave his owner a skeptical glance. The shaggy dog huffed, his lips flapping over his massive teeth. Then he stretched his legs out in a mighty stretch before easing back into a boneless heap. Giving up, Tristan snagged his travel mug from behind the counter and headed to the back of the house.

After a refill of his mug from the coffeepot in the main kitchen, Tristan headed out to the large terrace overlooking the Grange's rear gardens. The mist had turned to a light drizzle while he'd been in the kitchen, and the cold dew clung to his face and clothes, cooling him down slightly. Thankful for his heavy sweater, he leaned his elbows on the balustrade and brought his mug to his lips, taking a tentative sip at the hot brew.

"Your wolfhound is a waste of fur and bone." Mara appeared at his elbow, her mouth pursed into a disapproving moue. "And you should be wearing a coat. You'll catch your death from a cold."

The phantom housekeeper pressed her hands down into the pockets of her apron, her bony knuckles poking through the ethereal fabric. She was what a man would have called a comfortable woman a few decades ago, pillowy and soft where needed, with a face that could go from maternal to icy schoolmarm in a second flat. In a lot of ways, Mara'd been Tristan's mother, or at least his aunt, someone to talk to when he'd spent his childhood summers at the Grange.

His very lonely, odd summers during a time when he couldn't make heads or tails out of the people only he could see and hear, and his family certainly wanted to have nothing to do with his infernal nonsense.

To be fair, Tristan's adult summers and winters were pretty much repeats of his childhood ones, and there'd been no change in sight until a little over a month ago when hell came knocking at his door. Or rather— Hellsingers.

Doctor Wolf Kincaid of Hellsinger Investigations had turned everything upside down, then handed Tristan back his loneliness, its dusty corpse sucked dry like a dead fly on a windowsill in the summer. Wolf'd shoved his way into Tristan's life, screwed up his perfectly safe, bland existence, and then left him—alone and hurting all over again.

God, he *missed* Wolf. He missed everything about the man—from arguing with him about what a ghost really was to sharing a cheese omelet in bed after a long morning of sex. Sure, Tristan missed the sex—Wolf was his first and only partner—but most of all, he missed the connection, because he'd never *had* one before, and from all accounts, what he and Wolf experienced was almost magical. Or so he'd thought—until Wolf

Kincaid walked out of the Grange's front door, his anger leaving a hot trail behind him.

"Fuck him," Tristan muttered, and Mara lifted her eyebrows. "Kincaid. Not Boris. And hell, him—not Ophelia Sunday."

"I didn't think you were talking about the hound, even if throwing you over for a pretty girl is that dog's modus operandi."

"That's a new one." He contemplated the phrase. "What? You're reading Mickey Spillane? Wait, he's dead. Have you been *talking* to him?"

"Silly thing. Detective shows. Investigative shit. You learn a lot on those. They don't tell you all of it, but enough. I can probably hide a body better now, but it'd be useful if they'd share the chemical cocktail some of those crazies use to boil down the flesh. That would be mighty useful. I was thinking lye, but really, there's got to be better."

"Good," he grunted. "Maybe between the two of us we can hide Kincaid's body when I kill him."

"That's how you know you love a man." Mara reached out to pat Tristan's shoulder. The touch was a brief, feathery contact, but it made him feel a little bit better just the same. "You want to murder him as often as you want to fuck him. Maybe more. And from the sounds you two made in that bedroom of yours, I'm guessing you want to kill him a hell of a lot."

"Mara!" He gaped at her. "*Jesus! You watched us?*"

"Well, I'm dead, not… *dead*! Your doctor's got a nice ass, and God's sake, he's hung like a bull." Mara snorted. "But if you're going to be like that…."

She was gone when Tristan turned to look at her. Staring at the empty spot where the housekeeper'd been standing, he grumbled under his breath. "Would it kill you to stick around until *after* I came up with a snappy rejoinder?"

A damp red ball rolled across the terrace toward him. He couldn't see where it'd come from, but that never really mattered. Leaning down, Tristan picked it up and flung it out into the garden, then waited, anticipating its return to his foot.

The ball never came back.

Sighing with disgust, he brought his cup back up to his lips, hoping the coffee would warm up the cold lump forming in his chest. Swallowing, Tristan saluted the missing ball's owner and said, "Thanks, Jack. You might as well leave me too. Just like he did."

HOXNE GRANGE looked the same as it did the first time Wolf drove up to it. This time, however, his anticipation of its inhabitants had less to do with the spectral and everything to do with one pretty blond man whose hazel eyes turned a jade color when angry. And the last time Wolf'd seen Tristan Pryce, his gaze was Mayan jaguar green—and just as hard.

There were no guarantees it would be any different now, but Wolf knew he had to make an attempt to smooth over what he'd done. Because damn if he didn't miss Tristan.

The Muir Woods mansion seemed like it'd been built specifically to star in an episode of *Groovie Goolies*. Its *Gilded Age* extravagance and long wings boasted a luxury many people only dreamed of, but there was an air of still oddness about the estate. Even with a score of gardeners and a small cluster of household crew, the place seemed empty, because the staff seemed more shadow than people. The only spot of vibrant life in the place was Tristan.

And Wolf's angry parting words had been harsh enough to bleed that out as well.

"Shit, I should have brought flowers or something." It was too late to turn back. At least Wolf thought so. His mea culpa would have to be done sans bribe, and it probably was better that way. "Because he's a creepy fuck. I wouldn't know where to get black roses."

Down in the city, the morning fog was already gone, but up in the hills beyond where the Grange sat nestled among tall trees and brutally manicured lawns, a misty cloak clung to the mansion. Drifts of gray dew caught on the estate's elaborate cornices, creating paisley swirls in the deepening fog. The SUV's lights came on automatically nearly half an hour before, and the light blue beams caught on the piscine fountain situated in the circular driveway's greenscape. The flowers around the pool's base were now a raspberry hue, with a few dots of white at the petals' edges, a shimmering ring of color bright enough to serve as a beacon in the monochromatic scene.

The Grange was a wash of grays and shadows. Even the enormous wooden doors seemed to be muted down to a warm dusky tone, as if the only color allowed to the mansion's exterior was the wild beet ring around the fountain's marble base.

Parking his SUV in front of the mansion's front steps, Wolf counted to three before he got out. He had a short debate with himself about whether or not he should bring in his duffel bag filled with spare clothes and toiletries.

"Just do it. He's too polite to kick your ass out. Go with that." Wolf snagged the bag from the backseat and slung it over his shoulder, staring up at the Grange's grand front entrance. Squaring his shoulders, he took the steps two at a time. "Okay, Wolf, time to own your fuck-ups. Let's just hope Tris is in a forgiving mood."

The enormous green vase was gone from the foyer's massive table. Broken in the exorcism, it'd been replaced by a low scoop bowl nearly two feet across. Filled with roses and other flowers probably cut from the Grange's garden, the arrangement gave off a sweet, pleasant scent that mingled well with the lemony wood polish the house staff used on the mansion's walls and floors.

One thing the cerulean bowl also did, it gave Wolf a clear view of the Grange's mahogany reception desk Tristan's uncle had brought in from a hotel demolition. It was a gorgeous piece, heavily worked and massive enough not to be swallowed up in the mansion's main hall.

It'd been one of the places Wolf could find Tristan when he wasn't working on a book. Today was different, and Wolf stopped short, blinking at the woman behind the counter. Instead of the hot, innocently seductive blond man he'd been expecting, there was someone else instead, a young, slender woman with long black hair pulled back into a ponytail and blue eyes as bright as his own. She had the damned nerve to wiggle her fingers at him, as if he found his baby sister standing in his lover's place every day.

Clearing his throat, Wolf cocked his head at his sister, then asked peevishly, "What the fuck are *you* doing here?"

OUTSIDE PROVED to be too cold for Tristan. Especially after he ran out of coffee, and a steeped melancholy seemed to burrow down into him. Taking his cup inside, he debated getting another refill, then thought about Ophelia Sunday and wondered how long she'd been in the foyer. He'd lost track of time staring at the garden, and other than potential frostbite, Tristan hadn't come out of the experience any wiser.

Even as excited as she'd been about seeing a specter, ghosts were hard to come by in the Grange, and she probably was bored out of her mind.

"Probably should tell her we don't get anyone in the afternoon, usually. Maybe she wants something to eat. I should at least feed her." As he padded down the hall to the front of the house, Tristan's heart jumped in alarm at the familiar sound of a man's voice.

He stopped, wondering if he was going insane—finally—but no, it was definitely the arrogant rumble of the asshat who'd left him nursing a bruised heart after accusing him of drugging a batch of pastry.

"Oh no, not him. Not today. I can't—" Tristan's stomach gurgled, but he couldn't ignore the gleeful dance going on in some parts of his brain—and his dick and ass seemed to be quite happy at the thought of Wolf Kincaid being in the immediate area. It was annoying, this not-virginal thing, because now that Tristan knew what he was missing, his body could give him all kinds of ideas about what he and Wolf could be doing instead of fighting.

"It's not like I even *wanted* to be gay. I could have done without the sex. Okay, no. Not really. Not after Wolf," Tristan grumbled. "Shit, why did I have to want to be gay with him? Fucking hell. It's a choice, my ass."

Hurrying down the passage, Tristan handed his cup to one of the house staff workers heading toward the kitchen, asking her to put it in the sink. The woman looked startled for a second, as if Tristan was more ghost than real, but she nodded quickly and took the mug. His sneakers squeaked on the floor, and Tristan slowed his pace, not wanting to give Wolf the satisfaction of knowing he'd spurred Tristan to a near run.

"Walk. Act like—" Tristan realized he didn't know how to act. He'd ignored Wolf's texts, not wanting to give up the righteous anger he'd built up. It'd been one of the few times he'd known he was in the right, and damn it, Wolf owed him more than pixilated sweet nothings and purrings through a phone screen.

Better be careful what one wishes for, the saying went, and Tristan finally realized exactly how damning a wish could be. Confronted with the reality of Wolf Kincaid, he didn't know what to say or how to act, and he could have really used Mara's advice on the matter right at that moment.

Hitting the foyer at a good pace, Tristan's breath froze in his chest at the sight of the wide-shouldered man leaning against the reception desk.

Wolf's eyes were sharp, a blue deep enough to swim in, and his tousled black hair looked damp, probably from the moist air outside. His strong, handsome features hadn't changed, although Tristan'd wished someone'd punched Wolf's nose crooked in the week they'd not seen each other, but the only thing Wolf sported on his face was a light scruff of beard. His dark gray shirt fit in snug against his torso, its long sleeves pushed up to his elbows, exposing powerful forearms dusted with fine dark hair.

He looked good enough to eat. Hell, he looked good enough to fuck, and if anything, the lick of desire in Tristan's cock made him madder than ever before. It wasn't *right* to want the man who pissed him off as much as Wolf Kincaid could. There was a call to be a better man—a man Tristan could be proud of being. Instead, he opened his mouth, and something more visceral fell out.

Tilting his chin up, Tristan growled, "What the fuck are *you* doing here?"

"Funny. I just asked my sister that." Wolf's grin was a slow seduction of Tristan's senses. The damned man had the nerve to look Tristan up and down, his smirk growing lascivious when he finally settled on Tristan's face. "Damn, you look hot. How're you doing, Thursday?"

"You do not get to call me that—"

Tristan didn't get to respond with more because Ophelia Sunday cut in front of him, coming around the desk to shove her brother aside. Her foot hit a red ball lying near Wolf's feet, and the toy skipped across the foyer floor, bouncing against a nearby wall.

"I need something to eat. Why don't the two of you go fight somewhere else? You know, so I can have some peace and quiet. I have a lot of exploring to do. And tea. Lots of really cozy places I can tuck into, read a book, and sip tea, so you two go scream at each other some place I can't hear you." She studied Tristan with a curious look, then glanced back to her oldest brother. "*You* need to apologize better, Wolfgang. He was always horrible at it, Tris. Too much pride. Even when we were kids."

"Pride's not going to help him this time," Tristan promised darkly. "Seriously, Kincaid, what are you doing here?"

"Kincaid, huh?" Wolf's expression grew remorseful. "I thought we'd moved beyond that. And for your information, Ophelia Sunday, I *am* here to apologize. I just haven't gotten to it yet."

"Really?" Tristan blurted out. "What exactly are you apologizing for? Fucking up what's between us, or agreeing with my family that I'm nuts?"

"Wait, what?" Wolf pulled back, shock darkening his face. "What are you talking about?"

"Your report? The one to my uncle?" Tristan snapped. "Yeah, thanks to you, they've filed to get control over the Grange. They're trying to get me declared incompetent, Wolf, and it's all your damned fault."

Chapter 3

WOLF BECAME Tristan's shadow, at least for as long as it took the men to climb the long flights of stairs to the Grange's third floor. Not surprisingly, the Grange bore no evidence of the paranormal battle waged there a month before. Winifred left very little of her existence behind, other than a few broken pieces of furniture. Even the powerful, erratic spectrum readings the team registered before Gidget accidentally called up Matt's dead but murderous grandmother dropped down afterward to levels Wolf would expect he'd find at a local BART station. Sure, the Cook showing up brought a sense of relief to Tristan's worried mind, but the man'd fretted over his lack of guests before Wolf fought with him.

From the slump in Tristan's shoulders as they slogged up the stairs, things apparently went from depressing to worse while Wolf was in Florida getting his ass chewed on by gators.

Reaching the third floor, Wolf noticed the door to Mortimer Pryce's rooms were open. Up until recently, Tristan never ventured inside his deceased uncle's suite, choosing instead to let the man's memories steep into the walls like a very strong black tea.

They walked by the open doors without so much as a glance from Tristan, and if anything, that worried Wolf the most. Something was definitely wrong with the man, and Wolf's gut twisted, hating that he'd added to the press of problems Tristan seemed to be carrying on his shoulders.

"Hey, wait up," Wolf called out, hefting his bag up. "Tris!"

"God, I can't… deal with you right now." Tristan hit the door to his suite with a hard push of his hand. Unlatched, it swung open, slamming into the wall, then bounced back, nearly catching Wolf in the chin.

He snagged the door's edge before it struck him and entered cautiously. Never having actually been in a fight with Tristan, Wolf wasn't sure if Tris was a yeller or a thrower, and nothing said *I'm pissed off at you* like a well-aimed vase or plate.

Apparently, Tristan was a pacer, because he hit the length of the suite's main room in a steady stride, his beautiful face firm with anger. The man's eyes were hard and cold, glacially green against amber stars, and Wolf winced at the unspoken accusation of betrayal thrown at him in Tristan's heartbreaking expression.

"Talk to me, Thursday Addams." Wolf tried teasing the man out of his mood, but Tristan wasn't having any of it.

"You don't get to call me that. No Tris, no Tristan." He rounded on Wolf accusingly. "Shit, you don't even get to call me Pryce. God, do you know what you've done to me? You've made me *want* this thing between us, then—"

"Let's take this one thing at a time." Wolf crossed the room and dug into the cabinets of the wing's open kitchenette off the living room. He dug out coffee grounds and made up a pot to percolate. Tristan continued to mark off the length of the space, angling to avoid the scatter of couches near one wall. "What do you want to deal with first?"

"First? How about we go from last to the start? Your fucking report skewered me!"

"Tell me what's going on with your uncle—"

"Not just my uncle!" Tristan's finger waved about as furiously as a conductor's wand during an 1812 Overture performance. "My whole damned family! Because you told them—and I quote—*there is no recordable evidence of paranormal activity at Hoxne Grange.*"

"Wait!" Wolf abandoned the coffee watch and headed into the living room. "Tris, hold up. I didn't—"

"Not Tris. Sir. Maybe sir." He cautioned Wolf against hugging him with a light shove. "And not like in a leather harness kind of way."

"Okay, if we're going to hammer this out, I don't need the image of you in leather pants in my head." Wolf sighed. "Come on, let me explain. About the report first."

"What's there to say?" Tristan's voice grew deeper, a menacing growl Wolf didn't think Tristan was even capable of uttering. "You pretty much sent them a dressmaker pattern for them to make me a custom straitjacket. Do you think they'll at least let me choose what color canvas I'll be wearing? I'm thinking something in a heather tweed. Might as well be fucking comfortable and warm."

"Tristan, stop." Wolf grabbed at the man, holding him in place.

They had a brief battle, but Tristan's heart wasn't in it. A second later, he gave up the fight, but he snarled when Wolf tried to embrace him.

"Okay. No hugs, but shit, go sit down on the couch, and I'll bring you some coffee. We can work this out."

"Can I bash your head in with the cup? Because that's pretty much what would work for me," Tristan muttered as he pulled away, but Wolf was relieved to see him head over to one of the sofas.

"I'll bring you something heavy. Wouldn't want you to do something halfway," he promised. A minute later, he was carefully handing his lover a steaming cup of creamy coffee, cautioning him against its heat. "Now talk to me about what happened with your family. Shit, I was only gone a damned week. How much can happen in a damned week?"

"You and I happened in a week." Tristan sounded bitter as he sipped at his cup. "And you fucked *that* up in less than a day. So yeah, a lot can happen in seven days."

Wolf counted to ten. Looking around the room, he took in the whimsical artwork lining its walls and noticed how the watery sun turned the walls to a buttery hue. Taking a deep breath, Wolf counted again, down this time, before speaking.

He'd already fucked up his relationship with Tristan because he couldn't keep his temper. There'd be no going back if he let his anger rule the conversation and—being honest with himself—it gave him time to study the other man.

"Okay, let's get this thing between us off the table first. We'll deal with the family thing after." Wolf took Tristan's cup and set it down to the side. The table was warm where the mug'd been, a nice spot under his butt when he moved over to sit on the table, his knees on either side of Tristan's bent legs. Putting his hands on Tristan's thighs, he looked deep into his lover's eyes. "I am very sorry. I fucked us up. Beyond fucked up."

"Which time?" Tristan snorted. "The argument where you told me I imagined the whole thing with Winifred the ghost? The peeing on my foot when we were stoned off of your mom's whacked-out leftover honey? Or maybe it's the whole agreeing with my family that I'm nuts? Pick one. Let me know where to start."

"Yes. All of it. Except for the family thing. I did *not* say you were insane." Wolf sucked in a long breath and slowly let it out. "The pee thing was a mistake. The argument was—I got scared, Tris. *Really* fucking scared."

"*You* were scared? It wasn't you Winifred was trying to possess."

"Not Winifred. Forget about Winifred—"

"Not bloody likely in this lifetime."

"Okay, how about for the next half hour," Wolf said patiently. "Thing is, *you* scared me. Well, me wanting you. My track record with relationships is really shitty. I've been dumped more times than I can even count, mostly because, let's face it, I'm an asshole, and I get too far gone into my work."

"Agreed," Tristan interjected. "And not just your work."

"Thing is, with you," he murmured as he took Tristan's hands in his, "I'm scared. Shit, you and I went from zero to ninety in such a short time. I felt out of control, and then you made that baklava—"

"Still totally not my fault." Tristan eyed him suspiciously. "I've never had someone leave peyote-laced honey in my kitchen before."

"You think it was peyote?" Wolf thought about the odd animals he had dancing on his stomach that morning. "Could have been, but I don't know. She didn't tell me what it was exactly."

"I went with peyote because it was all I could think of." Tristan shuddered visibly. "You *peed* on my foot."

"To be fair, it did have flaming ants on it. I was worried you'd get hurt." Wolf shifted closer. "I've told my mom she's forbidden from leaving anything here again. Hell, if I had my way, I'd ban her from the Grange entirely."

"Can't. She loaned me your sister." Tristan let a small grin get past his anger. "And she can kind of see the ghosts. Well, what there are of them."

"So she told me. It explains what my mother was angling for when I saw her in the city."

"Your mom told you to come here?" Just like that, Tristan's faint smile was gone. "Really?"

"No, not really. I've been texting you, remember? I was going to head up here anyway." Wolf wished Tristan's smile would come back out. "She just came to me to ask me a favor for the family. She seemed to think I could get you to come with me."

"I'm pissed off at you. Remember that?"

"Yeah." Wolf grimaced. "I was kind of hoping I could beg for forgiveness, but I've got a feeling it's going to take a bit more than a few apologies."

"Pretty much." Tristan nodded. "Especially since you've made your bed with my uncle."

"That is not what my report said." Wolf's growl was impressive, a subtonal blend of anger and angst.

IF TRISTAN hadn't been so angry and pissed off about his relatives' hostile takeover bid of the Grange, he might have even spent some time seeing if he could get Wolf to make those sounds in bed. As it was, Tristan was more interested in skinning Wolf than kissing him.

"You wrote that you had no discernible evidence of paranormal activity." Tristan could almost recite the report from memory, especially since entire sections of Wolf's official documentation had been served up to him on a silver platter in his uncle's complaint against him. "Or something like that."

"Not discernible. Recordable. I had no documentation after Mrs. Killer Spook was done with my equipment," Wolf refuted. "Where was the part where I clearly documented the spectrum shifts in the ballroom? We had that data. You read the report before I submitted it. Where did I state you were ready for a loony bin? They're twisting my findings."

"Would it have killed you to say you *saw* a ghost?" Tristan leaned back. "Or even mention *some* kind of strange shit? Did you have to go all scientific?"

"I *am* a scientist, Tris." It was said apologetically, but Wolf was firm. "It's what Hellsinger Investigations is all about—the science of paranormal activity. It's what we do. It's who your uncle hired, but I did *not* say you were ready for an asylum. If anything, you're the sanest one of the bunch."

"If I'm so sane, then why do I keep hoping the ghosts come back to the Grange?"

"You don't have ghosts?" Wolf frowned deeply. "Since when?"

"Since Winifred," Tristan admitted. "Not even a handful, and it scares the hell out of me. Suppose this thing with Winifred broke the Grange? Hell, suppose *I'm* broken now?"

WOLF'S HANDS roamed, settling on his legs. Their heat was too tempting, especially when the man's fingers began making small circles up and down his thighs. He wanted to push Wolf away, but he was scared if he did it once, Wolf would never come back.

If Wolf was scared of their relationship, then Tristan figured he must rank as terrified because, between the two of them, Tristan knew next to nothing about interacting with another person. Hell, he didn't even have a relationship with his parents when they'd been alive, and Uncle Mortimer was as stiff-upper-lipped as possible. Wolf was the first person to ever really touch him—to hold him—and Tristan didn't want to jeopardize that.

But screw it, he wasn't going to be tossed under a bus driven by his Uncle Walter either. His uncle was intent on breaking Mortimer's will, and damn what Tristan wanted.

If only he knew what he really wanted.

"Shit, babe." Wolf let go of a long breath. "I didn't know."

"Suppose the spirits don't come back?" Tristan's brain apparently was tired of the back and forth and decided to take control. He hadn't expected to blurt out his fears to Wolf, at least not until he could work out how he felt about the man, but there he was—sharing. And it seemed he just couldn't shut up. "What do I do, then, Wolf? What if my family takes the Grange from me?"

So many fears clouded his mind, and Tristan couldn't find the end of one and the beginning of the next. Sitting alone in the dark after Wolf's stormy exit, he'd wondered if Wolf was ever going to come back. Then when the texts starting hitting his phone, he'd wondered if he should answer them. It would be better for Wolf if he wasn't attached to Tristan in any way, better for his career if not his life, but Tristan wanted the normal Wolf gave him, even if normal wasn't necessarily the term most people would use for what his life'd become with Wolf Kincaid in it.

It was one he'd come to use.

"I won't let that happen," Wolf said in his sweet, low voice. Sliding off forward, he hesitated for a moment before wrapping his arms around Tristan. "I'll testify in person. Anything you need. You're worth more to me than Hellsinger."

"You... I can't let you do it. I want you to do that. I'd be crazy if I said I didn't, but truthfully, you're right. It's what you fucking do, even if I don't agree with it." He relaxed into Wolf's arms, burying his face in the man's dark hair. Wolf smelled so good, felt so good, and for the first time since he'd been served with his uncle's papers, Tristan felt a glimmer of hope in his heart. "You've only known me—"

"I've known I've needed you since forever." Wolf cut him off with a whisper dropped into Tristan's ear. "It just took me a bit to finally meet you."

"I still want to kill you," Tristan admitted as Wolf risked giving him a tiny kiss on the side of his mouth.

"Yeah, but really, death is kind of what I've come to expect from Hoxne Grange," Wolf muttered as he stole another kiss. "How about if I cook us up some lunch, and you can tell me why my sister's moved in with you. The last thing this place needs is another Kincaid."

"God, you think?" Tristan groused, standing up to answer a knock at the suite's door. "I barely survived the first one."

WITH TRISTAN gone to check over the staff's work before they clocked out for the day, Wolf busied himself in the kitchen, looking for something to cook. He found a loaf of brioche, a few heirloom tomatoes, and enough cheese to drown a township in. Slicing the cheddar into thin planks, he set about to make grilled sandwiches. He had his hand on the back of a kitchen knife when Mara's voice broke the silence in the room.

"It's about time you got your ass back here," the ghost huffed. "Boy's been worrying himself sick."

The knife skittered across the chopping board, and Wolf let it go, not wanting to cut himself on the sharp blade. Giving Mara a dirty look, he inspected the cheese hunk and resignedly popped the sliver he'd cut off into his mouth, deeming it too unevenly cut for his purposes.

"I was only gone a little while, and it showed me I needed my head pulled out of my ass," Wolf pointed out. "And I tried to get a hold of him. Or didn't he tell you that? Besides, he had my sister to keep him company. You'd like her if ever you get around to meeting her. She says you two haven't met."

"She can't see me," Mara moved through the kitchen counter to stand on the other side so she could watch Wolf as he sliced cheese. "I've tried. I've even flashed her. And I've got some killer boobs. Want to see?"

"Gay. They won't do a thing for me."

"Pity, because they're spectacular." She hefted her breasts through her uniform. "Hell, I wasn't even sure *you'd* see me."

"Why? I'd seen you before." Wolf picked up a piece of brie, wondering if he shouldn't make the sandwiches out of that, when Mara's body flickered. "What the hell is going on here? Why can't my sister see you?"

"Same reason the Grange isn't getting any visitors, Kincaid," she replied sadly. "The place feels off, love. Something that woman did drained it—drained him. The one your two scallywags brought here. The Winifred woman, not your mother—although she didn't do us any favors."

"How can a place feel off?" Wolf put the knife down and stared at the now transparent specter. "Whatever Mortimer put on this place to make it... whatever the hell it is, that still works."

"You all drove Winifred out, remember? What did you think was going to happen to the rest of us? Those of us who aren't driven by rage? We don't have the power to fight that pushing out." Mara's hands moved like frantic doves in the air as she spoke. "I keep hoping it will heal itself, especially since that girl came, but so far, nothing. Only a few very strong spirits have crossed the threshold, and those are few and far between."

"Fuck." Wolf's heart lurched, then sank. If what Mara said was true, he'd destroyed everything Tristan lived for. That thought set his mind reeling, and he mutely stared out into the living area, wondering what the hell he could do. "And here I was kind of hoping he'd consider coming with me down to San Luis Obispo to my cousin's place. I thought if Ophelia Sunday could see the... shit. Shit!"

"What were you going to do there?" Mara wandered about, sometimes crossing through the counter as she walked around the room. "It might not be a bad thing for him to go if it's something that would take his mind off of things. The boy needs some time away from the dead. I love him, but talking to ghosts and dogs all day has got to be bad for your belfry."

"Sey—my cousin—has this toy hospital thing. Well, used to be a bed-and-breakfast her grandma started. Now it's a farm for wayward animals and a house with a lot of old dolls and teddy bears. Sey's one of the more normal Kincaids—steady, you know? But she told my mom there's been some odd things going on over at her place." Wolf shrugged. "And by odd, she meant boo-wigglies. I figured Tristan might want to take a break and go on a road trip. Now I don't know if that's the right thing to do."

"It's more than the right thing," Mara insisted. "You *have* to get him to go. Do you have any idea when the last time that boy left this place for longer than a day or two? You'd think he was guarding the crown jewels or feeding the Tower's ravens."

"If the Grange is—" He didn't want to say it, but there weren't a lot of words to choose from. "He won't want to go with me. Hell, I'm not even sure if he's forgiven me yet."

"He hasn't stabbed you with a pencil, so that's a good sign." Mara made a face at Wolf's lifted eyebrows. "He did that once to that milquetoast of an uncle of his. I don't think that man ever forgave him for that, but the boy was six, and Walter *is* such a fricking ass."

"I'll try, but it'll probably turn out to be a bust. They usually are." Wolf leaned on the counter. "Hate to tell you this, Mara, but a lot of times people see ghosts when it's nothing more than a house's foundation giving way or bats up in the attic. The real attic. Although there's been a real belfry or five too. Never discount the crazy."

"You have to get him to go." Mara sounded almost desperate, and Wolf frowned at the distress in her voice. "Maybe doing this—with you—will give the boy some kind of purpose. Maybe getting out there, into the world, instead of waiting on the dead in a dying heap of stone and fog."

"I'll do my best," Wolf promised her. "It's all—"

Boris's toenails clicked on the hallway floor outside of the suite, and the door creaked as the enormous wolfhound pushed his way in. Spotting Wolf in the kitchen, the dog ambled over and bumped the man's leg, peering up at him through scruffy eyebrows in the hopes of getting a piece of whatever Wolf was cutting.

Tristan came in on the dog's heels, tossing a pack of staff papers onto the table by the door. Looking about curiously, he smiled tentatively at Wolf. "Who are you talking to? Boris?"

"Um...." Wolf glanced at Mara, floating a few feet in front of him. She shook her head, and he cleared his throat. "No one. Just talking some things out. I've got something I want to ask you, if you've gotten around to forgiving me yet."

"I'm thinking about it." Tristan snagged a piece of cheese, his hand cutting through Mara's midsection. After taking a bite out of the orange square, he broke off a piece and offered it to the dog. "Here you go, Boris. Just no farting, okay?"

Wolf watched Mara drift through the blond's body, her face wistful as she passed into Tristan's skin and out the other side. She shook her head and sighed, but Wolf wasn't sure if Tristan felt even the typical chill of a nearby ghost, especially when he leaned over to ruffle Boris's ears and neither reacted to Mara's presence.

"Convince him, Kincaid. *Please*." Mara's form began to thin, and a moment later, he was left with only the burn of her face in his memories, but her voice crept past him with a chilly whisper. "Get him to go with you, and show him a bit of the world. Before he dies here alongside this house and the rest of us."

Chapter 4

"HEY, LITTLE sister, what have you done?" Wolf sang and lifted his lip at Ophelia Sunday as he strode into the room she'd apparently claimed as her own.

Hoxne Grange was set up as a maze of halls and rooms, and he'd explored nearly every square inch of the mansion when he'd been investigating Tristan. There were names and labels attached to every damned corner of the place, and his head swam trying to remember where the family breakfast room was or if the Thistle Room was on the first or second floor.

He was pretty sure there was a map of the place or at least something Tristan might have shown a ghost or three, but like getting lost while driving, he wasn't going to man up and ask for directions.

Sadly, the only reason he'd found Ophelia Sunday was because she was singing an old show tune at the top of her lungs, and Wolf simply followed the off-key rendition of "Hello Dolly" until he stumbled on the right room.

"Great, now I have to burn the rugs," she muttered, rolling her eyes before going back to the thick book she had balanced on her lap. "Someone let a Yeti in, and it's shit on the carpet."

He wasn't sure what defined a drawing room, library, or sitting room. From what he could tell, they all pretty much looked the same, with the exception of the main library, a cavernous two-story room situated at the back of the house. *That* room was a bibliophile's wet dream, and he'd dug into a few of the antique anthropology books before he'd gotten waylaid by Tristan's deep green eyes.

For all he knew, the books he'd taken back up to his room were still there. And from how he and Tristan left off, he'd have ample time to read them when he retired to its chilly confines later that evening—the *very* chilly confines.

The library or study, whichever this room was called, seemed to fit his sister's style. An eclectic mix of Egyptian and Victorian Orient, the furniture looked comfortable, if a bit worn. Tall arched windows looked out onto the front lawn, and she'd pulled back all of the heavy burgundy drapes to let as much sun as she could into the room. The mishmash of tapestries and patterns shouldn't have worked, especially not the beige-toned Persian rug under her feet, but the room not only suited her, she seemed to be more relaxed than he'd ever seen her before.

Until she opened her mouth. Then the bratty younger sister he'd grown up with emerged in full Valkyrie form, ready to do battle with a sharpened tooth and a wicked tongue.

"Piss Tristan off yet?" Ophelia Sunday smirked at his uncomfortable throat clearing. "Not bad. I owe Mom ten dollars. She said you'd do it before sundown. He's so mellow. I thought it'd be at least tomorrow."

"Good to know you've got my back, Ophie." He dodged the small stack of Post-it Notes she chucked at his head. They flew past him, skipping over a table like a stone on a lake. "Your aim is shit."

"So's your love life. I'd tell you not to call me that, but that'll just egg you on," she countered. Her eyes, so much like his own, peeled away the thick layer of smug and cockiness he'd spackled on himself. "I like him, Wolf. Not romantically, but he's a sweetheart. A bit weird, but really, look at our family—not like we can throw stones."

"Yeah, I like him too," he admitted.

"Then why did you fuck it up?"

"Because I'm an idiot. Because I'm new at this." He sprawled onto a sofa across of her, studying the stylized cherrywood alligators the set had for legs. "A whole bunch of becauses. Why are you here?"

"Because I'm sick of working at a crystal shop—"

"You own the crystal shop," Wolf pointed out.

"But I'm not doing anything… vivid with my life." She held up the book she'd been reading, tossing her long black hair away from her face. "Do you see this? *An Examination of Spectral Activity* by Archibald Pryce. The library has a million of these kinds of studies, and Tristan needs… help."

"Can you do that? Help? How much do you see here?"

She'd always been a sensitive, someone the family could count on to feel paranormal activity, but like most people, actually seeing a manifestation was rare.

Until he'd come to Hoxne Grange—then he saw all manner of things, including some he'd rather forget.

"It's getting stronger. The shapes are more defined." Tucking her legs under her skirt, Ophelia Sunday laid the book down next to her and studied her brother. "I think it has something to do with what Mortimer Pryce did to the place, and well, Tristan's… strong."

"Yeah, I got that," he agreed softly. "Too strong. And he's been stewing in this shit for too long because he can't get away."

"That's where I come in," his sister replied. "I've got a couple of managers to run the shop. Hell, I barely go there most days. I need to do something different, Wolf. Something more than saying have a nice day and yes, hematite is good for canceling out negative energy. And I'm all for smudging, but is that all there is to life?"

"There's also tea parties." Wolf grinned at Ophelia Sunday's defiantly flashed middle finger. "Seriously, you're really going to stay here? And do what?"

"Help with the hotel—"

"It's not a hotel," Wolf asserted.

"There are guests, even if they aren't alive. And admit it, the whole thing is fascinating! Tell me you don't want to dig right into it and see why this place attracts the dead."

"He won't let me—dig, I mean." He stole the bottle of ginger ale his sister had left on a table next to her, nearly toppling off the sofa when he reached for it. "I've been forbidden to study the Grange. He's afraid I'll fuck something up."

"I think Mom's already done that." Ophelia Sunday smoothed her skirts. "There haven't been a lot of guests arriving."

"Yeah, I heard." He didn't want to tell her about Mara struggling to get Tristan to see her. In true Ophelia Sunday fashion, she'd jumped right onto the sore spot he'd been hiding. He sipped at the bubbling soda, then held the plastic bottle out for his sister. "I'm really worried about him."

"I know Mara's been a bit scarce too," she remarked, taking back her ginger ale. "He's mentioned it. Kind of in passing, but he's noticed."

"Shit, she was hoping he wouldn't." He swore lightly, rubbing at the fatigue clinging to his eyes.

"Mara's been pretty much the only—person—he's interacted with on a consistent basis for the past ten years. You don't think he wouldn't notice if she wasn't around as much? He's quirky, not stupid."

"No, he's definitely not stupid." Wolf couldn't stop the smile spreading across his face, but hiding it was the next best thing. Pity his sister was as sharp-eyed as a Catholic nun, because her snort was nearly elephantine.

"You should see your face when you talk about him," Ophelia Sunday teased. "You're all rainbows and unicorns. It must be so humiliating for my big badass brother. Poor Wolf, falling in love."

"I never said I couldn't fall in love. Just that it didn't seem possible," he corrected.

The siblings had that particular conversation more times than he could count. Their brother, Bach, believed in true love, while Wolf sat on the other side of the spectrum, claiming everything was chemistry and personality. Ophelia Sunday was somewhere in between, so it'd been a kick in the teeth when he'd found himself drawing hearts over his *i*'s when he thought of Tristan.

"You guys are so cute. And so mad at each other. The make-up sex is going to be awesome!" His sister was merciless, and her toes were like daggers when she dug them into his shin. He made a grab for her ankle, but Ophelia Sunday jerked her leg back before he could catch her. "Oh, is this your way of asking me if I'll cover for your sorry ass while you eat crow and apologize for being a dick?"

"I've apologized. I'm going to keep saying I'm sorry until I'm blue in the face," he replied. "I wanted to see if you'll be here—if you'll stay here so I can drag him down to San Luis Obispo. Sey thinks she's got a little bit of a gremlin—"

"You're dragging him to a haunting?" Ophelia Sunday rolled her eyes. "Really? Why not down to the city? A five-star hotel—because your place is shit—some romancing. Wolf, you've got rocks for brains. Next you'll be telling me you got him a vacuum for his birthday or something."

"Look, Sey's place is nice and relaxing. The town's pretty mellow, and we can eat ourselves silly down there. And he's good with it. I think he's even looking forward to it."

"Only you, brother." His sister sighed. "I'm not planning on going anywhere. I'm already helping him out, and yeah, he needs to get the hell away from here for a bit. But please tell me you're going to up the romance and not spend the entire time trying to make those machines of yours beep."

"Promise." He held his hand up to swear he'd behave. "Besides, it's Sey's place. What's the worst that can happen?"

"YOU ARE stupid in love with him. Just get over your shit and forgive him."

If there was one thing Tristan could count on, it was Mara's plain, blunt speaking. He looked up from his Wacom tablet and stared through her.

Literally stared through her. He stood up, unsure about what to say… what to do. Mara'd never been translucent, or at least not in years.

"Mara?" The stylus he'd been holding dropped and rolled someplace. He didn't care where it landed. Hell, he didn't care if he never found it. He could see *through* Mara as if she were one of the unsure, indeterminate guests who'd wandered into the Grange in the hopes of finding peace.

"Oh good, you *can* see me. I wasn't sure if you'd be able to, but I pushed as hard as I could." She went through the motions of sitting in one of the fluffy-sided chairs he'd dragged into his apartment because they reminded him of beanbags with legs. "Sit down, kiddo. You're looming."

His knees buckled, and she flickered when he sank back down into his computer chair. Boris grumbled at him when Tristan's foot nudged his side, but the wolfhound didn't bother opening his eyes. Tristan's breath was tight in his chest, and there seemed to be a distinct ringing in his ears, as though someone was playing with a bicycle bell a few doors down. His vision seemed to be full of speckled dots, and Tristan blinked, trying to push away the clotted darkness swarming him.

"Put your head down between your legs, Tristan. You're going to faint." Mara patted lightly at his hand, but he didn't feel her touch. "I wanted to talk to you before you left with Wolf tomorrow."

"I'm not so sure I'm going with him." Dropping his head down made him dizzy, and the blood rushing to his forehead was making his ears hot. "How long do I have to do this? And what is… why are you… like that?"

"One thing at a time," Mara replied. "Fine. Sit up. You look like your dog licking his balls when you do that."

"You're the one who *told* me to do that." He swallowed and peered into his coffee mug. It was empty, and his throat felt like he'd swallowed a ream of papyrus. "Shit, I'm losing it. I won't be able to see the guests anymore. Fuck! Or you. Or Cook—"

"Get a hold of yourself there, kid," she scolded lightly. "You're not losing anything. I'm here to talk to you about the Grange and, well, to ask you to go with Kincaid."

"He thought I drugged him," Tristan protested. "On purpose. Then he said I made up all the shit that happened."

"I didn't say he wasn't an asshole—"

"There was a tongue! A big black sticky tongue coming at me like a spongy slinky, and *he's* the victim?" He threw his hands up in surrender, and Boris woofed in his sleep, either alerting Tristan there were shenanigans going on or, more than likely, to lead an intruder to the silver drawer so they didn't have to search the house for it. "Fuck him, Mara."

"Honey, it's about time you fucked him," she said baldy, and his face caught on fire. "You were the oldest virgin in the state. Hell, I've got shoes who've had more sex than you have."

"I didn't need to know that," Tristan protested loudly. "Shit, you're going out again. What's going on? Do you know?"

"I think you're burning out," Mara admitted slowly. "That's what they call it, right? When you start to lose your mojo?"

"How can that be? I'm not doing anything different than I was before." He refused to accept Mara's explanation. "It's got to be something about what they did to Winifred. It broke Uncle Morty's ritual."

"They strained it," she agreed. "But it's not broken. Maybe once the ley lines recharge the Grange, everything will be back to normal. It's just going to take time. At least I hope so."

"Is that why you're—" He waved his hand in the air. "—like this?"

"Partly. It's harder for me to come over here in the afternoon, and there've been times when I've come to see you, and you haven't seen me. It was happening before the Kincaids did—well what they did here. It's just a part of how things work, Tristan." Mara smiled at him, a gentle, beatific expression on her face. She was so familiar to him, from her cotton-floss silvery hair to the spray of freckles on her slightly wrinkled left cheek. "I tried really hard today, because I *do* want to convince you to go with Wolf. It's important."

"How is it important? You just said the Grange is going to recharge."

"But you're not," she explained. "You haven't left the Grange for longer than a day in how many years? When was the last time you went down to the city and stayed overnight? Or the weekend?"

"I went to that conference in Vegas...." He couldn't remember when that was, but it'd been a disaster. By the time his agent found him holed up in his hotel room, he'd drained the minibar and eaten every single candy bar he could find just to avoid going downstairs to the buffet. "It was different then. I was younger."

"You're not much different, honey." Mara was gentle but firm. "Your Wolf is good for you. Whether you realize it or not, he challenges you—"

"Challenge is not always a good thing. Maybe I get tired of arguing with him."

"You love fighting with him." She scoffed at his small protesting noise. "Admit it. He makes you feel alive. More than living in this tomb does."

"Hoxne Grange isn't a tomb." It was something his Uncle Walter said all the time, and hearing it come from Mara's lips felt like the deepest of betrayals.

"Not for you, kiddo, but for me and Cook? It is. For the ones that come through those front doors, it's a path to elsewhere." The ghost bent forward until she was nearly nose to nose with him. "You sit here in this house waiting for death, and it comes to you. Little bits and drabbles of the dead who share their lives with you. You are living *through* them, Tristan. Can't you see that? Mostly everything you know about the world is what you heard from the dead. That's not healthy, kiddo. Not at all."

"So I'm just supposed to say fuck it and climb into a car with him?" He sat back, sending the hydraulics squeaking. "And dump all of this on Ophelia Sunday?"

"She'll be fine. And whatever she can't handle, I'll do," Mara insisted. "You need to get some air. Some sun. Hell, eat something other than your own cooking or delivered pizza."

"I get Chinese sometimes." He knew he sounded petulant, but there was no helping it. There suddenly was a corner behind him, and he'd been backed up into it. "I just don't like... leaving you here. Not like this."

"I'm going to leave you some day, honey," she reminded him softly. "One day that might happen. Even the afterlife has to end sometime. You've got to start living now, while your body can enjoy that man you've got in your back pocket. You need to drink some wine, eat crusty bread, and watch a sunset. Hell, go fuck in some place you could get caught, like under a bridge or in a park."

"Are you nuts?" Tristan shuddered. "I'd catch something. Or get arrested. Probably both."

"See, that's what I mean. You need to learn how to live a little bit, Mr. Pryce," Mara teased. "So what if you get caught? What's the worst that can happen?"

"I get arrested for indecent exposure and lewd behavior. I write children's books, Mara. That is *not* something my agent or publishing house wants to spin."

"Okay, so you don't get your groove on in public, but go *do* something. Hell, eat something from a street taco truck and get food poisoning."

"Your idea of a good time is a hell of a lot different than mine. I'm beginning to wonder what you're watching on television," Tristan shot back. "Can't I just… shit, I don't know, Mara. It's… too big, you know? Wolf—he's overwhelming sometimes."

"You give as good as you get, honey," she replied. "I taught you that. You've got everything you need to make it out there in that too-big world. You just need to take that first step out of the front door and go."

"What if… you aren't here when I come back?" She was his mother and savior all in one. An incorporeal, flimsy echo who'd taught him how to cheat at poker, make an omelet, and swear in at least fifteen different languages. There was a fear inside of him, a fear of loss, and Mara was the only family he had—or at least counted. Losing her—hearing her admit she could be lost shook his soul, and his eyes stung with tears. "I can't come back and find you gone. I can't—"

"I'm not going to promise I'll stay. None of us have that kind of power over life and death." Mara firmed, and now he felt the brush of her fingers on his arm. "You'll have your memories of me. That's all we have. Whether someone is alive or dead, that's what keeps us going—the remembrance of people we love. There will always be some part of me with you, just like I will always have a part of you with me, whether I am here at the Grange or gone to the beyond. It's how we fill our souls." Mara pressed a kiss to his temple, a light, feathery touch on his skin. "So, yes, you silly thing, go and have a good time, and don't worry about what you leave behind. Go make memories, and promise me one thing."

"What?" He wiped at his eyes with the back of his hand.

"That the two of you fuck like bunnies," she said, her eyes twinkling. "Wild, mad fucking bunnies."

Chapter 5

"I CAN'T believe I let you talk me into this," Tristan said for the third time. "I must have been drunk or something."

Wolf kept silent. In the hours since they'd left San Francisco, Tristan spent most of his time staring out the window at the fog-shrouded Pacific. Wolf chose to take the coast highway, especially after hearing Tristan'd never been on a road trip. It'd been a long morning, a challenging one—for Tristan's stomach, anyway.

He'd liked the Blue Raspberry Slurpee, and although the Sno Ball was a challenge for him to eat, Tristan devoured its layers and probably was riding a sugar high from the coconut-marshmallow-covered chocolate cupcake. Wolf, however, would be left eating pork rinds alone for the rest of their lives. Tristan took a piece of bubbly crackle and nearly gagged at the pop of skin on his tongue.

No, cheap pork rinds were definitely not on Tristan's list of things to put into his mouth.

Now, if only Wolf could somehow convince him that *he* was something Tristan could put back in his mouth, because the way things were going between them, the pork rinds weren't going to be the only thing spending their lives alone.

They'd slept apart the night before. Way apart, because Wolf was in the far wing, back in the room he'd originally slept in. It was a small act of penance on his part—one Wolf wasn't all too sure Tristan even acknowledged.

"How long are you going to be mad at me?" he ventured softly. "Remember, my family doesn't do tantrums—"

Tristan threw him a cutting look. "I don't know. You seemed to throw a pretty good one yourself."

"Okay, I'll give you that." A sign announced they'd arrived in San Luis Obispo, and he guided the SUV up toward the canyons. "I *am* sorry."

"Are we going to do this here? In the car?" A flash of green stormed in Tristan's eyes.

Any warmth they'd built up the night before had burned off as quickly as a thin bay fog under a hot rising sun. Wolf'd known Tristan was hurt. Hell, if he could, he'd take back every damned word he'd flung at Tristan before he ran off to Florida.

"I'd like to work things out, babe. I fucked up. Hell, you and me—we're flailing through this relationship thing." The streets were a blur, and Wolf had to concentrate on the road, finally spotting the turnoff he wanted. "I like sharing a bed with you. I like laughing with you. Hell, I like arguing with you but not hurting you. I prefer loving you more."

"Do you think we're sharing a room at your cousin's place?" Tristan raised his eyebrow. "And don't mention the Slurpee again. Yeah, I liked it, but there's only so much you can milk a blue raspberry slush."

"Your tongue still looks like a jelly bean." Wolf laughed. "I'd say yeah, I can milk it a bit more. And tell me the truth, Thursday. Did you miss me?"

"You were gone maybe a week," Tristan pointed out. "And so many messages—"

"But did you miss me, Tristan Pryce?" They'd come to a red light, and Wolf leaned over to steal a kiss from the corner of Tristan's mouth. "Admit it. You did."

"If I do, are you going to sing?" Gesturing to the intersection, Tristan said, "Light's green."

"I promise. No singing."

"Then yeah," Tristan sighed resignedly. "I missed you."

SAN LUIS Obispo—SLO—was larger than Wolf remembered. It began with a typical suburban sprawl and eventually led to a Disneyfied downtown district. Every other sign read organic or natural, although there were a few digs of carnivore pride scattered here and there. Tris counted five tea shops in the first ten blocks of quaint storefronts and got into a spirited debate with Wolf about if the natural juice store counted as well, since they boasted freshly brewed matcha.

The sidewalks were crowded, mostly wandering tourists or groups of young men and women burdened with backpacks. Wolf told him SLO was a college town, and it showed its demographic with pride. Scattered here and there were cheap eateries promising a hefty portion of fresh greens and filling wraps. A Mexican food place smelled promising, giving off a lingering aroma of grilled meat and refried beans done with real lard. Tristan's oversugared stomach growled, reminding them both it'd been hours since he'd last eaten anything with protein in it.

"There was a ghost back there. She was staring out of the window." Tristan tried to keep the excitement out of his voice, but more than a little bit of it snuck in. He actually bordered on gleeful, and Wolf quirked a smile at him. "And she didn't look like she was planning on killing me. A repeater, I think."

"Not a bad thing. The repeater part. Not the killing." Wolf exhaled. "Let's see if we can avoid the whole killing ghost thing again, okay?"

"If my uncle has his way of things, I won't have to worry about any ghost, killing ones or otherwise."

Wolf reached across the car and put his hand on Tris's thigh, patting him gently. "Don't worry about it. We'll take care of your uncle."

"Did you forgive me about the baklava?"

"What?" Wolf's brow creased. Then he nodded in understanding. "Yeah, I was an asshole. I admit it. Fuck, I should have… hell, I should have done a lot of things, but more importantly, I should have listened to you. Or at least suspected my mother of something stupid like that. You'd think I'd know better by now. And you? Forgiving my asshole behavior?"

"I'm thinking about it. My magic mushrooming you was an accident. You screaming at my head was on purpose." Tristan pursed his mouth. "Tell me about your cousin Sey. And why the hell does she have a toy shop?"

"Actually, I don't know what to call it." Wolf had the grace to look sheepish. "I think it's more of a doll hospital gone over the edge. She's an artisan, really—learned it from her mother. Fixes antique toys for a living. The place started off as an inn a long time ago, but when my aunt—Sey's mom—took it over from *her* mother, it kind of became a place for the family to go to when things got a bit rough."

"Did things get rough for you? Your mom's kind of nuts, but I didn't think she'd put you guys in danger."

"Not us. For Hellsingers." Wolf thought of the times he'd watched as members of his family crawled back to their safe houses, beaten down and bloodied from battling things no one else believed in. "Sometimes, yeah. Things can get rough. But Sey's place, it was good to go to. Kind of like summer camp except with fake body parts all over the place."

"And you call *me* Thursday Addams?" he scoffed when Wolf nodded at him. "You're the weird one."

"I thought it was cool when I was a kid. There were eyeballs everywhere. Now? Okay, yeah. Still kind of cool."

"Really?" Tristan shuddered. "Like Winifred's tongue?"

"They're not *real*. Okay, they're doll eyes. Some of them are human sized. I used to put them in my mouth and scare my cousins by spitting them out at their faces." Wolf laughed at Tristan's horrified look. "Swallowed one once when I was seven. I didn't want to tell Mom about it, but I looked at my poop for days for it but never saw it. For all I know, it's still rattling around inside of me, looking for the doll's head it used to be in."

"Great. That'll help me sleep at night." Wrinkling his nose in disgust, Tristan shook the remains of his slush to mix it back together. "But what's she like?"

"Cool. She's older than me by about maybe ten years, and sharp. Sey always tinkered with things. When I was a kid, she could fix anything. Probably still can." Wolf slowed the car as a marker announced the entrance to San Luis Obispo. "Sey's place is outside of SLO. You kind of liked the older part of town. I saw you smile. It's very tree-hugging otter scrubber."

"It's like you speak English, but the words are not making any sense."

"Granola town. SLO—San Luis Obispo—we just drove through it? That kind of very hipster douche kind of downtown. Lots of organic sandwich shops and fair trade coffee places with gluten-free biscotti. You even counted them."

"And you think I'm like that?"

"Not so much the organic, but I'm pretty sure you'd scrub an otter if it needed it. There's also a fantastic home-style sausage shop." Wolf shot him a smirk. "Of course, I can give you a sausage—"

"Shut up. I'm still working on the forgiveness thing."

"Hey, I've been saying I'm sorry since back at the Grange."

"And what about the Grange? Do you really believe it's haunted?" Tristan shifted in his seat to study the passing buildings. "Or do you think I'm crazy?"

"Babe, I was there. I can't document what Winifred was or even explain it. Hell, I can't explain what any of the things at the Grange are," he admitted. "But I know I can't measure them and present it as evidence. That doesn't change the fact that I believe you. Hell, I didn't at first. I'll cop to that. And I'd love to study the Grange more—if I could make sure that none of my equipment was disrupting the energy of the place."

"Do you think that's what happened? To my ghosts?" Tristan chewed on his upper lip. "Your equipment? Your mom's botched séance?"

"Truthfully? Everything spectral operates on frequencies. So does my stuff. That séance slash exorcism my mom hacked her way through? That could be only the tip of the iceberg. I've had some time to think about a few things, and I am wondering if something I did disrupted things somehow as well. I don't know."

"Do you think it'll come back? Hoxne Grange *had* a purpose, and I liked how it was."

"It still does have a purpose. Yeah, it got kicked in the teeth—hard, but I think it'll be okay." Wolf turned the SUV down a treelined drive, and the street began to wind around back toward the highway. "It's a bit of a drive still. I wanted to show you the town since Sey lives out in boonfuck Egypt. It's kind of isolated."

"Worse than the Grange?"

"Oh, hell yes," Wolf snorted. "I think that's part of the problem. Sey's out there without any day-to-day contact with anyone but a couple of farm guys who come by for a few hours. Sometimes a couple of my aunts drop by. They all move around too much to keep track of. Oh, and if my Aunt Bertha is there, whatever you do, don't drink anything she gives you. She's where my mom got the honey from."

"Great," Tristan sighed. "I'm going to Underhill. Next you'll be telling me she's married to Oberon."

Wolf laughed once, then sobered up. "Well, actually—"

IT TOOK them another forty minutes to get to the canyon road Sey lived on. A sign announced they were heading onto a private road, something clearly evident by the cracks in the blacktop and a thick overhang of tree branches above the SUV, but Wolf drove on. Tristan was tiring, coming down from a sugar high, and overwrought with worry about his home. Ophelia Sunday assured him she could keep the Grange in its odd business while they were gone, but Wolf had his doubts. Sure his sister was sensitive. She'd always been a dowsing rod for spirits back when he'd considered a career as a Hellsinger, but dragging his kid sister around on hunts wasn't exactly what he'd had in mind for a life.

Instead, he'd taken advantage of his paternal grandparents' generosity and gone to school—to become someone his mother's side of the family viewed as a traitor to his own kin—a paranormal investigator. Explaining he wanted to *prove* there were ghosts fell on deaf ears, and he'd been met with more skepticism by his blood relatives than he brought with him on a job.

Tristan's home, Hoxne Grange, was the most intensely active site he'd ever worked, and now it seemed to be faltering—its spectral activity fading quickly into the mundane before he could capture actual documentation of its paranormal essence.

And there wasn't a damned thing Wolf could do about it.

He could, however, take care of the man who owned the place, especially since Tristan seemed to have not slept the entire time Wolf'd been gone.

The tree line hugged the road, and white stiles separated the woods from the shoulder. In some spots, the brush thinned, and they could see older farm homes, complete with rust-painted barns and the occasional livestock. Most were cows, but when they turned a corner, a mottled alpaca peered out from behind a willow tree, keenly interested in the SUV's passing.

Sey's place emerged slowly, creeping out of a thick copse when he turned up into a gravel road. A large, sprawling old two-story house, it wore its past as an inn on its grounds. A large circular driveway led off to a cement pad marked with cracked, worn lines for parking spaces.

The house itself was a clapboard colonial with a few touches of Victorian styling, complete with a turret and rotunda off the side. Painted lemon yellow with a blinding white trim, it loomed out before a backdrop of hills and forest, shouting a welcome to anyone passing by, with its wraparound porch and yards of flower beds stretching out from its river-stone foundation. Its many rippled glass windows shone as best they could in the winking sunlight. The house sparkled and flirted with them as the SUV pulled up.

A massive spread of trees climbed up the hills behind the property, and acres of cleared land stretched out on either side of the house. An enormous old-style barn, complete with hay doors and white accent beams on its crimson paint, crouched behind the yellow house, and to the right, a thick white fencing corralled a small herd of enormous shaggy red cattle.

The bovines paid no attention to the SUV, although a fuzzy rust-colored calf lowed at the vehicle before scampering off to join the others.

"Those are awesome. They're like… bantha!" Tristan was fascinated by the cattle, and he watched them closely as he got out of the car. Peering over the roof at Wolf, he looked both alarmed and intrigued. "She doesn't eat them, does she?"

"No, they're freeloaders. All of them are. We'll get eggs from the chickens, but that's if they're in a good mood. Sey's a sucker for lost causes. Things here die of old age or boredom. Last I heard there's a camel around here too, but that was a while back. He might be gone, but you never know." Wolf grabbed their bags and then dropped them on the ground as a slender red-haired woman rushed down the house's broad porch. "Hey, there's my girl!"

Her hair was rooster bright, and while a bit on the slender side, the handsome woman had a raw-boned strength to her. And if anything, her broad smile was as brilliant as her coxcomb shock. Dressed in worn hiking boots, khaki cargo shorts, and a formfitting white tank top, Sey Kincaid was the picture of health, her long limbs tanned a dusky gold, and she moved effortlessly across the lush lawn, her arms spread wide to embrace Wolf.

"Ah, Wolfie!" She launched herself at him, delight written all over her face.

"Sey!" Wolf grabbed at the woman, catching her in midlaunch. She felt good in his arms, a solid piece of Kincaid, as familiar to him as his own skin. "God, it's good to see you."

"Wolfie?" Tristan's drawl dripped with amusement. "That's cute."

"Ah, is that the boyfriend?" Sey whispered into his ear before slapping Wolf's shoulder for him to release her. "God, he's hot. Are you dying? Is he taking pity on you? Do you have consumption, Wolf Kincaid, and didn't tell anyone? Or are you lying to the boy so he'll sleep with you?"

"Tristan Pryce, I want you to meet one of my favorite cousins, Sey Kincaid. Sey, this is Tris." Wolf bent over to murmur in her ear. "Behave. I like him. Don't scare him off."

"Boyfriend might be debatable but something for certain." Tristan yelped when Sey embraced him, her sinewy arms wrapping around him tight enough to make him squeak. "Uh, hi."

"Ah, love, you are simply too gorgeous to be stuck with that one." Sey winked, her eyes bright with mischief. "Tell me you like older women too."

"Why? Do you know one?" he managed to squeeze out as she hugged him again.

"Oh, you I am going to like." Letting Tristan go, she put her hands on her hips and examined the duffel bags they'd brought with them. "So, one room or two? How does someone ask that without hinting around things? I'm thinking I need to put the two of you far away from my room, or I'll hear you through the walls, but that bed's one of the old iron ones. It'll probably scream up a racket the moment either one of you gets going on it."

Tristan's face went red, and she burst out laughing, startling the cattle behind the stiles. The calf galloped about, bouncing through the herd, and bellowed loudly. Muttering a pardon under his breath, Tristan fled for the fence, his head down low so his shaggy blond hair covered most of his blush.

"Ah, Sey. He's new to this," Wolf admonished. "Go easy on him."

"What? Being a boyfriend or Kincaids?" She grabbed at one of the bags, exclaiming at its heft. "What have you got in here? Shrunken heads?"

"No, you're the one with bits and bobs lying about the house." He liberated the bag, slinging it over his shoulder. He hit the release for the back hatch, and the SUV's rear door popped up. "And Tris is—special. To me."

"Then why is he over there cooing at the cows instead of over here making puppy eyes at you?" Sey frowned at him. "Did you fuck it up already?"

"Oh, how you know me so well." He'd only packed the barest of necessities for a ghost hunt in the car, but it would still take him two trips to get his equipment into the house. He set the largest case down on the driveway, then elongated its handle so it could be wheeled in. "He's a medium. Probably one of the strongest I've ever seen."

"And you've brought him here?" Sey's slate-blue eyes practically boggled out of her head. "Are you insane? Didn't your mom tell you I've been having problems?"

"Yeah, that's why I wanted him to come." Wolf stopped unpacking the car and stared down at his older cousin. "They speak to him, Sey. He sees them. Hell, I think he actually accentuates their existence in a lot of cases. He also needed out of where he was for a bit. Someplace different than where he's grown up. Mom said she told you about Hoxne Grange—"

"Holy shit! He's *that* medium?" Sey tsked in sympathy. "God, that poor kid."

"Okay, I don't know what she told you, but stop with the poor kid thing. It'll piss him off." Wolf craned his head to study Tristan scratching the young calf's nose. "He's strong, Sey. Solid but kind of fragile in a lot of ways. I don't think his folks treated him right, and shit, I didn't do him any favors a couple of weeks ago."

"Lost your temper, then?" She sniffed at his nod. "Hotheaded Scot to the core."

"I'll own up to that," he replied. "I brought him here because Ophelia Sunday seemed to operate on his wavelength a bit, and he needed to get the hell out of the Grange for a while. It'll be a change of pace for him while I hunt down your problem."

"I'm not one of your cases, Wolf. This isn't rats or some crazy rabid bat. Things are moving around the house, and now I swear to God I can almost hear whispering." Sey shifted her hips, her expression serious as she stared off at Tristan's distant form. "I know there's something wrong here. I can't pinpoint what it is, but I'm not one of your hoaxes. The only reason I told Meegan I'd let you have a crack at it first is because it's not so bad. Just a little worrisome, but really—"

"I don't think you're a hoax, Sey." It was bad enough most of the family thought he'd crossed the line into full-blown skeptic. Wolf didn't want to piss off one of the few relatives he had who still liked him. "I'm here to see what I can find. And maybe Tristan can help me figure it out. He's *good*, Sey."

"And you love him. He's kind of fond of you. He keeps looking back here, and it's not because I've got a great rack." She nodded her chin at the blond. "Only you would bring a guy on a ghost hunt. What happened to dinner and a movie?"

"Tristan's not a typical kind of guy, and hell, we didn't exactly ever…." Wolf paused suddenly and swallowed. "Fuck me. I've never ever actually taken him on a date."

"And he's already met your mother." Sey whistled softly. "He *must* really like you, because Meegan? She's a deal breaker in my book. I'd run screaming for the hills if you brought that hippie around me and said welcome to the family—and I'm already related to her. Tell you what, let's grab your shit and get it into the house, and you and Tristan can go canoodle in the barn or something. Go take a roll in the hay. It'll be good for you both. Nothing gets the juices going like a night in the country."

"With my luck, he's allergic, but it's worth a shot. Hell, I'm desperate, Sey. I *really* fucked up."

"What did you do?"

"Kind of accused him of doping me, but really, it was something Mom left behind. He was innocent, and I sort of lost my shit. Totally on me," Wolf confessed. "I don't know how much of it was me seeing pink elephants or how scared shitless I am about loving him. Fuck, Sey. I think about him all the damned time. Every other guy I could just walk away from. Not him. Not Tristan. And it scares the wrinkled skin off my ball sack."

"Well, then, you better pray he goes easy on you, because, Wolf, you've got it bad, and there's no way in hell you're going to get out of it alive."

There had to be a little hope, because Tristan looked his way just as Wolf stared down the length of the lawn at the paddock. Tristan gave him a smile—shy and faint with a touch of lust in his eyes. Wolf knew that look well. He'd lived for that look, and his heart did a little jig when Tristan brushed as much of the calf hair as he could off his hands and walked toward them.

It didn't take Tris long to get to Wolf's side, and Wolf grabbed at Tristan's hips before he could slide past. Tristan smelled like sugar, sunshine, and a bit of the farm. Wrinkling his nose in gross exaggeration, Wolf leaned over to sniff at Tristan's skin.

"Mmmmm… eau de baby cow. My favorite." Wolf chuckled as he nipped at Tristan's neck. "Saw you made a new friend."

"Yeah, he seems to like getting his head scratched." Tristan ducked to block Wolf's teeth, but he didn't pull away. "Is there a bathroom inside, or am I going to have to go look for a tree?"

"Outhouse," Wolf lied with a broad grin. "Half-moon on the door and—"

A loud boom shook the air, and the SUV's passenger side mirror blew off, bits of metal and glass pebbling up into the air around them. Wolf shoved Tristan down behind the side of the vehicle, and he shouted as another shotgun blast went off, shot peppering the fender and the dirt near their heads.

Hooking an arm around Tristan's waist, Wolf pulled his lover back to the rear, trying to keep the thick tires between them and whoever was shooting at them. The cattle were bellowing in terror, and off in the distance, something screamed in a high-pitched wail. The air grew thick with the smell of trampled grass as the Highland cattle fled the front of the paddock, quickly becoming shaggy red dots on the far hillocks, with the calf clustered in on all sides by the protective herd.

Sey lay on the dirt behind the SUV, her smile wavering a bit when Wolf reached her, dragging a stunned Tristan behind him. Another blast hit a mock-orange bush, and the air went fragrant with green and blown-to-bits flowers.

From the house, a quaking old voice called out to them, feeble but menacing. "I'm going to run your fucking fed asses off our property! You ain't got no business here! I've got my rights."

"You hurt?" Wolf ran his hands over Tristan's prone body, checking for injuries. The blond shook his head, but he sounded winded, and his face was pale with shock. "Stay down. Sey and I have to have a little chat." Glaring at his cousin over his lover's long legs, Wolf cocked his head toward the house. "When the fuck were you going to tell me Aunt Gildy was here, and who the hell gave her a shotgun?"

Chapter 6

"YOUR FAMILY is nuts." Tristan was talking to himself. Wolf wasn't even nearby, but the sentiment remained. He didn't need his family to commit him. He'd found his own loony bin, right there in a place called SLO. Turning around, he shook his head at the insanity surrounding him. "Really. Wow. No words."

Tristan stood in the house's main living room and stared. It was all he could do—stare. And everywhere he looked, something stared right back at him.

And only one of those things was alive. But the gray Persian he thought was stuffed blinked just as he looked away, so he upped the live body count to two.

The house was a ramble, rooms connecting to other rooms and a long hall off the foyer with a staircase curling up to the upper floors. Pale gray walls did their best to lighten up the miles of dark cherry floor, but it was a losing battle. The house's furniture appeared to be mostly castoffs thrown down from a beanstalk, because everything seemed enormous and upholstered in the oddest fabrics, ranging from a cow print to tapestry, and there was no rhyme or reason on style. A mission-style table sat in a dining room off the main space, its utilitarian plainness surrounded by Victorian armchairs dressed in various shades of velvet.

The oddly comforting furnishings paled into the background with the sheer glut of antique dolls and teddy bears bristling and poking out of nearly every place possible. Wide worktables were placed against the room's one long wall, and almost every inch of flat surface was covered with bits or tools.

But mostly bits.

And eyeballs. Lots and lots of eyeballs or things with eyeballs.

Sey and Wolf were off hiding the shotgun they'd found Aunt Gildy wielding, leaving Tristan alone with the short silver-haired old woman. If anything, Tristan wasn't really certain the fey-faced woman wasn't one of Sey's creations, because her bright beady eyes followed Tristan about the room as he moved.

"We sure Sey's name isn't really J.F. Sebastian?" Tristan offered the old woman a weak smile. "Because I think we're one marching soldier doll away from finding an origami unicorn on the porch."

Up close—and unarmed—the elderly woman seemed innocent, even harmless, if he didn't take into account the cunning I-can-kill-you-with-my-mind look in her eyes. Her floral housedress was a bit too big for her slender frame, and she swung her bare feet back and forth as she sat on the too-tall couch, her toenails painted lime green to match the leaves on her dress. Gildy's gamine face was nearly as bare as her feet, embellished only by a smear of shockingly pink lipstick against her thin crepe skin.

"So you're one of those kind of boys? Like Meegan's oldest boy?" Gildy quizzed Tristan while he studied what looked like a stuffed squid on a nearby shelf. "You fancy the dick? Sey told me you like the dick."

He gave up trying to make sense of the cephalopod once he spotted a toucan beak hidden among its tentacles. The only elderly person he'd actually interacted with before was his Uncle Mortimer, and he'd never even whispered the word penis, much less any of its nicknames.

"Who, Wolf? Yeah, he can be a dick sometimes." Tristan went with being obtuse. It was safer that way. "Actually, he can be one a lot of the time. But I *do* like him when he's less dickish."

"Aunt Gildy, leave Tris alone." Wolf strolled in, then bent over to kiss the woman's cheek. She slapped at his leg, her eyes twinkling at him. "You okay, babe? Talking to Gildy can sometimes be like bartering with a used car salesman."

"I'm a Hellsinger—or used to be," the old woman grumbled back. "Always know who you're up against. Best advice I can give you. If I like you, anyway. Otherwise, I'd just shoot you."

"Tristan's one of the good guys. No shooting him." Wolf hooked an arm around Tristan's waist, and he let Wolf pull him in. Bending over, his whisper tickled Tristan's ear. "Gildy was a horrible Hellsinger. Don't let her tell you anything different."

"I'm old, Wolfgang Kincaid, not deaf. I was a *great* Hellsinger. I just had some problems with the ghost part of the job." The old woman's gnarled finger poked at the air. "I took down the Chicago Seven."

"That was a milk delivery theft ring." Wolf nodded. "Very fierce—for kids who skimmed buttermilk off of the morning deliveries."

"Only two of those kids walked with a limp afterwards. Life lessons!"

Wolf snorted. "You also shot up the Albuquerque Wells Fargo in '66 because you thought you saw a repeater."

"It was an honest mistake!" She sniffed imperiously. "The same man kept going into the bank vault over and over again."

"So she unloaded two rounds of rock salt into everyone inside the place." Wolf rolled his eyes at Tristan, but it was obvious he was only teasing the older woman. "They were triplets."

"Common mistake." Gildy pulled at the hem of her dress, picking at the eyelet. Fixing a steely eye on Wolf, she sniped, "At least the family still talks to *me*. Which is more than I can say about you."

Wolf stiffened against Tristan, and his expressive face shut down in an instant. Every inch of his large frame tightened, and Tristan automatically slid his hand up to rub at the spot between Wolf's shoulder blades.

There was a story there, an achingly rough tale lying just beneath the surface of Wolf's skin, and Tristan pulled away just enough to stare up at his lover's face. A raw vulnerability flashed over Wolf's expression, as if the old woman had taken a hot blade to his gut and twisted it deep into his stomach. Tristan could almost taste the pain in Wolf's eyes, and a bitterness lingered in the tight smile he'd affected to put Tristan at ease.

"Hey, it's okay, babe," Wolf reassured him, but Tristan wasn't buying it. Especially since Gildy immediately began to babble away her sharp, thrusting remark.

"I didn't mean that, boy." She began to struggle to her feet, but Wolf shook his head. "Wolf—"

"It's okay, Aunt Gildy. You're right." If anything, the man's expression grew more brittle before it flashed away into the cold, hard mask Tristan saw when Wolf first walked into Hoxne Grange. "The family *doesn't* want to have anything to do with me. Hell, I should be happy Cin and Sey are still talking to me."

"Wolf, I didn't—"

Tristan lost track of Gildy's voice. The living room walls slanted in on him, and he blinked, trying to shake off the dizziness swamping him. Something chattered nearby, and he turned to see what it was, surprised to discover the noise was coming from his own jaw as his teeth rattled together. Pinpricks ran over his skin, and under his shirt, his nipples drew in, growing taut with a chill. The house was getting colder by the minute, and his spine ached from the encroaching frostiness.

"Shit, it's cold all of a sudden." Shivering in Wolf's half embrace, he leeched as much of the man's warmth as he could. "I need to grab a sweater or something. Where did you put my stuff?"

Time slipped back into its easy flow, and Wolf turned, worriedly glancing at Tristan. "Babe, it's almost eighty outside. You getting sick, maybe? A fever?"

"Don't feel sick." Tristan exhaled, and his breath frosted the air in front of his face. "Just… crap! What the hell?"

Not only was the room cold, it was breathing. The walls moved in and out in time with Tristan's own breathing, and when he gasped, the room shuddered along with him, its pictures chattering against the plaster like a man's death rattle.

It became a struggle to get air in and out. With each breath, Tristan had to fight harder and harder to keep going. The pressure on his chest grew, and with each stuttering shake in his lungs, the house quaked with him.

The glass in the living room's double sash windows rattled violently, and a pane creaked, spiderwebbing a crack across its face. The army of half-assembled toys on a long table jittered across its surface, a few careening over the edge and hitting the floor below. The sound of porcelain shattering filled the room. Then somewhere in the house, something large fell, a thumping boom echoing through the floorboards.

Sey yelled from outside of the room, screaming at them to get safe, but Wolf was already on the move. Grabbing his aunt, Wolf looked around for someplace safe and settled on a large table. A vase on a nearby sideboard skittered across its length before falling over and rolling against the undulating wall. Cracks appeared across the room's plaster, dark lightning shapes forming through the paint and kicking up small plumes of dust into the air.

"Gildy, get under there!" Wolf guided the old woman under one of the tables, then shoved couch cushions at her to protect her fragile bones. "Tris! Get under the other one!"

He was too cold to move. His joints were frozen up, and Tristan fought to stretch his hand out to Wolf. The cold fog of his breath grew thicker, and he could taste something foul and rotting on the mist. When he finally inhaled, he choked on the dank fear closing his throat.

"Babe? Tristan?" Wolf's voice seemed so far away, and the room was turning black on its edges, speckles of shadow eating away its walls and moving to the floor. "Babe, you've got to move!"

He couldn't say anything. As hard as he tried, Tristan couldn't form any words, and even worse, the air he'd gotten in clotted in his lungs in a sour storm. Wolf's mouth worked in silence, but the fear on his face was nearly as heavy as the rot forming in Tristan's chest. Wolf moved toward Tristan and reached out to grab him.

As Wolf's hand touched his arm, the rattling stopped as suddenly as it began, and the plumes of frost coming from Tristan's open mouth whispered away, leaving the air without a trace. There were small tremors of sound throughout the house as items settled down or rolled up against something solid, but for the most part, the air was heavy with a silence so deep Tristan thought he could hear the cattle breathing outside.

Or, he thought, looking about the room, the shushing noise could have been Gildy hyperventilating from where she crouched under a thick oak table.

"What the hell was that?" Gildy called out from her hiding place. "That was sure as shit no quake."

"I don't know, Gildy." Wolf rubbed at Tristan's arms, his hands moving quickly to create as much friction as he could. "Shit, Tris, you're freezing cold. Are you okay? Did you see anything? What the hell happened?"

"I don't know, but it wasn't an earthquake, Kincaid. Definitely something else." Tristan shivered violently as the day's heat rushed back into him. "I think Sey's place *is* haunted."

"You okay?" Wolf put down the last of their bags. "Better?"

The house had settled down, back to normal, but he still wasn't certain Tristan was fine, especially since it took nearly three minutes before he stopped feeling like an icicle inside.

They'd cleaned up the sparse damage as best they could. There was no fixing the spiderwebbed walls or glass pane, and Sey declared the damage to her toy pile was kept to a minimum. Gildy's insistence on being armed was loudly voted down, and the old woman sulked for a few minutes on the couch, then loudly pointed out they could have been killed by a poltergeist in the time it would have taken her to find her weapon, load it, and fire.

While they were all in agreement about keeping Gildy shotgun-free, none of them had a clue about what triggered the event, and Tristan's flagging energy concerned Wolf enough to press him to lie down for a little while.

It concerned him even more when Tristan readily agreed.

Wolf talked them all into spending some down time before having dinner and talking about the possible reasons for the house's odd behavior. Whatever went down in Sey's living room, it'd also been enough of a rattle for Tristan to agree to sharing a room—and a bed—with Wolf. He even hugged Wolf tightly before following Sey upstairs to one of the sun-filled master suites.

"Yeah. It was just weird. It's been a long time since weird happened to me outside of the Grange. Guess I wasn't expecting it, and it was... okay, *weird*." Tristan bounced experimentally on the room's king-sized bed, cocking his head as if to listen for something. "No squeaking. Good. Although I'm not sure I'd feel comfortable having sex in your cousin's house."

"Shit, wish Gidget and Matt felt like that. I about tore them new assholes for groping each other in the Grange's ballroom." Wolf rubbed at his face, feeling the miles he'd driven crawl over his skin.

"They had sex in my ballroom?" Tristan gaped at his lover. "Really? Weren't they supposed to be working?"

"Trust me, we had the conversation. And thing is, not only do I really like them, qualified techs willing to work crazy hours and on ghost hunts are kind of hard to find." He sat down next to Tristan, testing the feather top's softness. "Besides, it would have been safer if they'd kept to sex. If they had, Gidget wouldn't have tossed Winifred's ring into the pond."

"Okay, sex wins," Tristan agreed as he flopped back onto the bed. He lay there for a moment, then twisted onto his side and sat up to stare at Wolf. "What was that about? Downstairs with your Aunt Gildy? What did she mean about the family not talking to you?"

"How about if we focus on you instead?" Wolf lay down on his side next to Tristan.

He didn't want to talk about his family—not with Tristan's enormous hazel eyes looking bruised around the edges. The man's pupils were still blown out, swallows of black against flecks of green and gold, but they were clear, and Tristan's uncanny ability to see right through him seemed to be in fine working order.

"Less bullshit, Kincaid." Tristan shifted a bit. "More talking. And not about what happened downstairs. I need to take my mind off of that for right now. I'm still a bit freaked out."

"I don't know if I'm comfortable…."

The blond he'd fallen for definitely wasn't going to be denied, but Wolf needed a bit of time to get his brain kicking in. His mind raced still with the excitement from downstairs, and he wasn't quite ready to delve into the depths of his relationship with the rest of the family. Not just yet.

It didn't look like he was going to be given much more time, because Tristan grabbed at his hand and tugged, maneuvering around on the bed so they lay with their heads on the pillows and their bare feet tangled together.

"There. More comfortable." Tristan nudged his shin with his toes. The man's feet were practically prehensile, because his toes nipped and pinched like fingers when Tristan wanted them to. There'd been a moment when Wolf accused him of being able to fold them together like praying hands, and Tristan gleefully showed off he could do just that. "Talk. Or I start tickling."

"Fuck, hon. I don't know where to start." Wolf nudged closer, pressing his body up against Tristan's long length. The connection anchored him, and there was some part of him that lightened when Tristan snuggled in even closer.

"How about at the beginning?" Tristan's breath was hot on Wolf's face, a welcome change from the frosted exhale he'd been sporting down in the living room. "What happened? Is your family really not talking to you?"

"Yeah. It's kind of like the Kincaid clan's version of Amish shunning." Wolf tried to lighten the heaviness growing in his chest. "I've kind of become He Who Shall Not Be Named. Kind of cool in a way."

"Wait, why?" Tristan sat up suddenly, and Wolf immediately missed his touch. "What the hell does that mean?"

"Hey, lie back down. You're supposed to be resting," Wolf urged, guiding his lover back onto the bed. He waited until Tristan nestled against him again, but the man's limbs were taut with tension. "Hey, it's no big deal. Not really. I'm just kind of not welcome at any of the family things—like the yearly get-togethers. Not something I miss. And there's a small thing of the older ones kind of cussing me out when they see me, but that's rare. Most of my sane cousins still talk to me. The ones I like, anyway. Like Cin and Sey. My sister and brother are cool, but they're not—Hellsingers."

"That's fucked. I thought you guys were like this huge Gypsy clan," Tristan whispered, and his face drooped with a painful sadness. "Why didn't you tell me this sooner? And why would they do that?"

"Tell you what? That my whole family pretty much disowned me for becoming a paranormal investigator?" Wolf shrugged off the pangs of regret stinging through him. He longed for the Kincaid camaraderie he'd grown up with, and he'd not thought he'd miss one moment of his boisterous, brash clan until it was suddenly yanked away from him without any real chance to argue his case.

"Yeah, that." Tristan reached up and traced Wolf's mouth with the tips of his fingers. "God, that's shitty. Why would they do that?"

"One of my grandmothers—I've got three because they have this lesbian threesome going—she thought I was going to be a Hellsinger. Like Cin. Hunting down hauntings and freeing spirits. Thing is, I don't know if I believe they're actually doing that. That thing with Winifred—with you? That was the first time I'd really *seen* that kind of activity. Shit, everything I'd learned up until the official shunning was theory, and even that was kind of shaky."

"So what? They don't actually see ghosts? The ones they're supposed to be sending off?"

"See, remember when I told you I wanted to *prove* the existence of ghosts? Of having some way of actually verifying spirits?" Wolf lightly kissed Tristan's wandering fingers. "For as long as I remember, I've always wondered if ghosts were real or if it was just some sort of scam the family was pulling. I mean, I'd seen things I couldn't explain, but I was a kid at the time. And for all of their badass ghost hunting, it's not like they can come back with a pelt or something. So I started really studying up on the paranormal—and not just what the family told me."

"They didn't like that?" Tris cocked his head. "Okay, now it's sounding like a cult."

"No, they're not a cult. Mostly they're fortune tellers, kind of. Like my mom. Owning crystal shops or reading tarot cards, but there are a few of them who actually go out and hunt spirits. Like Cin." Wolf quirked his mouth in a sardonic grin. "Cin's kind of intense and shit. I used to want to be like him when I was a kid, which is kind of stupid since he's only a couple of years older than me, but he was always—leather jacket cool. Probably even when he was in diapers. He can sense ghosts—like Ophelia Sunday—and can tell when something's malevolent. He's the only Hellsinger who'll talk to me. Hell, he's the one who supported me when I told them I was going to be a scientist because I wanted documentation of spectral existence."

"So you were tossed out because you didn't have blind faith?"

"Pretty much," Wolf conceded. "And then you came along, and the whole paranormal thing took a left turn into reality. Now I don't know what to do or what to think. Do I still believe most hauntings are bullshit? Yeah, because it's been few and far between when I've run across something I couldn't explain away. Hell, I'm kind of glad I'm a skeptic because sometimes people are scared—paralyzed by it—and I come along and show them it's not real. I don't think I want to stop doing that."

"What if you come across something that *is* real? What then?"

"Then—shit, I don't know," he admitted softly. "Maybe that's where I need to really stop and think about what I'm doing. Do I study the place? Because, God, I want to go balls-deep into the Grange to see what makes it tick, but suppose I fuck it up? That place is important to you—"

"And I'd kick your ass," Tristan reminded him with a nip on his nose.

"Yeah, there's that. Is my research—my want to prove spectral existence—worth losing you?" Wolf rubbed his thumb over Tristan's high cheekbone. "I've already decided that it's not. So, where does that leave me? Is what I'm doing really going to matter in the long run? Or am I just pulling wings off of faeries?"

"But suppose you *do* find a way to prove there's a ghost? And suppose it's something like Winifred?" Tris sighed. "Shit, we barely survived that. And you guys kind of knew what was going on."

"Okay, I have no idea if my mother knew what she was doing." He nodded at Tristan's wide-eyed stare. "Trust me, babe. Meegan's idea of research pretty much is reading whatever pages aren't stuck together in her cookbook most of the time. The only reason I agreed to her supposed séance was because she'd gotten the info from one of my aunts. I wouldn't have let her take a stab at it otherwise."

"And it's not like they would have spoken to you about how to get rid of the ghost." Tristan shook his head. "Fuck, isn't that like cutting their noses off to spite themselves?"

"They look at me being a scientist as a betrayal." Wolf slid his index finger over Tristan's parted lips. "I'm not saying all of them do, but most. Especially the ones who hold the purse strings. They're suspicious and clannish—where the hell do you think I got it from?"

"Your mom—I mean, Meegan's not exactly the most suburban person I've met. Okay, hell, most of the people I've met are dead and lived before there were suburbs, but still."

"My mom's considered a family radical. None of her kids really cleave to the Kincaid ways. Hell, Bach's a damned chef and owns a restaurant with tablecloths and candles. Definitely not a family way of life." Wolf laughed. "We were raised to have everything we own fitting in one suitcase and being able to skip out on a motel bill at the drop of a hat. The Kincaids walk a fine line between charlatan and exorcist, with very few of them actually being able to shove a ghost off its rocker. But it's what we do, and I, my darling Tristan, rocked that boat so hard you'd have thought they were all on the Titanic and I was the largest, iciest mofo they'd ever seen."

"So you going out to prove things aren't things that go bump in the night is kind of like a slap in their faces? Because you're saying what they do is bullshit?"

"Yeah, pretty much," Wolf murmured. "But see, most of the time, I used to think that. I didn't have *proof*. I couldn't provide any proof, and I still can't. That's what's frustrating about this whole thing, Thursday. If I can just find a way to get evidence, *irrefutable* evidence, I'll be validating everything any Hellsinger past and present has been doing with their lives."

"You're as much of a Hellsinger as they are," Tristan snorted. "You're just working at it from a different point of view. That's all. God, they're fucking stubborn. They should want you to do this. They'd have nothing to lose and everything to gain."

"Yeah, I guess so." Wolf laughed. "So maybe in the end, I'm a Kincaid whether they want me in their clan or not, because I'm just as stubborn about wanting to do this as they are wanting me to quit. I'm not going to give up on this if you're willing to tough it out with me. Not until I can show the world ghosts do really exist, and I'm kind of hoping—if you feel up to it—you'll be willing to help."

Chapter 7

"How long have you known him?"

Sey was sneaky. And for some reason, Wolf'd forgotten exactly *how* quiet and stealthy his cousin actually was. Especially when she wanted to corner someone in a place he couldn't quite run away from without seeming like a yellow-bellied skink.

Her patented ninja ways, however, were a good way to give a guy a heart attack at three in the morning as he watched his sensors flatline with not a peep of phantom activity since the house finished its Linda Blair impression.

"Jesus fucking Christ, Sey! Put some fucking bells on or something!" Taking a deep breath, Wolf got his heart back under control. "Are you *trying* to kill me?"

"If I'd wanted to kill you, I'd have plugged that toaster in and tossed it into your bathtub when you were ten." His cousin refilled his coffee cup from the spare machine he'd found in her pantry. Pulling up a chair to sit next to him, she looked around the house's former maid quarters, taking in the dizzying array of monitors and sensors he'd hooked up. "This is a lot of shit. It's like living in a video game."

"Yeah, sometimes," he admitted sheepishly. "But honestly? It's a fuck of a lot of fun when I get a hit. It's like... a car chase where I can't see anything but the fog."

"You the cop or the thug?" Sey returned his broad grin and crossed her legs on the chair's seat. The rubber soles of her purple footie pajamas scraped on the lounge's plaid fabric. "And don't think I don't know what you just did there. You're avoiding my question—how long have you known Tristan?"

"I wasn't avoiding it. I was ignoring you." Wolf saluted her with his mug of black coffee. "And I told you about Tristan. It's been over a month."

"Moving kind of fast, aren't you?" She studied him, expertly peeling back his protective layers.

"He met Meegan and survived to tell the tale." He grimaced, remembering the anger he'd unleashed on Tristan once the doctored-up honey finally left his system. "I'm not sure *I* did, but he took it like a champ. Between the two of us, he's the one who deserves better, but Tris is still willing to give me a go. So yeah, I'm going to move fast before he changes his mind."

There was more to say—mostly about how Tristan made him happy inside and how Tris and his quirks somehow touched the dark, cold bits in him, left behind when he'd been ripped up by the roots when his family turned their collective backs on him. Everything he was warmed in Tristan's presence, and short of sounding like one of those cards that sang when opened, Wolf didn't know where to begin telling Sey how much Tristan seemed to fit into him—and around him.

The words never reached Sey's ears. As Wolf began to open his soul to his cousin, every piece of equipment on the table lit up and began to sing.

"Shit, here we go." He spun around to focus on the bank of flat screens he'd set up on the other side of the *L* he'd made. The cameras he and Tristan set up hours before flickered and spat back images turned lime green by night-vision lens. A microphone picked up the creaking of someone's weight on the front hall's floorboards, and the camera tracked a shimmering white form gliding toward the living room.

An agile form that looked remarkably like their Aunt Gildy.

The cameras tracked the old woman's progress as she paused long enough to glance up the stairs leading to the upper floor bedrooms, then gleefully skip-hopped over to the study. Sliding something out of a pocket in her nightgown, she jimmied open a glass-fronted china cabinet set against one wall and threw the doors back with wild abandon.

"What the hell is she doing?" Wolf cocked his head. "Isn't that where you keep the booze?"

"Shit, she's not supposed to drink. It screws up her meds." Sey muttered curses under her breath and rose up in her chair. Wolf put a hand on her shoulder to set her back down, and she snarled back, "Look, no one wants her living with them—well, I do. She's weird, and she might shoot my head off, but I like the old bat. I don't want to see her pickled to the gills, and damn it, she's been faking this whole 'I'm an old woman' bit. The only reason I put her on the first floor is because she said she couldn't move well enough to climb the stairs. She's like fricking Ginger Rogers out there."

"You can deal with that in a bit," Wolf said softly. "Look behind her."

A spray of orbs bobbed along behind Gildy, dancing as if pulled by an invisible string. The sensors in the study sent back modulating screeches and clicks to Wolf's equipment, and his EMF meter sang a merry little tune perky enough to inspire an Irish jig.

"I'll be damned. You *are* haunted." He exhaled, glad to see the sensors' response.

"You doubted me?" Sey nudged him hard in the ribs with her bony elbow. "Fuck you. I *told* you I wasn't hoaxing."

"I wasn't thinking you were, but it's not outside of something Gildy would pull just to get attention." Rubbing at the spot, Wolf ducked another dig. "Hey, you're not the only one who's been taken in by the old lady."

"I'm going to have a serious talk with her." Sey frowned. "And shake her down. For all I know she's got an Uzi in her bedroom."

"Shit, she's probably got a tank in there." Wolf jotted down the time of the activity as the camera recorded their aunt's movements.

"This is a damned sight better than walking around the house with an EMF reader and holy water," Sey admitted. "This shit picks stuff up you can see!"

"Problem is, it's infrared, so really, it could be a lot of things. Ambient energy bursts or light specks reflecting off a source we can't see. I'll have to do some spectral analysis. If it repeats night after night in the same spot, then that kind of debunks the activity. Those kinds of things usually prove to be someone coming home at the same time every night from work and their headlights bouncing off of something or a power surge cycling through the grid."

"And if it doesn't repeat?"

"Then you're still kind of screwed because you can't accurately replicate the event. So you've got one instance of orbs, and that's not enough data to be definitive." He reached over and tapped a metal box with a digital gauge running up and down with numbers. "This is an ultrasound monitor. A lot of spectral activity operates on a sub-spectrum below light, so that's something I'm working on getting reliably documented. If I can match up a good tonal record timed to your orbs, it'll reinforce the data a bit."

"Does all of your geekness turn Tristan on?" She pulled her fingers through her hair, making its ends stick up all around her head. "Because you sound like a really badly written porn novel right then."

"Tris outgeeks me any day, and yeah, it's a huge fucking turn-on." He scribbled down notes for his timing check. "You should hear him talking about monster origins. Makes me harder than one of your badly cooked biscuits."

"Hey! My biscuits are fine!"

"Archeologists look at your biscuits and wonder if they're not remains from Pompeii." Sey's elbows flashed again, and this time Wolf couldn't avoid her strikes. Red stars sparked over his vision, and his ribs ached enough he wondered if she broke one. Rubbing at the spots, he scooted his chair a few inches away. "And stop with the praying mantis jabs. Jesus, do you rent your elbows out to ninja or something? Fuck, they're like knives."

"Quit your whining and take it like a man. She's going to get drunk off her ass. I'm going to find her on the floor if we don't say something." Sey sighed. "Really, she's like five pounds soaking wet. My cat's bigger than she is."

On the monitors, they got a clear view of the older woman sipping from a cut-crystal glass, both of her hands folded around its faceted sides. She'd found a thickly upholstered chair to sit in, and with her knees drawn up, she was almost lost in the darkness if it wasn't for the flash of light catching her eyes as the night-vision camera scanned the room.

"You have a cat?" Wolf cocked an eyebrow at her. "Where is it? On the mantle somewhere? Tell me it's stuffed and there's a squirrel dressed in a union suit and a top hat riding it into battle."

"Shut the fuck up, and no, Crowley's just lazy. Most of the time he's sleeping off his breakfast or dinner on my bed. It gets the best sunbeams."

"You named your cat Crowley?" He spared his cousin a glance, then shook his head before returning to watching the monitored study. "That's kind of fucked up."

"Hey, not—God, you're a dick." Sey punched his arm, and Wolf turned to bare his teeth in response.

Laughing, he hooked his hand under the edge of his chair and scooted another few inches away. "Ah, but I found someone who likes my—"

The monitors gave them their first indication something was off. Gildy's chair skittered across the floor, and the woman yelped in surprise.

Her shout jerked Wolf's attention back to the screen just in time to see all hell break loose.

TRISTAN KNEW he was dreaming. Or at least it felt like a dream. His face was numb, and the bed he was lying on seemed to creak under him as he moved. A sliver of moonlight stretched over the unfamiliar white eyelet duvet covering him, and Tristan wondered who moved the window, because he'd never had a gloaming hit him from that side of the room before.

None of the shadows were familiar. His sleek-lined furniture was gone, replaced with heavy bulking forms looming menacingly from spots along the wall.

Even the air smelled different, slightly dryer and less green with a hint of salt in it. There was something earthier beneath the sage and pine, a pungent otherness he couldn't quite identify. It smelled like—livestock of some kind.

He was also cold.

Again.

His limbs were stiff, frozen and tight. At some point in the middle of the night, his spine had crawled away. Probably after Wolf, since it seemed like the bed was empty of one skeptical blue-eyed Scotsman. His Scotsman, in particular.

"Simooooooone…."

The howling started low, then built up, echoing through the suite. It was a child's voice. One burdened with a sadness as deep as the cold in his bones. He'd grown up hearing the laments of children. Sometimes in English. Most often in Chinese. He'd be counted fluent in Cantonese if he only spoke of sorrow and pain.

This child, however, surpassed them all.

There was movement to the side of him, a flicker of white and then a pale blur of something against the darkness. It took every drop of energy Tristan had to move his head, and the muscles in his neck screamed in agony with each inch he gained, but eventually, his cheek hit the pillow, and he could see the thing standing next to the bed.

It was definitely a child.

Or at least the remains of one.

He'd taken care of enough guests at the Grange to know dead children in the past often wore long dresses regardless of gender. Still, something about the nightgown-swaddled form standing next to his shoulder screamed little girl—even if her skull only boasted a few wisps of thin hair. He'd have guessed her to be about seven or eight, but it was difficult to tell since she looked stunted and drawn in. Even draped in a voluminous shroud, he could see the press of her skeletal rib cage through the thin lawn fabric, its sharp shelf curving in over a cadaverous belly.

Sunken, wrinkled skin covered where her eyes should have been, and for the life of him, Tristan couldn't see any seam where she should have had lids. Instead, the concave space was unbroken from the top of her skull down to the thin slash of her lips. Her cheekbones stood out in painful juts, and dark lines webbed out under her skin, mottling her complexion. She looked parched, as if every drop of moisture was leeched from her skin and flesh until the only thing remaining was a husk of rattling bone wrapped in parchment.

And she certainly rattled when she moved, because Tristan heard her bones clacking against one another when she lifted her hand to stroke at his hair. Her fingers were cold and oddly elongated, tipped with broken nails nearly as long as her palm. They ran under the strands along his hairline, feeling less human and more like the scramble of a roach's legs as it fought to clear itself from a spiderweb.

He would have shivered if he could move, but turning his head had depleted Tristan more than he'd have liked to admit, so he lay there, as trapped as the imaginary roach dying in his hair.

"Simone…." Her mouth barely moved, but the word creaked out of her lips. Her throat spasmed with the effort of speaking, and her body swayed back and forth with the effort of standing. "Kiiiiilll yooooooooooooooou."

"I'm not Simone," Tristan croaked over his swollen tongue.

He couldn't be sure the ghost even heard him. There was no reading her eyeless face. Nothing changed on her features. Even the crooning whispers from her slightly parted cracked lips slithered out with a smidgen of movement. Her hand and arm continued to move—stroking down to tangle in Tristan's hair, then sweeping back in a circular motion where she jerked to a sudden stop, only to replicate the motion time and time again.

He would have thought she was a repeater, but there was something anchored about the child, something darker than a flashing bit of personality embossed over the ether. She'd come looking for someone—a Simone who'd left her—and most of the repeaters he'd seen in the past didn't interact with the corporeal world at all.

The little girl shouldn't have been able to touch him if she were an echo. And he certainly wouldn't have been pinned in place by a frigidity so deep he feared his legs would be broken beneath its weight.

"Think, Tristan." Scolding himself seemed to at least jar his brain into some sort of forward motion, because suddenly it scrambled for a way to get off the bed and out of the room. If he could just edge out of her touch, he might be able to break loose.

If being the operative word of his plan, because so far, his legs and arms seemed reluctant to respond, and the nearly mummified little girl was quite content to play with his hair until he eventually joined her.

Fear played with his balls, rolling its icy fingers along his thighs and knees. His spine seemed to be back, locked into a hard line, much like the ghost's lips. Grunting, Tristan tried twisting his shoulders to break contact with the girl's hand, and he was rewarded by the slight squeak of the bed beneath him.

The jostle was enough to pull his head farther away from the young ghost's touch, and she responded by cocking her eyeless head, and her thin mouth pulled back, forming a thick seam that began to stretch inhumanly far back under her sharp cheekbones. The line stretched and stretched until its end points were nearly to her tiny earlobes. Her skin suffered for the pull, thin crackles appearing on her face, and bits of broken skin flaked off. They peeled away from her dry face, catching on some unfelt wind to spiral away from her in a scabrous cloud.

"Hurt meeeeeeeeee." While her expression remained fixed, the rise of her howl grew in screeching steps. Terror filled Tristan's belly, and he choked when a flood of bile rushed up from his guts. She shuffled forward, and her serpentine fingers grabbed a chunk of his hair, wrapping the strands tightly around her bony knuckles. "Simooooooooone."

His mouth worked hard, and he gurgled around the sour pressing on the back of his throat. Coughing, he finally was able to spit out the obstructive fluid, horrified when it bubbled down his chin and over his chest in an oozing black spill.

"Goooooooooooo!" Her head unhinged, broken open at the seam of her exaggerated lips. Broken teeth studded her rotted jaw, and cankerous sores dotted her stretched inner cheeks and tongue. Her throat cracked open, pulled apart nearly to an obtuse angle, and her uvula flapped back and forth in a flaccid dance against the pocked roof of her mouth.

Tristan couldn't find his breath, although the furls of cold mists coming from his mouth told him otherwise. His screams were trapped behind his own tongue, unwilling or unable to make it past the chunk of meat. The ghost's threadbare skull crackled with energy, and her thin strands of fine hair stood out around her face in an unholy halo. The black lines beneath her skin thickened and thinned, gathering in spots along her cheeks, arms, and neck only to scatter out again, much like a spider searching its web for prey.

Tight with rage, the ghost began to scream, an endless brightly pitched howl high enough to make Tristan's ears bleed. He felt something pop along his left eardrum. Then his face started to lose sensation, a numbness creeping down his cheek and lips.

The furniture against the walls shook, and the bed thumped despite his weight. It jumped across the floor, pushed by the ghost's rage. Pictures flew across the room, glass shattering when the frames careened into anything solid. Beneath him, the floorboards buckled, carrying the bed off in its tidal wave flow. Somewhere, someone was crying out, and Tristan wondered if it was his own sobs he was hearing.

Another burst of pain along his eyes hit him, and Tristan knew for sure this time it was his own voice he was hearing. His throat bled with the sound of his pain. The house quaked, twisting into an Escher landscape around his screams. Tristan tried blinking, but his lids refused to move, and dust pummeled his bared gaze, a thousand pinpricks driving down into his eyes.

Just when he thought the pain couldn't get any worse, the little girl mounted the bed, and her spittle-flecked maw hung over his face, spraying him with acidic drops. Her tongue lashed out, winding up around her nose and temple to lick at the flakes coming up off her chafed skin, and when it drew back down into its hollow, its blackened surface glistened with translucent specks as bright as newly fallen snow.

Raising one arm, the little girl slithered up over Tristan's torso and patted his cheek with her gnarled fingers. Bending down, she hissed into

Tristan's aching ear, the edge of her tongue flicking along his lobe as her hand moved down his throat, finally resting on his chest.

"Not living with me again, Simone," the specter whispered. Then she plunged her hand through Tristan's chest, shattering the ice in his veins into a prickled anguish through his blood. The world tilted, and as everything went black, the little girl kissed his cheek and murmured beneath his keening scream, "Not ever again. I won't let you."

"Shit, grab Gildy and get out!" Wolf screamed at Sey as he headed to the door. "Going to find Tristan!"

He barely had time to get out of the room when another rattle grabbed the house. A flash of thin moonlight from the window outlined the tree line, where nothing moved, not even a rustle of wind through the leaves of the oak growing in the side yard. One of the cows mooed sleepily from its stall in the barn behind the house, and a nighttime bird called out, a peaceful croon totally at odds with the chaos tumbling through Sey's home.

Taking the stairs two at a time, Wolf nearly stepped on a puffed-up gray Persian hissing on the landing. The feline's eyes were wild, and it curled back, arching up when Wolf ran past. A tug on his sweats told Wolf the cat snagged him with a claw when he went by, but he kept going, hoping the Persian got loose, or it was going to be pulled behind him like a water skier.

His bare feet squeaked on the polished floor when he turned down the hallway at a jog. A few long strides took Wolf up to their bedroom, and he grabbed at the knob, turning it back and forth, but the latch didn't give. Putting his shoulder to the door's solid heft, Wolf tried the latch again and shoved hard. The door remained stuck in its frame, refusing to budge.

"Fuck this." The floor buckled under him, and Wolf lost his footing, slamming into the landing's high railing. One of the pointed newels dug into his side, and he huffed at the sudden pain. Wolf pushed off the handrail and slammed back into the door, and it cracked under the push of his weight.

Another hit left him reeling, but the door gave, splintering from its frame. Wolf's momentum carried him into the bedroom suite, and he stumbled in, rolling onto the floor before coming to a rest at the foot end of their wrought iron bed.

He lay there for a stunned second, drinking in the silence, until he realized he not only ached along every inch of his body, but the house was quiet, with only the minute sounds of things settling back down echoing through its winding halls.

Standing up took a little bit of effort, but it was worth it. Especially when he realized the heavy panting he heard was coming from the blond man lying on the bed. Staggering to get to his feet, Wolf grabbed at the foot of the bed frame and pulled himself up.

Tristan lay under the duvet, his eyes screwed shut and his fingers fisted into the linens. The covers were wrapped tightly around the man's body from twisting in his sleep, cocooning him in place. If the blond's pained mewls weren't alarming enough, what Wolf saw arranged around his lover's twitching body made his blood run cold.

Every inch of space of the bed was covered, packed in tight with cracked porcelain doll heads, their fragile ivory skulls crazed from impact, and just as Wolf reached over to peel the shattered heads away from his lover's prone body, Tristan's eyes snapped open, and he began to scream.

Chapter 8

"HEY." WOLF nested up behind his lover and slid his hands around Tristan's waist. Pressing his chest into Tristan's shoulders, he laid a kiss on the man's long neck. Sighing contentedly, Tristan relaxed, leaning into Wolf a bit as he stared out into the fog-shrouded pastures beyond the old house.

It was funny how the mere push of Wolf's weight on him made Tristan's heart skip. He couldn't decide if it was because they were touching or just the simple trust the other man had in him, but after a moment of wondering, Tristan realized he didn't care one way or another—so long as Wolf was there, fitting into him as easily as breathing.

Then from the mists, a moo belled, and the sound made Tristan laugh.

It was not just any moo, but a delicate, sweet undulating singing of bovine origin. It warbled and wove about, riding the breeze to the house's wraparound porch.

Unfortunately, so did the particularly ripe smell of a bovine's grass-fed expulsions.

"Ah, you gotta love the country." Wolf rested his chin on Tris's shoulder and snuggled closer. "So romantic. So… pastoral. So—"

"So stinky," Tristan cut in. "I never guessed how stinky the country could be. 'Course all of those barnyard jokes should have been a clue."

"Yeah, I loved coming here as a kid." The man's murmur was wistful, but Tristan wasn't fooled. "I'm glad you got to see it."

"Is this where you do Eddie Murphy's old act and say 'it's a pity we can't stay'?" He snorted when Wolf pulled back a little bit to object. Tristan turned around in the man's embrace, rested his butt on the porch railing, then hooked his arms around Wolf's shoulders. "I can hear you thinking, Doctor Kincaid. You're busy flogging yourself for what happened to me and are trying to figure out a way to get me to go home."

"I was thinking maybe a hotel nearby," Wolf admitted softly. "I can't abandon Sey, but I *did* want to spend time with you."

"Yeah, not going anywhere. I'm not willing to go back into the tower and grow my hair so you can climb up on it whenever you want to show up." He would have laughed at Wolf's offended expression if he didn't think the man'd been quite serious about trying to shield him from what happened. "You can't protect me from myself, Wolf. Because what happened here isn't because of you. It's because of me."

"If I hadn't brought you—"

"Things like what happened today—well, whenever we're counting it—have been going on around me since I was born." Out of the fog, another low belling echoed, followed by an answering call. Wolf refused to meet his eyes. The man's gaze drifted over Tristan's shoulder, so he gripped Wolf's chin to recapture the attention. "*You* didn't do this to me. *I* did this to me. It's been a long time since I've had an event, because the Grange is kind of set up to channel passing spirits or something, but before then, this kind of shit happened all the time. Hell, Wolf, do you think this was the first time I've been woken up by something wanting to get in my mind?"

"Not like this." Wolf shook his head. "This was…."

"This was just like a few hundred other times. Why do you think I ran away to Uncle Mortimer's?" He cocked his head to match Wolf's confused tilt. "San Francisco is probably one of the most haunted places in the state, and there I go, being born right into it. Hell, one of my first memories was a ghost. Pretty sure it won't be my last."

"I don't want that for you, babe." Wolf sighed, wrapping his arms tighter around Tristan's waist. "I want you to be happy and… I don't know what else."

"You want me to be normal," Tristan corrected gently. "Hate to break it to you, Kincaid, but that's *never* going to happen."

"You *are* normal. *Your* normal." Wolf's lips left a butterfly kiss on the corner of Tristan's mouth, and he couldn't help but smile at the wistful tone in Wolf's voice.

"Did I tell you I had an older brother?"

"No, you didn't." The cattle were moving closer, their soft rolling calls growing louder. "What happened?"

"I don't know. He died way before I was born. I think he was maybe one or a little bit older when he passed." Shrugging, Tristan tried to remember anything he'd heard about the child who'd come before him. "No one in the family talks about it. Something went wrong, I think. No one says *anything*, but see, I remember always hearing a baby crying.

Like it was in pain. I'd tell my nannies I heard it, and they told me it had to be cats outside or something."

"Nannies?" Wolf's eyebrows soared up across his forehead.

"Yeah, I had a few. They kept leaving for saner kids," he said with a chuckle. "The point is, that's one of my first memories. Hearing a baby wailing in the middle of the night. When I was about four or five, I told my mother about hearing the crying, and I asked her if we could make him feel better. See, I knew he was my brother. Something inside of me *knew* who was crying even though no one'd told me about him—about Percival. I think it was the last time my mother was alone with me. She was…. I don't know if she was angry or scared or maybe a little bit of both, but after that, she avoided me like I was a shambling leper with bells on."

"You were her kid!" Wolf let loose a few curses under his breath. "Shit. Babe—"

"That's what I love about your mom. She'll never turn away from you. And yeah, she leaves hallucinogens around the house, but really, easily avoidable," Tristan teased.

"I told you not to eat her cooking," Wolf pointed out. "It's something in the family, I swear. It's like they all channel Sweeny Todd or something. But Tris, your mom probably loved you. She just hurt for your brother."

"No, she didn't love *me* enough. When she and my father died, suddenly Percival wasn't the only one crying in our house. I'd lay in bed listening to her crying and calling for him." He had to close his eyes, hoping to drive away the pain laden in his memories, but it stung anyway, an angry, vicious scorpion hidden among innocuous underbrush. "The rest of the family already thought I was crazy, so it wasn't like I could go to anyone and say my mother was there in the house. But she would roam the halls and call for the baby. I never saw her, but she'd walk by my room, and I used to wonder why I hadn't been enough for her. My mother couldn't stand me. I was too weird—too different—too *me*."

"Shit, Thursday—"

"See, I knew I was broken. From an early age. Because dead people visited me or walked through me. I was the only one who saw or spoke to them. I learned Chinese from murdered prostitutes, and really what I got isn't useful for normal conversation, but I can certainly ask if you want a reverse jade dragon or a phoenix rising threesome." Tristan slid his hands up to Wolf's cheeks, rubbing at the scruff he found there. "And it was okay to be weird at the Grange because I couldn't get hurt."

"You're not broken, Tris." Wolf kissed his palms. "You're *not*."

"That's not the point," he said sadly. "I've been hiding in that tower, and whether I knew it or not, I grew my hair long enough for you to climb up it and visit me there, but Wolf, I don't want to stay there. I want to be with you. Out here. And it's time I kind of embraced the weird I've been given. Even if it scares the fucking hell out of me. I've got to start living. I can't be my mother and spend my afterlife looking for something or someone I'll never have again. I need to have this now—I need to have *you* now."

"You have a life, babe. You do." Wolf shook his head, and Tristan laughed. "Don't mock your life. It's a good one."

"It's a bookmark. Mara was right. It's like I'm waiting for Death to come to me, and hell, it has. In little bits and drabbles, Death visits me. I live through the ghosts that come to me. I've got to *not* do that anymore, Wolf. And I'll either do it with or without you, but I'd rather do it with you."

"So what are you asking me?" His smile was nearly as wistful as the sound of the cattle mooing behind them. "What are you saying, Tris?"

"I guess I'm asking you to do a little bit of living with me. What do you say, Kincaid?" Tristan took a deep breath and plunged in. "Want to go ghost hunting with me?"

THE CAMEL made his appearance from over the rise a few moments after Tristan went in to get some sleep. Wolf was saluting the ungulate's arrival with a jaunty wave of his hand when the screen door behind him squeaked open. A second later, Sey edged up next to him with a mug of steaming hot coffee, tiny dollops of cream dancing across its swirling surface as she set it down on the porch's broad rail.

"Here you go, kiddo. Drink up." Sey gave her pet camel her own salute, lifting her mug as he chewed a mouthful of grass.

"Anything boozy in this?" Wolf sniffed at the cup. "Because I could really get drunk right now."

"It's six in the morning," Sey scoffed.

"Right, it's got to be at least six thirty before we can get hammered. How could I forget?"

"How's your boy doing?" Sey rubbed at Wolf's shoulders, and he tried to shake off the tension building down his spine. "Tristan certainly can take a kick to the balls. Wouldn't have thought that about him."

"Tired as shit, but he's passed out," Wolf replied wearily. "Fucking hell, Sey. This is insane."

It had to have been the last bit from the third pot they'd brewed, and it was as bitter and sour at the end as it was at the start of their long morning, but Wolf didn't care. It was hot, and the acidic, oily sting would at least keep him awake for a few more minutes.

That's all he needed. A few more minutes, then he could go collapse with Tristan in the bedroom next to Sey's. One thing was for certain. Even if he'd been able to fix the door he'd broken, he wasn't going to have Tris sleep in that room again. Not after what he'd gone through. With Gildy safely asleep and Crowley the cat once more laying claim to Sey's windowsill, he'd needed some time to think before joining Tristan, watching the sun valiantly fight a losing battle through the morning fog.

He'd kind of grown up in the house. With Meegan's nomadic lifestyle, it'd been a safe haven—someplace permanent he could always find in the same condition as when he left it. Visiting his paternal grandparents every once in a while hadn't been the same. Their too prim and proper estate made being a kid uncomfortable, and Wolf was always very aware of how grubby the Kincaid brood was when compared to the fine china and sideboard set his grandparents ran with.

If Sey hadn't moved into her mother's house when the old lady took off for—knowing her—warmer climes, he would have offered to buy it. It was *home* of sorts—solid and dependable.

And now under siege by an entity Tristan described in horrifying detail.

"I shouldn't have brought him here, and now he's arguing with me that he *should* be here because he wants to live more." He took another sip of coffee, taking penance in its taste. "Jesus fucking Christ, it's like I'm *trying* to kill him, and he's just skipping along like it's a visit to grandma's house with his picnic basket."

"You didn't know, kiddo." Sey snuggled up next to him, leeching some of his warmth. "I asked you to come down because stuff kept moving around when no one was here. Who the hell expected some angsty evil ghost cosplaying Geordi La Forge? I sure as fuck didn't."

"Yeah, she was missing the banana comb. Shit, Sey, all I have is my fucking—" He needed to kick something, something with lights that maybe beeped when something changed on a spectrum no one but him gave a shit about. "I went to school for this kind of crap—"

"You went to school to become a scientist, honey." Sey's tone was gentle, but Wolf heard the thread of reproach woven through it. "You're not a Hellsinger. You walked away from that, remember? No one expects you to know what to do with this kind of thing. Hell, *I* don't know what to do with this kind of thing."

"I *know* how these things work." Suddenly the coffee in his stomach churned, curdling in his guts. "I've spent my entire—well, not life—but a pretty good chunk of it trying to parse out the *why* of ghosts, and I know jack shit about turning them. Fucking hell, I had to ask *Meegan* to help me get rid of a poltergeist my people brought to Tristan's doorstep. And now this?"

"I'm going to say it again, Wolfgang. You are *not* a Hellsinger. Sure, you've picked up some stuff from the family. We all have. But this kind of crap is out of our league. We're going to need to call in the big guns, but I don't know who'll come. Maybe one of the younger ones, but we definitely need help." Sey stroked at his hair, soothing away the prickles of anger tightening his neck. "Can your ego handle that?"

"*My* ego? Probably not. I *am* a Kincaid," he admitted. "But I know Tris. If he's got his teeth into something, he's not going to back down. And hell, I'm not sure I'd want him to. He's strong, Sey. He can do things—see things—and he got the rug yanked out from under him because—"

"Of you." Sey rolled her eyes. "Yeah, I got that part of it. Question is, what are we going to do about this shit? And are you *sure* we can't ship him home? Maybe drugging him so he's out of it when we pack him up. Oh I know, he can take Gildy with him too."

"Yeah, good luck on that." His laugh was nearly as bitter as his coffee. "He won't go. Hell, he pretty much told me to pull up my big boy boxers and get ready to do battle. How do I deal with that? How do I keep him safe?"

"He's not yours to keep safe, Wolf. He's yours to love and maybe have fights with, but Tristan's sure as hell not a pushover. You, little cousin, are going to have to learn how to compromise, but it was good to dream." Sey drained her cup, then set it down on the rail. "Hell, the ranch guys will be here soon. I'm going to meet with them and then head to bed. I'm getting too old for this shit."

"Sleep sounds fantastic. Let's just hope we don't get another visit from Blind Dog Betty. I don't think my heart can take it." Wolf watched the camel dip his head down for another mouthful of damp grass. There was one person he could call. Someone more dangerous than his mother, that was for sure, but all in all, he'd be safe from accidentally waking up next to a hookah-smoking caterpillar. Glancing at his watch, he sighed, "Shit, it's way too fricking early."

"Early? For what?" Sey covered her mouth, her jaw cracking in a yawn. "Not bed, that's for sure. It was past bedtime about three hauntings ago."

"No, for a phone call," he grumbled and rubbed his face.

"Not to sound like a cliché, but who are you going to call?"

"The one person with mojo in the family that I *know* will come help me." Wolf gave his cousin a hooded glance. "I'm going to call Cin, and I hope to God he's someplace nearby."

STEPPING OVER the bin filled with shattered doll heads he'd pulled away from Tristan's sleeping form, Wolf sat down on one of the living room couches. He'd gone upstairs to check on his lover, making sure to leave a thick line of rock salt along the sills and across the doorway before he came back down. Fatigue trailed after him, running to catch up with his bones and seizing him every so often, like a game of tag he'd never win. His skin even felt tired, and Wolf wondered what had happened to his orderly world and why he never wanted to go back to it.

Tristan.

Damn it, his life had been perfectly fine before Tristan Pryce, but fine wasn't how he'd ever wanted to live. Growing up as a Kincaid, he'd learned to despise pedestrian and safe, but there he'd been, resting on laurels while chasing after a nebulous dream.

"But am I using him?" Wolf played with his phone, turning it over in his hands. "Shit and hell. What the fuck am I going to do?"

He'd spent his career searching for viable, documentable paranormal activity, and now he had a lover who pretty much called ghosts out to play everywhere he went. Sey was talking to someone outside, but he tuned everything out except what he needed to say to Cin.

His slightly older cousin had been born cool; Wolf was sure of it. Stronger willed than any of the bossy women who ran the family, Cin soaked up every bit of Hellsinger knowledge offered to him, strapped on his own brand of raising Cain, and headed off to the world to fight demons—his own and others'.

But would he be willing to fight Wolf's demons as well? Wolf stared at his phone, wondering if his big bad cousin would cross very firmly drawn family lines and come to his rescue.

"Only one way to find out," he scolded himself. Then he made the hardest call he'd ever had to make in his life.

"'Lo?" Cin picked up before the first ring even faded from Wolf's ear, and the man's rough, deep voice sounded dragged down with sleep. "That you, Wolf? What fucking time is it? Where the fuck are you?"

"I'm at Sey's." He wasn't going to waste time with formalities. "And I need you here, Cin, if you can."

"What's up?" Cin's sleepiness was gone, and Wolf imagined, by the sounds coming through the phone, Cin was up out of bed and shoving things into a duffel bag. "Whatcha need?"

"I need a Hellsinger, man." Wolf took a deep breath, breaking a vow he'd made to himself decades ago. "And I need you to teach me how to be one."

Chapter 9

THERE WAS salt across the doorway to the small room off the back porch entrance, and Tristan was very careful not to break the line as he stepped across the threshold. Elsewhere in the cavernous house, voices bounced back and forth as Wolf and Sey wasted their breath trying to convince Gildy to relocate to another relative's house until they could dislodge the spirit haunting the former inn.

Gildy, much like he had himself, pretty much found different ways of telling them both to fuck off.

The tiny room glittered where the sun hit its salted sills, small prisms kicking up through the open lace curtains hanging on either side of the room's wide windows. Even with the wraparound porch's overhang, the sun seemed determined to reach into the space, lighting up a sea of dust motes hanging in the still air.

Like much of the house, the room was thick with paint and steeped in history. The walls were aged, whispering to Tristan of past conversations and liaisons. His imagination ran with the possibilities of what could have happened in the tucked-away room at the back of the former inn. Had someone slept here and dreamed of bigger things? Or had it been a place to shove the debris of others' lives?

Whatever purpose the room might have once had, Sey used it to store fabrics and a few pieces of furniture too heavy to lug up to the attic—including a deep-seated, battered antique divan upholstered in an ugly mustard jacquard they'd been all too happy to cover with a sheet.

They'd piled all of the dolls' parts on one end of the divan, carefully arranged so everything could be gone over at a later time. For Tristan, that time was now, especially since the other two were busy fighting a losing battle with an old woman barely tall enough to ride a car in Autopia.

"Okay, Tristan, let's see what we can find out about this stuff here. Maybe something's written on one of them." He rolled his eyes at the thought. "Right, because this is just an episode of *Angel*, and everything

I need to know about this week's episode, I'll find written on the back of a doll's head."

Frowning, he took a step across the wood floor, pausing when it creaked beneath him. But after finding out Wolf's mother copied what they needed to banish the Grange's malicious spirit from a book marked Banishments and Curses, for all he knew, the back of a doll's head was exactly where he needed to look.

"Stranger shit has happened," he muttered, remembering his epic battle with Winifred's rogue tongue. "Hell, I've been some of that stranger shit."

He didn't know what he was going to find, but it gave him something to do other than fret.

Not wanting to sit on the bed with the doll bits, he grabbed a high-backed wooden chair and dragged it over to the edge of the sofa. Pressing his knees into the beaten-up cushions, Tristan reached for the largest piece, a doll head, nearly perfect except for the large Y shaped crack across its cheek and ear.

It was old. He didn't need anyone to tell him that. The doll's eyeless sockets were chipped on the edges, and it felt gritty in his hand, a fine powder clinging to his fingers when he rolled it around on his palm. Tristan couldn't imagine the delicate, tangerine-sized head would have been able to stand up to the rigors of a little girl's playing.

But then, he reasoned, the only experience he'd had with little girls were the ones who punched and teased him in elementary school—a particularly vicious breed of child only found in the hallowed halls of an educational institution.

It was a standard head, or so he imagined. The glue marks along its skull hinted it might have had hair at some point, but he couldn't make out the color of its wig. Faint lines of paint clung to the creases in its lips and ears, dark smudges on its crumbling gray face.

"Okay, remember, I have no idea what I'm doing here, so be gentle," he told the doll head. "Supposedly a medium can see things when they touch something. Let's see if that actually works."

Cupping the doll head in both hands, Tristan stared into its emptied eyes, reaching down into himself and closing out any stray thoughts he might have.

He lasted about thirty seconds before his brain tickled back with a question about what kind of cookies Sey might have in her kitchen.

"Oatmeal, I think, mister. Maybe some of those cinnamon chocolate ones she makes sometimes."

A deep voice behind him startled Tristan, and he dropped the doll head. It seemed to bounce off his fingers as he tried to catch it, but the head was determined to die, and it continued its deathly descent, arching almost gleefully to hit the floor. It shattered, breaking into tiny bits and powder, with only a single forlorn ear left of its existence.

"What the fuck?" Tristan turned, the chair scraping on the floor as he shoved it back.

He could see through the young black man. Filmy and translucent, the man was broad and thick-bodied, sporting a short bristle cut over his square head. Although shorter than Tristan, he appeared to loom in the room, his ghostly overalls sticky with viscera and mud. Despite the nearly bestial jut of his features, the man's eyes were soft and his movements were gentle, as if he would take special care with anything he touched.

"Sir?" The man was younger than Tristan initially thought. "Are you okay? I can get the missus if you want me to."

Although muscular to the point of massive, his downy cheeks and faint mustache put him barely at the dusk of adolescence. The button-up shirt he wore under his overalls was worn at the collar, and he'd rolled the cuffs up to expose his thick forearms. His hands were scarred, and his knuckles were barked with small cuts, bled dark over his ghostly pale flesh. Heavy work boots left a trail of faint muddy prints behind when he walked toward Tristan, but they faded after a few seconds.

He followed Tristan's gaze to the floor, and a horrified look transformed his rugged face from Samarian to ashamed teenager. "Gawd, Mrs. Kincaid's sure to lose her head if she sees me tracking mud across her floors. Can't graduate without a head. Where'll they put that hat?"

"Wait!" Tristan stood and, without thinking, reached for the young man's arm when he turned to leave. His hand passed right through the specter's bicep, but the ghost didn't seem to notice. Instead, he paused and looked curiously back at Tristan. "Promise I won't tell anyone you left the mud behind."

"She'll know," the young man said in his soft rumble. "It's because she's a mom. My mom always knows. But she pays good, and she don't mind me coming after classes. The missus wants me to graduate college. Says it's as important as me playing ball. Football's a heck of a lot easier than engineering, but I like knowing how things work more than I like taking other guys apart."

"What's your name?" Tristan knew he had to seize the ghost before he whispered away. The young man didn't seem like a repeater, not with as much as he interacted. Maybe someone more like the Grange's Old London Cook, a spirit tied to caring for others in the afterlife.

"Raymond, but most people call me Raygun or Ray." He shrugged. "They say I kind of look like Flash Gordon—well, if he were a black man from the valley. I don't think so, but it makes my ma smile, so I don't mind."

"Can I ask you a few things?" Dusting off his palms, Tristan saw the ghost flicker momentarily. "Shit, that's what's keeping you here. That doll head."

Bending down, he tamped his hands into the head's gritty remains and focused on the young man in front of him. Raygun was definitely clearer. The denim of his overalls gleamed a faint blue, and his crew cut had a definite silky sheen to it.

"Whatcha need to ask? Because I've got to get my work done soon. We're taking the bus up to San Francisco this evening. Going to be playing Bowling Green State out in Ohio the day after next." He cracked his knuckles, an ominous sound despite his cherubic smile. "Gonna whip some Toledo butt. Show them Cal Poly Mustangs are something to be reckoned with."

If Raygun was a specialized repeater like Cook, Tristan was hoping he'd retain some memory of the other ghosts in the area who were around while he was haunting.

"Have you seen a little girl around here lately?" he ventured softly, only partially relieved when the young man's expression turned to one of sheer terror. Nodding, Tristan reassured him with a gentle tone. "Yeah, I got that from her too. Why don't you tell me everything you know?"

"I'M NOT going anywhere," Gildy insisted.

She'd come out of her room dressed for battle in khaki cargo pants too long for her short legs and a flowery pink bathing cap. After stomping past the cousins, she sat down at the kitchen table with a pair of scissors and began to hack off the ends of her pants to make them fit. The rubbery flowers on her cap bobbed as she moved, distracting Wolf as he tried to reason with her.

Unfortunately, he'd come too close to the woman, and her bad habit of gesturing with her hands as she spoke ended up with Wolf gaining a shallow stab wound in his side and Gildy's sorry-not-sorry apology being lost beneath Sey's scold.

"It's not safe," Wolf said for the fifth time. It probably would be safer for *them* if Gildy was gone. Spotting a pair of butterfly knives sticking out of a pocket of her oversized pants, Wolf leaned down and relieved her of her weapons. "You *cannot* go around with weapons. You're going to hurt someone with these."

"Those are perfectly safe! And I've never accidentally...." Her gaze drifted down to the bloody spot on his T-shirt, and her face flushed slightly. "Well, shit. You should know better than to come at someone when they've got something sharp in their hands. You'd think it was your first time around a pair of scissors!"

"What have you got on you, old woman?" Wolf moved to check her other pockets, but Gildy fended him off with the shears.

"Come near me, and I'll shiv you like the dog you are," she grumbled. "I'm not going out there without something to defend myself."

"Ghosts can't hurt you!" Sey muttered as she filled a coffee filter with ground beans. "Just give him what you've got, Gildy."

"Can't hurt me? Tell that to your boy toy, Trixie." Gildy snorted at Wolf.

"Tristan," he corrected absently, shaking each of her pockets and pulling out what he found. "Trixie was... is my intern."

The haul was another two knives—one paring and one Swiss Army— as well as a set of brass knuckles and a handset from a vintage seventies phone, a sawed-off connector cord dangling from the speaker bulb.

Holding up the phone remnant, Wolf quirked an eyebrow at his aging aunt. "Really, Gildy?"

"Those things are fucking awesome," she piped up. "You can do some serious damage with one of those. I once took out three bank robbers with just a phone and a knitting needle. Use what's around you, boy. First rule of being a Hellsinger."

"The first rule of being a Hellsinger is to reassure people you're not crazy," Wolf replied caustically. "And cut the addled old lady act. You're about as fuzzy as a bowling bowl."

"Do you *want* people to know I've got all my marbles?" Gildy leaned over to whisper as she elbowed him in the side she'd stabbed earlier. "I've waited decades to be able to pull off the old lady shtick so people underestimate me. You *trying* to get me killed by blowing my cover?"

"At least lose the swim cap." He tugged at one of the flowers. "You reek like an old bathmat wearing that shit."

"Kind of don't want to." Gildy jerked her head toward Sey. "I kind of found some of the girl's crazy hair stuff and tried it out. You know, just to see how it'd look."

"You know I can hear you, right?" Sey flicked the coffeepot on, then turned around, crossing her arms over her chest. "Okay, Aunt Gildy. Let's see it. What did you do now?"

"How bad can it be?" Wolf's jaw dropped when the elderly woman slowly tugged off her cap and her hair sprung up around her head, a riot of blues and purples tipped with dark oranges and red. "Holy fucking shit, you're a damned were-parrot."

A slamming car door jerked their attention away from Gildy's kaleidoscope hair, and Sey craned her neck to see out of the kitchen window toward the front of the house. "You expecting someone?"

"Just Cin, but not for hours yet. He had to wrap up a few things." Wolf tossed Gildy's contraband onto the kitchen table. "Leave it there, Gil. I mean it. I'm not having you walk around like a Ginsu commercial while we're trying to deal with this ghost shit."

"Well, *someone's* here." Sey muttered as she crossed the kitchen floor. "And it better not be another reporter looking for the famous Gildy Wallenda. You've milked that old chestnut for the last damned time."

"Hey, that story's always good for a drink in Vegas!" the old woman shouted at Sey's back. Shooing Wolf with a wave of her hand, she grumbled, "Might as well go after her and see who that is. I'm not going to touch any of it."

"Yeah, like I believe you." Wolf scooped up the weapons he'd found and shoved what he could into his pockets. The handset was a problem, but tossing it on top of the fridge was as good a place as any to keep it out of Gildy's reach. "Try to stay out of trouble for at least ten minutes. And whatever you do, don't *kill* anybody."

The sky changed in the time it took Wolf to go from the kitchen to the front hall. One moment he was walking through sunbeams. Then in his next breath, the light in the house shifted and he was walking through a pearly gray, with a threatening rumble rolling around at the edges of the sky. With every step he took toward the front door, the light dropped, until he was forced to hit a switch on the foyer wall to turn on the old chandelier hung from the hall's high ceiling.

The faux candlelight bulbs hummed and threw off a soft golden glow bright enough to be captured in the antiqued tin medallions surrounding its cord. At the end of the hall, Sey stood with the door wide open, ushering in a tall faux-bookish man carrying two old-fashioned pieces of luggage.

Wolf recognized the type. SLO catered to that kind of man—and women as well. His thick black glasses weren't functional if the lack of distortion behind the lenses gave Wolf any clue. Unlike Tristan's formerly functional glasses, the man wore the spectacles as a statement rather than to see through. He was the kind of man who could speak eloquently about artisanal sugars and which indigenous animal shits out the best coffee beans to produce the perfect brew.

With his artfully tousled brown hair and expensive, carelessly draped clothes, he was the perfect embodiment of every asshole Wolf went to college with—an entitled pain in the ass who would one day drown like a turkey if he stood in the rain because he was too entranced with the water coming down from the sky rather than seeking shelter.

And Wolf hated him on sight.

Irrationally perhaps, but he'd always been right in following his instincts, and right at that moment, his gut told him to grab the man by the seat of his perfectly rumpled corduroys and toss him back out the front door.

Sey's nervous but welcoming smile forestalled *that* idea, but Wolf didn't take it totally off the table—not yet.

"Wolf, I want you to meet Daylen Lee-Smythe. He'll be staying here with us for a few weeks. Daylen, this is my cousin, Doctor Wolf Kincaid." Sey hashed out a quick introduction. "Wolf is a parapsychologist— among other things."

"Ah, one of the soft sciences," the other man drawled. "It's good to meet you, Doctor. I hope I won't be too much in the way while I'm working with Professor Kincaid."

"Yeah, I doubt that." Wolf cocked his head, debating where he'd start breaking bones in the man's slender body. "Can't imagine you'll be getting in the way for all of the five minutes you'll be here."

"Hold on a moment, Daylen." Sey motioned toward the general direction of the living room. "Why don't you put your bags there, and we can get you sorted out in a bit."

"Charmed." Daylen clipped the word off with a brittle iciness that didn't match the pleasant expression he'd plastered on his handsome face. The young man's aristocratic nose tilted a bit as he cruised Wolf, a flicker of interest firing up in his blue eyes. It died nearly as soon as it appeared, and he smiled with a patented fake warmth at Sey before trundling his bags into the other room. "Thank you, Professor Kincaid. I'm looking forward to working with you."

"What the hell?" Wolf hissed under his breath. "Who the hell is that? And when the fuck have you been called Professor Kincaid?"

"He's an exchange student from Canada. And I've been a Professor at Cal Poly for years, mostly graduate students. How the hell do you think I pay for all of this? Fixing broken dolls? Well, okay, I *teach* about history and restoration, so I guess it does pay the bills a bit," Sey muttered hotly. "Really, Wolf. You're not the only one in the family with a brain."

"I never said that," he protested. "What is he doing *here*?"

"I agreed to an exchange program—one where the student would stay with me and be immersed in reconstructing fragile porcelain antiques. With Gildy staying here and this damned haunting, I forgot he was showing up today."

"Well, send him back!" Wolf grumbled. "We're trying to figure out what the hell is wrong with this place! Do you want people to know you think you've got ghosts?"

"It's only Ontario." Gildy popped her head up around Wolf's elbow. Both cousins jumped, and Sey put her hand over her heart, patting her chest. "What? That's only a couple of hours to drive. Hell, knock him over the head and dump him in the trunk. I'll take him down myself."

"Ontario in *Canada*, Gildy. Not the one by Chino," Sey corrected. "You didn't notice the accent?"

"Nah, I just figured he was being an asshole. Putting on airs and all that kind of shit." She snorted and jerked her thumb at the living room. "Tell me he doesn't come across as an asshole."

"Well, I can't get rid of him. You're just going to have to act like this is one of your jobs, Wolf." His cousin held up her hand before he could protest. "Look, you and Tristan can work this out, and Cin's going to be here in a bit. I'll keep Mr. Lee-Smythe busy while you guys figure it out. It's not like I can do anything. I'm about as useful around a ghost as Gildy here is."

"Damn it, I was a very good Hellsinger!" The old woman shook her bathing cap under Sey's nose, grazing Wolf's face with rubber flowers as she swung her arm about. "I came here to relax between jobs!"

"You threw holy water on the mayor of Sacramento because you said he was possessed by an onion demon," Sey reminded her. "It was either come here or stay a few months in jail."

"Shoulda chosen jail," Gildy muttered.

"Still an option!" Sey replied cheerily. "Seriously, Wolf. Just… figure out whatever this thing is. I want to go back to my normally scheduled life. Or as close as I can get to with Gildy here."

"Hey, I found something—" Tristan came out of the back of the house just as Daylen Lee-Smythe emerged from the living room, an impatient look on his finely drawn features. They nearly ran into each other at the juncture in the hall, and Daylen threw his hands up to capture Tristan's shoulders as the blond swayed unsteadily to a stop.

"Well, who do we have *here*?" Sey's exchange student purred. Any hint of conceit faded from Daylen's face, and Wolf watched in abject fury as the young man's hands roamed down Tristan's arms and came to rest on his lover's slender hips. "Are you studying with Professor Kincaid too? Tell me we're sharing a room."

"Yeah, Sey, tell you what—you keep your damned student away from me and Tristan, and I promise I won't fucking kill him," Wolf growled at his cousin. "Because right now, that looks like it would be the solution to *all* of my problems."

Chapter 10

"THAT'S TRISTAN. He's my… partner," Wolf drawled, walking past Sey's newly minted intern to slide his hand across the small of his lover's back. "He's here visiting with me."

"I think I've lost something in this conversation." Extracting himself from Daylen's grasping hands, Tristan stepped back. "Um, who are you? Is this Cin? And what happened to Gildy's hair?"

"Toucan skull-fucked me. It stained," the old woman muttered.

"Gildy!" Sey and Wolf barked together.

"Let me introduce myself. I'm Daylen Lee-Smythe, late of Ontario. Canada, that is. Apparently, California has one as well," the stranger offered up, and his hands were back, this time stuck out in front of him for Tristan to shake. "I'm here to learn about antique restoration from Professor Kincaid."

"You restore antiques?" Tristan poked Wolf in the ribs, teasing. "You never told me that."

"Not me, Sey. I'm Doctor." He fended another stab off, grabbing Tristan's wrist. "She's the Professor."

"If I were you, I'd rather be Ginger," Gildy complained. "She was hot. I'd have gone gay for her. Maybe even Mary Ann too."

"So you investigate ghosts too?" Daylen sidled up to Tristan. His fingers were back, going places only Wolf had been. "You're going to have to tell me about it."

It felt… odd having another man's touch on his skin, and Tristan fidgeted, putting as much distance as possible between the man's roving hands and his own body. Another step made him feel better, then another. Before he knew it, he'd slammed Wolf up against a hall table and still felt like he needed another mile or so away from Sey's student.

The photographs on a Queen Anne table rattled when Wolf's hip struck its edge, and Gildy jumped. Reacting quickly to the noise, the old woman shoved her hand down a pocket and came up with a handful of rock salt, which she flung at the rocking table.

Unfortunately for Wolf, she caught him full in the face as he scrambled to catch the frames before they hit the floor.

"Are you fucking insane, Gildy?" Wolf followed up with a string of blistering Gaelic Tristan was sure could be heard back a few generations.

"Don't give me any of your shit, boy," the old woman growled back. "I've got cayenne on the other side."

"Kitchen," Tristan ordered Wolf. "Let's wash your eyes out. And don't antagonize her. She'll saltpeter you next."

"Don't give her any ideas," he mumbled. "I'm going to see if I can guide dog my way to the kitchen."

"I'll get Daylen settled. Then I'll come help." Sey ran her hands through her hair, tugging it with her fingers in frustration. She looked like Tristan felt—overly tired and needing a good meal or at least something strong and alcoholic, but the woman shook her head when Tristan offered to help with Daylen. "No, you go on."

"I certainly can assist," Daylen pronounced loudly. "I'm certified in first aid and common emergency medical procedures. It was a requirement for the trek I made through Nepal and Tibet. You'd be fascinated to find out how similar many exotic insect infestations in the human skin resemble salt burns. I would be glad to—"

"We're good." Tristan smiled tightly at Sey. Wolf was already gone, having disappeared down the hall toward the kitchen. "Maybe Gildy can help you too."

"She'd better, or Wolf's going to skin her alive." Sey nudged her aunt. "Come on, lady. You and I need to have a serious talk."

"Look, with all the ghosts and earthquakes, you can't blame a woman for being a little jumpy!" Gildy protested. "Look at what that scamp did to blondie here! Do you think I want to wake up packed in like I'm a skull in a Paris catacomb? I think not! Better safe than sorry."

"Ghosts, you say?" If anything, Daylen's glowing smile brightened to nearly nuclear levels, and Tristan wondered if they made lead sunglasses so he wouldn't lose his eyes. "I *love* haunted houses! This place is haunted? Is that what you're studying? Is it a White Lady or something more sinister, like a rejected suitor coming to kill his rival?"

"We don't know what is happening, per se." If possible, Sey's sigh seemed to get heavier with each passing second. "Wolf's here to study what might be a phenomena. The house is a historical landmark of sorts, so there might be something to it, but honestly, we don't know."

"The boy woke up from a dead sleep with doll heads staring up at the ceiling!" her aunt proclaimed loudly. "Phenomena my ass! That's a full-out fucking haunting. First class spooky. Half of those damned things were clown dolls. It doesn't get any more scary than that."

"Gil, get upstairs and help me get Daylen's room ready. We'll put him in the back bedroom," Sey ordered. "And don't give me any shit about not being able to move well. I watched you sneak easily enough to the liquor cabinet the other night. Daylen—"

"You can call me Dayle if you like. Everyone in the family does. Although my father calls me Quad because I'm the fourth. Odd man. Thinks it's funny because his nickname is Trey. Mother keeps telling him—"

Tristan fled before he couldn't shake himself loose from the man's polished, hypnotic meanderings.

He found Wolf in the kitchen, bent over the sink with the faucet's spray hose pointed at his face. Tristan waited until Wolf finished washing the salt off, handed Wolf a towel, then instinctively winced in sympathy when he saw Wolf's bloodshot eyes.

"Wow, what was in the salt?" He took the towel back and patted at Wolf's damp shirt, trying to blot out some of the water spots spreading through the cotton. "Acid?"

"Wouldn't surprise me in the least," he muttered under his breath. "She's going to kill someone, Tris. If I don't kill her first."

"Sit down. I'll get you a beer. Unless you want something stronger?" He was already rifling through the refrigerator before Wolf grunted that a beer would be fine. After popping open two Tsingtao, Tristan slid one over the kitchen table toward Wolf as he eased down into one of Sey's chrome and vinyl diner chairs. Plopping down across from Wolf, he swallowed a foamy sip, then said, "That really wasn't Cin?"

"Did he *look* like a Kincaid?" Wolf's nostrils flared in offense.

"Having only seen four of them—and one of them was your mother, who dresses in early rainbow—so I couldn't say," Tristan shot back. "Now who is he?"

"No one." Wolf rolled his eyes when Tristan nudged him in the thigh with a sharp jab from his bare toes. "He's some guy Sey's supposed to teach about antique toy restoration. She forgot he was coming because she was in the middle of this shit. And she can't send him back to Canada. They've already made the hostage exchange, one of her students for one of theirs. She's stuck with him for three weeks, and that means *we're* stuck with him."

"Shit, and I thought the worst thing I had to worry about was something like Winifred." Having someone around—*a mundane* Meegan called them—would muck things up tremendously. Or would it? He wasn't sure. "Sey probably doesn't want the academic community to think she's crazy, so—"

"Ixnay on the ostghay," Wolf concurred.

"I have no idea what that means," Tristan admitted. "Wait… pig Latin. Is that pig Latin? So old school. Much mocking. Do you know leet speak? I hear it's the rage with all the kids."

"I hate you so much right now. And yet, when you're surly, I want you even more." Reaching across the table, Wolf snagged Tristan's hands, wrapping their fingers together. "And yeah, no ghost stuff around the civilian. But I think it's already too late. He got one look at your ass, and now he's going to be as much of your shadow as that useless wolfhound of yours. We're just going to have to get Sey to keep him really busy. Now tell me what you found out. Did you find something in the doll heads?"

"Better…." Tristan knew he was grinning like a silly idiot. "I got a ghost to talk to me."

"The little girl? Tris, you shouldn't have—"

"No, not her. Another one. A young man from the sixties. He's kind of a repeater like Cook." Tristan described the young man he'd been able to keep with him for a few minutes. "He used to work here, but I don't know when he died…."

"Don't they—the ghosts—normally show up the age they died at?" Wolf's beer bottle hovered at the plump of his lower lip, pressing the flesh down into a moue. "You know, I never ever thought of that."

"If that was the case, maybe I'd be running a senior center instead of a hotel. I think people become ghosts at an age they felt happiest at or maybe even when something really big happened to them. I don't know, but I don't get anyone that old."

"Unless they died young?" Wolf took a sip and licked at a speck of foam left on the rim of the bottle. "No, I think you're right. We know Winifred was oldish when she died, but she looked middle-aged—"

"But crazy," Tristan interjected. "Don't forget the crazy. Maybe that's when she went crazy—middle age."

"Crazy is what made her a ghost." He gestured out at the world in general, a graceful dip of wrist and fingers. "Middle age just probably made her bitter."

Tristan felt a burn start up in his cheeks when his brain whispered to him about what those fingers did to him the last time he'd had sex with Wolf. The beer wasn't cold enough to quench the fire under his skin, but it went a long way in shoving it aside, especially when he nearly choked a mouthful of foam up his nose.

Outside, the wind howled a moment before its voice was lost in the pound of a sudden rain. Wolf got up and closed the kitchen's open windows, dousing the hush of falling water. The shifting daylight bled silver over Wolf's features, but his lascivious wink at Tristan provided enough of a glow to set sparks off in Tristan's insides.

On his way back to the table, Wolf stopped only long enough to leave Tristan gasping from a hot kiss, their tongues sliding up against one another in a melting velvet push before the other man pulled away. He was still struggling to catch his breath as Wolf sat down, his heavy-lidded eyes sparkling with a smug satisfaction at taking Tristan's wind from him.

"Okay, now tell me about this kid. How much can he tell you if he's a repeater?" Wolf cocked his head. "I've only seen your Cook ghost when she comes in, and not all that well. How alike are they?"

"I'm only guessing. Not like I got a manual or anything." Tristan eyed his lover. "Did you? Do the Hellsingers have something we can use?"

"Dunno, babe," Wolf admitted slowly. "I'm not on their loaning-books-to list. Hell, I'm barely tolerated at funerals. Have you seen this kind of ghost before, elsewhere? Are they weekly like Cook?"

"No, it's all different. I don't know why." He shrugged. "There were Chinese prostitutes when I was a little kid, but they weren't constant. Just shifted in and out once in a while. Shit, my great-grandfather falls down the Grange's stairs every Christmas Eve and breaks his back. He lies there for about five minutes shouting at people to kill him because he can't walk anymore, but he just broke his legs and hips. Took him a while, but he healed up. Hell, he refused to live on the first floor because that's where the servants slept. It's why the Grange has an elevator, but that's the moment his ghost repeats. Not his death but that one moment. And only once a year."

"Okay, so you can die and haunt a place that you might not have died in, but it was significant to you," Wolf mused. "Can we take a chance on your guy being more like Cook? Do you think you can pull him up again for Cin? A full manifestation would go a shit ton of a way in convincing him we mean business here. Shit, I wonder if you're the only one who can see him. Channeling instead of entity realization."

"I'll try. He got stronger when I had some doll head dust on my hands. It might work again. I left it there, just in case." He'd been worn out when he'd finished talking with Raygun, but the ghost at least gave him some kind of place to start looking for answers.

"So talk to me, Thursday. Now that I've got your attention." Wolf wiggled his eyebrows at him. "And Raygun? What kind of name is that?"

"Dick," Tristan muttered. "It was a nickname. He was a football player for Cal Poly, and he was going on a plane trip to Ohio, I think— Toledo, he said Toledo."

"That would be Ohio," Wolf agreed sagely. "How does that connect to our Little Girl Dead?"

"I think Ray—that's his real name—is like Cook and remembers what happens only during the time of his current haunting. If I ask Cook about a guest she'd seen yesterday, she'd remember, but if she'd left and come back, she wouldn't know who I was talking about."

"Do they retain—your guests—do they hold onto memories of other ghosts there?" Wolf studied him curiously. "Is there a resonating consciousness in the specters?"

"I don't know. Mara seems to remember things." Tristan was ashamed to admit it, but he normally just checked the arriving specters in and left them to their own devices. There was a shift of something in Wolf's face when Tristan spoke about the deceased housekeeper, but it was gone before he could comment on it. "I haven't really tested it. It's not like we talk about anything that's happened in the past. Mostly she talks about things that happened to me recently. We don't even talk about Uncle Morty, but I know she goes into his rooms."

"Something we actually can investigate," Wolf said softly. "I haven't seen anything manifest outside of your presence, Tris. Sure, I've seen some orbs and other stuff, but most of the big flashy stuff happens only when you're around."

"I don't *do* these things—" He bristled, but Wolf shook his head, cutting off his tirade.

"I didn't say you did. What I'm saying is that you might be a catalyst of some kind." The man's tone was gentle, but the implication still rankled. Wolf scooted his chair over next to Tristan, and their knees bumped, jostling both of them in their seats. "It's a good thing. Babe, if we can somehow pinpoint—"

"For you, it's a job. For me, it's my fucked-up life." Tristan knew he sounded bitter, but he couldn't help it. Not after years of listening to his relatives talk about him as if he weren't even in the room. Called everything from delusional to insane, talking to the dead drove him further and further from his family until he was left alone, rattling about in a large mansion with only ghosts to keep him company.

"Hey, Tris." Wolf's arms came up, and Tristan let himself be wrapped into a tight embrace. "This isn't about making you some kind of experiment or shit like that. I want to help you to learn to control this thing you've got. On a lot of levels, it drives you crazy. Wouldn't you like to be able to turn it on and off?"

"God, yes," he grumbled. "I can't even walk across the Golden Gate."

"It isn't just about working with the dead. Yeah, that's what I want to prove." His lover coaxed a smile out of him with a brush of a thumb over Tristan's chin. "But to me, figuring out *how* you do things isn't as important as you. Okay? If you want to stop—just walk away from all of this—we can. Don't ever feel like you can't. I'll walk with you. Whenever you want."

"I don't want to walk away," he confessed. "I just don't want to feel like a freak."

Wolf quirked his mouth, "You kind of *are* a freak, babe. But see, that's what makes you interesting. Nothing wrong with being a little freaky. I wouldn't mind being a little bit more weird myself."

"You get any weirder, and we'll have to share a straitjacket," Tristan scoffed, but he gave Wolf a quick, awkward hug. "Thanks for… talking stuff through with me. I think I just get a little tired or something when I'm done talking to dead people I don't see all the time."

"Shit, I get tired talking to *live* people, so I'm not going to throw any stones from over here in my glass house. Now tell me about Ray. Then we can go rescue Sey from Gildy and Octopus Boy. Does he know anything about our resident soul sucker?"

"He thinks she's a hotel guest staying here with her parents." Tristan nodded at Wolf's confused look. "You've got to remember, when he was alive, this place was an inn, so he doesn't know it's a private residence now."

"Does he think Sey's... shit, her grandmother owned this place back in the sixties. Does he think Sey's her grandmother?"

"I don't think he sees anyone who is alive." Tristan thought back to the too-short conversation he had with Ray. "He said the missus. Sey's not married, and in his mind, there were kids here. He didn't want the missus's kids playing with the little girl staying here. He tried talking to her, but she was looking for something—a doll."

"Is the doll Simone? The name she was saying when you saw her?"

"I don't know. He didn't tell me." He shrugged. "I didn't have a long time with him. He was worried about staying too long. But Ray said he *had* to go look for the doll. It might be why he was attracted to the doll head I broke. She was screaming at him, and it hurt him—"

"Sonic transference? Could she have pushed her reason for haunting onto him? That would be interesting. Weird but interesting. Consciousness contagion." Wolf leaned back in his chair, pulling at his lower lip as he thought. "Shit, I need to make notes. Keep talking. There's got to be pen and paper in here someplace."

Tristan stared at the window for a few seconds, watching the rain grow heavy and hard. The porch's embellishments dripped from the torrent, and the walkway was already slick with puddles. A gust of wind hit the house, rattling the windows in the kitchen, then died off, angling the rain in yet another direction. Beyond the back garden, one of the property's workers struggled to hustle a shaggy red cow into the barn, the Highland moseying along as its thick coat repelled the storm's beating.

"And yet, you are not talking." Wolf tapped the table in front of Tristan, yanking his attention back into the room. "Keep going. I want to get this down while it's fresh in your mind."

"There isn't much beyond that. She started screaming at him to find her doll, and he hurt everywhere. Like he'd been playing football for three days straight. That's how he put it." His beer was empty, and Tristan debated grabbing another one when his stomach grumbled, reminding him he hadn't eaten anything since breakfast. "He ran off to help her search. I think he was scared of her. Hell, *I'm* scared of her, and I'm not sharing the ether with her."

"So the screaming hurt?" Wolf wrote something down on the notepad he found. From what Tristan could see, it looked more like squiggles and numbers than anything legible. Catching his lover's skeptical glance, Wolf winked. "I'm postulating frequencies. Based on what I found out from Winifred—"

"'Cause that whole thing worked out so well," Tristan grumbled under his breath.

"Hey, I didn't get a chance to try anything on her. I wasn't expecting my mother to suddenly break out an exorcism. It was *supposed* to be a séance." Another few scribbles, and the paper became a labyrinth of graphite and smears. "I think we can isolate tones and spectrums to capture activity or, hell, even maybe exorcise her. Some of your music disrupted her, so tonals work. I just don't have enough data. We'll need to replicate her appearance. Shit, I wished I'd had more time with Winifred."

"That scares me. More than the ghost." He looked around the kitchen. "Does Sey have someplace else to live? Because you guys tore the shit out of the Grange."

"The Grange was fine."

"That's because it's mostly stone. This house is wood. All you're missing is one of straw, and you'd have a whole set," he pointed out. "God, your mom knew what she was doing when she named you Wolf."

"Baby, the only blowing I intend to do is you, not a house," Wolf shot back. "Now let's go over this again and see if you can remember anything else."

Chapter 11

THE HOWLING woke him.

Outside—in the dead of night—the storm screamed and wailed, tearing apart the country silence in a fit of endless rage. Tristan reached across the bed, only to find it empty and cold. His heart felt alone, as desolate as the bed next to him. Closing his eyes, Tristan let his mind drift and let the storm rage around him—to listen for the voices hidden within the tempest's howls.

This time, he heard nothing. No one was hiding in the pitchy whine of the wind slamming into the house. No familiar voices calling out to him. Not even a whisper of an unearthly little girl with flesh scallops in place of eyes.

And he seemed to be missing the comforting breathing of the man he'd fallen for just a few weeks before.

There were no lights on in the room. Either the storm was so deep it swallowed up everything around it, or they'd lost power, because nothing shone through the dark outside, not even the spotlight set up over the barn's double doors.

He lay a few moments longer, marinating in flashes of sparks inside of the roving clouds and listening again, satisfied there was nothing in the storm but the wind and its pounding rain.

A creak echoed softly from the direction of the bedroom door, and Tristan tensed uncontrollably for a second before chuckling to himself. The floorboards did their own random squeaking, and a dark shape approached the bed, a Wolf-shaped shadow emerging from the milky darkness.

"What are you laughing at, goof?" Wolf stripped quickly, then eased into the bed, pushing the mattress down enough to make Tristan roll into him. Their bodies rubbed together, naked skin on skin, and Tristan shivered at the damp cold of his lover's flesh.

"I was thinking you were the ghost coming to get me. Because maybe the salt doesn't work in the dark." He shivered but wrapped his arms around Wolf's chilled chest. Wolf smelled of lightning and rain, and Tristan's fingers came away moist when he ruffled Wolf's unruly damp hair. "Where were you? And you're kind of soaked."

"I heard Sey get up and went to see why. She was worried about the barn doors being locked down tight enough in the storm." The man nuzzled against Tristan, turning until Wolf was nearly lying on top of him. "God, you feel good. It's fucking cold out there."

"So you went instead?" He shifted, parting his knees so Wolf's legs could slide down between his. It didn't take long before his cock noticed the other man's warmth. Hell, his nipples were already pulling in tight from Wolf's bare skin brushing over them. "You're a good cousin."

"Yeah?" Even in the dark, Tristan could see Wolf's wicked, gleaming smile. "How about a reward of some kind?"

"I've got some chocolate in my backpack," he whispered. "Might not even be melted."

"Not the kind of sweet I was hoping for," Wolf murmured back. His fingers roamed down Tristan's side and then slid between Tristan's legs to ripple over his sac.

Tristan yelped, and his balls pulled in, suddenly shocked by the cold touch. His cock, once raring and on the verge of pearling, retreated as well, fleeing the scene like a mugging suspect caught with a handful of gold chains. His legs drew in automatically, pushing up to protect his crotch, and Tristan felt something soft give way under his left knee— something squishy and vulnerable.

He didn't have to ask Wolf what he hit because Wolf made a sickening gurgle and rolled off him, taking the blankets with him.

"Fuck. Shit, I'm sorry." Tristan sat up, shivering. Without the blankets, the cold ate its way through his skin, and he reached for the lamp on the nightstand. It took a few seconds of frantically clicking the switch before he remembered the power was out. Wolf lay on his back, knees raised and hands cupped over his crotch. "Are you okay? I am so sorry. I didn't—"

"It's okay. I probably deserved it," Wolf gasped. "Damn, I hate when that happens. It's like puking in your chest. Can you let me lie here for a bit, Thursday? I might have to cough my balls up my throat and put them back where they belong."

"How much time do you need? A day? A month? How hard did I hit you?" From the panting and gasping coming beside him, Wolf sounded like he'd need a lifetime. "It was a knee. Not a knife."

"Sous chefs wish they could use your knees in their kitchen." Wolf exhaled hard, then sucked in another shuddering breath. "Okay, almost getting the feeling back in my cock."

"Can you roll over a bit? It's really cold." Tristan tugged at the blankets trapped under Wolf's weight. "Maybe you'll feel better if you're warmer?"

"Just keep those knees of yours under control." Wolf whimpered dramatically but allowed Tristan to free the duvet and cover them. "Fuck kitchen knives. Your damned knees are like halberds."

"My legs aren't that long," he snorted back. "Some help you'd be in battle."

"I don't know." Wolf made a show of lifting up the covers to peer under them. He moved a little bit gingerly but seemed to be recovering quickly enough from what Tristan could see. "I might have to have them wrapped around me for comparison."

"I just kneed you in the balls, and you want to have sex?"

"I could be five days dead, and I'd want to have sex with you." Sliding closer, Wolf wrapped his arms around Tristan's waist and snuggled in until they were lying on their sides with their noses, chests, and cocks pressed against each other. "Of course, it would be kind of icky for you, but you love me, so I know you'd power your way through it."

"You think I love you?"

"I know you love me," Wolf boasted softly. "How can you not? I make you laugh."

"So does Boris," Tristan drawled. "When he farts in his sleep and he scares himself awake."

Wolf tilted his head back and studied Tristan thoughtfully through the shadows. "I might do that too, but I don't hear you laughing. You're telling me you love the dog more? At least I don't drink from the toilet."

"You drink from the milk carton. That's much worse." He was still a bit cold to the touch, but Tristan edged in closer. "You're too cold. My dick's going to fall off."

"Totally my fault. My fingers must be like popsicles." Wolf rubbed his hands on the fitted sheet, then touched Tristan tentatively. "How's that?"

Unlike the last time, Wolf's fingers were warm, and Tristan nearly purred as his lover fondled him with slow, deliberate strokes. He stretched out to return the favor, but Wolf pressed his mouth onto Tristan's and murmured a soft no.

"Let me just enjoy you. I could have fucked this up. Hell, I did fuck this up," Wolf continued to whisper. "Then I didn't know how to fix it."

"So you made up a ghost story at your cousin's?" Wolf's fingernails scraped over his taint and hole, drawing out a gasp from Tristan. His brain bubbled at the sensations coursing through his body. "Kinda slick on your.... Shit, I can't think when you do that, Wolf."

"Sometimes, Mr. Pryce, you think too much." Wolf's mouth left his to travel down to his chest, stopping there only long enough to nip at one of Tristan's nipples. "Stay right there. I brought—"

"Taking a chance you were going to get lucky, Dr. Kincaid? Even when you knew I was pissed off?" The man's weight was gone, and the mattress buckled a bit as Wolf got off the bed. "Kinda cocky."

"I was hoping," Wolf corrected from across the room. He must have hit his toes or leg because he let out a short curse when he thumped into something. "Shit, where did I put the lube?"

"Got some in my duffel. On the chair." Tristan pushed himself onto his elbows. "Over there."

"Yeah, I know where the chair is. It just jumped out and bit me," Wolf grumbled. "Wow, what the hell did you bring here? Looks like you bought out a sex shop."

Muttering into the darkness, Tristan shot back, "Fuck you. I didn't know what to get."

They'd not been fighting when Tristan ordered lubricant and condoms from an online store. Too embarrassed to ask Wolf about what to get, he clicked on anything that looked interesting. What he'd gotten seemed more like a how-to manual from a scientist bent on populating a new world than sex aids for a newly minted gay man. Still, he remembered how he'd dumped the entire box when he was trying to figure out what to pack while Wolf waited for him in the Grange's lobby.

It seemed like a lifetime ago. An entire emotional universe ago. Their seesaw relationship was tilting back up, but how long would it be before he came crashing back down again, hitting the ground hard enough to drive splinters into his tender soul?

"I can hear you thinking from here," Wolf said as he climbed back on the bed. "Stop. Thinking. Thursday. Or better yet, tell me what's got your brain firing on all cylinders. Because there's smoke coming off of those slick gears in that head of yours."

"Suppose we fuck this up again?" Tristan let Wolf pull him into a hug, and something plastic rolled against Tristan's arm as he tightened his embrace around Wolf's torso. "One of the things... what is that? Lube? It just hit me. It's huge. Did you bring a dildo? I sure as shit didn't order one."

"Forget about that. Let's talk about us—fucking this up, okay?" The cold had returned, but it was held back by Wolf's heat and the soft cotton duvet he'd thrown over them both. "We're both going to mess up. Hell, I'm going to say it'll be eighty-twenty, with me fucking up 80 percent of the time, and you'll probably growl and snap at me because you're working, and I'm getting in your shit."

"You do get annoying." Tristan spat a piece of his own blond hair out of his mouth. "And you chew on my pencils."

"You've got some great-tasting pencils." Wolf sniffed imperiously. "All hard and sweet, dangling erotically from your—"

"Pencils. Not dick."

"Fingers," Wolf finished. "I like watching you play the pencils."

"Well, stop biting them. It fucks them up, and they feel weird when I use them."

Tristan didn't think Wolf needed to know it was because the bite marks made him think of other things Wolf's teeth were good for. The man's ego was inflated enough as it was.

"Duly noted," Wolf said gravely. "No biting pencils. Only Tristan. Tell me what's really bugging you. Deep down inside. And don't tell me nothing. Just because you've never had anyone to talk to before doesn't mean you don't have me to listen to you now."

He lay there, breathing and listening to Wolf's body move and shift. Since he'd first seen Wolf stroll into the Grange as if he owned the ghost-infested mansion, Tristan knew his life would change because *that* man had walked into it. He just didn't realize how much it would—or how much he'd need the man lying next to him. Tristan couldn't come up with anyone he'd spent more time with than Wolf. Even now, with the possibility of Ophelia Sunday helping him at the Grange for extended periods of time, Tristan was scared—frightened of stepping out into the world and finding Wolf was no longer by his side.

"You make me stronger," Tristan admitted. "Kind of. No, you do. I like having you with me. Even when you piss me the fuck off."

"Bullshit about the stronger part," Wolf snorted. "You're one of the most stubborn sons of a bitch I've ever met. Pull the other leg, Tris."

"I'm serious." He lifted his fingers up to Wolf's mouth to shush him. "Just shut up for a moment and listen."

"No, babe, *you* listen." Wolf's hands were warm on his face when they cupped Tristan's cheeks. "You kick ass. In your own way. In a pretty geeky hot-bodied artist way."

"You can't ask me to talk to you, then tell me I'm saying things wrong," Tristan pointed out. "Kind of defeats the purpose of this talking thing."

"Fair enough," he conceded. "Can I keep your face? I can kind of make out the squish I did with your mouth. It's kind of cute."

"Let go of my face and let me talk." He gave one of Wolf's palms a kiss before they were pulled away. Tangling his legs around Wolf's, Tristan got comfortable and gathered his thoughts. "You make me feel like I've got wings. Sure they're just wax and feathers, and I don't know what the fuck I'm doing with them, but I can go places… or at least try to go places with you. You make me want to see what's outside in the world. Hell, I've been thinking it would be cool to go see other hauntings—maybe even help you figure this whole thing out. I couldn't have done that before if I hadn't met you. Your family, and I know they drive you crazy, but Meegan and Ophelia Sunday really make me feel… good. And normal!"

"Well, that's got to be the first time my mother and the word normal have ever been uttered together in the same sentence." Wolf didn't avoid Tristan's light smack. "It's true. But it's nice for Ophie too. She's always been—sensitive. We just never had any way of really kind of proving it. Hell, she was stoked when you asked her to be there. Thank God you're gay, or I'd be fitting you for a tuxedo and helping you pick out rings."

"She said a lot of your family is sensitive to ghosts. And don't call her Ophie."

"Secretly, deep down inside her blackened little Smurfy heart, she likes it. And yeah, they are attuned, or some of them are," Wolf admitted softly. "And a lot of them are fakers too. That's what really made them kick me out. I didn't want to perpetuate the family's charlatans. There are real ghost hunters out there, Hellsingers like Cin, but a lot of them are like Gildy. They tell a family their problems are over, when in reality, the place might never have been haunted, or worse, they're left with a very pissed-off ghost like Winifred."

"That's… messed up, Wolf."

"Yep. Liars on either side of the fence. And I hate to admit it, but there are quite a few in my family. It's how they make their money. We're pretty much what people imagine as gypsy stereotypes but without the whole covered caravan nonsense. A few Winnebagos, though. And you can never go wrong with an Airstream." He kissed Tristan's nose, leaving a small wet spot behind. "It's complicated. There are so many reasons I want you to be with me, and there's one really big reason I don't."

"What's the really big reason?" Tristan asked softly, dreading what the man's answer would be.

"Because I don't want you hurt, Thursday," Wolf whispered into Tristan's ear, then nipped down his throat. "I'd rather die than see you being hurt."

THE STORM raged outside, but Wolf heard only Tristan's soft cries for more. They'd grabbed a bottle of lube, driven more by need than by design. In the dark, it proved to be a crapshoot. Wolf was hoping for something utilitarian. What they got was a self-warming tropical scented oil Tristan playfully referred to as Fruit Lubes.

While the coconut and mango were a nice scent on Tristan's pale skin, the slick oil helped Wolf ease his fingers into Tristan's tight body.

The man's hole was greedy, sucking him in with every twist of Tristan's hips. Wolf slowed his exploration, concentrating on wrapping his lips around the base of Tristan's shaft, then gliding slowly up to its head. He daubed at the slit he found there among the velvety skin, sucking at the salty pungency of Tristan's burgeoning seed.

He played at Tristan's entrance, sliding in a tip of his finger, then two, drawing out the process while Tristan writhed on his hand and in his mouth. They'd gone from playful to serious in the span of a few kisses. His mouth still burned from the heat of Tristan's lips, and the already storm-broken silence was now filled with their soft murmurs.

Wolf couldn't imagine what he'd been thinking when he'd stormed out of the Grange. Except perhaps he'd been driven more by fear than any sense of anger. The blond man had burrowed under Wolf's skin, too deep to shake off, even if Wolf really wanted to. After a lifetime of drifting on the edges of relationships—hell, on the edge of his own family—Tristan had become *home* for him.

A home he was so scared of losing, like he'd lost every tangible thread tying him to permanence before he'd met the quirky, stubborn artist he was playing like a fiddle.

Quite the loud fiddle with strong fingers, Wolf thought as Tristan yanked on his hair.

"Want me inside of you, babe?" Wolf murmured around Tristan's cock head. "Or maybe to play with you a little bit more?"

He slid his finger around Tristan's rim, a slow skim over the tight muscled ring. His own cock was dewing as much moisture as the storm beating at the room's windows. A flash of lightning poured silver over Tristan's splayed-out body and burned the image of porcelain, shadows, and sweat into Wolf's mind. His lover's mouth was parted, lips pulled open as if mirroring the gaping acceptance of his entrance as Wolf delved even deeper into his passage. The musky, sensual tang of Tristan's body rode over the lingering sweetness of the lubricant, and Wolf grinned, knowing he'd have to lather himself up in the fruity concoction soon.

Tristan's body was primed, begging to take him in, and Wolf didn't want to waste any time plunging into the man's hot clench.

He rolled a condom down his cock, and it snapped at the base. Wincing slightly at the sting, Wolf scrambled for the bottle they'd left somewhere on the bed. He found it near Tristan's hip, then used his teeth to open the cap, keeping his fingers riding Tristan's rim.

"Now, Wolf," Tristan groaned and reached for him. "God, just fuck me already."

"Such a poet," he laughed, capturing his lover's mouth in a punishing kiss. "Hold onto me. And don't let go."

It felt so right to have Tristan's legs snug over his hips. Wanting to go even deeper, Wolf raised Tristan's knees until his legs rested on Wolf's shoulders. Then he reached down to part the man's firm, round ass. More light from outside, a distant glow this time instead of a skittering bolt, but it was enough for Wolf to see the dip of his lover's hole. The plum shadow invited him in, peeling back into a begging moue as Tristan shifted his hips.

When Tristan's fingers dug into his forearms, Wolf knew Tris wouldn't be able to hold on much longer. Palming himself with one hand, Wolf guided himself to the brink of Tristan's body and pushed in, parting the tight ring with the tip of his cock.

It was hard going. The soft retreat of Tristan's body was at odds with the man's needy mewls, and Wolf had to work carefully through, rocking his hips in a glide forward while pushing in. He felt the moment his cock breached Tristan's inner sanctum because the sudden engulfment of silken fire around the spongy head was enough to drive him insane.

He wasn't going to last. Neither of them were. It'd been too long since they'd done this dance, shared the salty kiss of their sweaty bodies or tasted the bitters of each other's seed. Wolf knew then he was mad—a sure sign of the insanity pulled down from generations of Kincaids—because he walked out on this man. This beautiful man lying beneath him, spread open wide and taking him in like no other had done before. Trusting. Sweet. And most of all, stubborn enough to give back as good as Wolf dished out.

Just like he was doing right now.

This was no passive lover under him. Tristan's hands roamed over Wolf's body, plucking at his nipples until they were nearly stiff enough to leave red trails on skin. His nails scraped, catching on sensitive areas. Then he found the plump of Wolf's ass, digging into the hard muscle. He'd have bruises tomorrow for sure. Long, slender hand marks he'd wear under his clothes. More intimate than a love bite and sometimes just as hard won in pleasurable pain.

He pounded into Tristan's cleft, pushing the man's asscheeks apart with every thrust. Any rational thought Wolf might have had shattered beneath the rolls of thunder building up inside of him. Soul-breaking booms rocked the house, rolling over it in a tumbleweed of sound, but Wolf kept going. He was driven by one thing: bringing his lover to a peak so they could fall off together.

Wolf knew Tristan was close. The man's hands were still, a death grip deep into Wolf's biceps, and the tightness around Wolf's cock fluttered and danced. Trapped between them, Tristan's cock bobbed along as well.

The first splatter of salty spill on Wolf's hard stomach was enough to drive him over the edge. Resting his weight on his knees, Wolf continued to drive into his lover. Reaching between them, he took hold of Tristan's cock and began to milk the man's shaft. The web of his thumb caught on the thick ridge under Tristan's dick, and Wolf slid his grip around, twisting up into a spiral, then palming the already wet head.

The second shot struck him in the face, and he caught a drop on the edge of his lip. Dabbing his tongue out, he drew in the speckled splash from the edge of his mouth. With Tristan's heady, intense zest overloading his senses, Wolf came, hard and fast, pouring as much of himself into Tristan as his body could wring out.

Ensnared in the web of Tristan's heat, Wolf didn't see the shimmering malevolent glow until it was too late to do anything more than completely shield his lover's body. Throwing himself over Tristan, Wolf fought to shake off the roiling lethargy of his climax as he batted away the heavy iron lamp flying across the room toward their vulnerable heads.

The lamp's heavy stand hit his arm, and he felt the bitter, sharp strike down in his bone. Shoving at the antique, Wolf choked on the shock of pain running from his wrist to his shoulder. Beneath him, Tristan tried to extricate himself from Wolf's weight. They'd parted, the wet slither of their bodies coming too quickly for Wolf's liking, and he could only hope he hadn't hurt Tristan in the process.

"Noooooooooooooo!" The shimmer grew a face—of sorts. It dangled at the end of the bed, a sheath of bluish white and a widening black maw. The lower edge of its cavernous maybe-mouth dropped farther and farther down the length of the glow until it became an impossibility of a mouth, draping down past what would be the elbows of a young child.

Wolf didn't need Tristan to tell him the specter was angry. In a blink, the phantom flew at them, its terrifying scream rending the air. He threw his injured arm up, more out of habit than anything else, and used his body to protect the struggling man partially beneath him. As the glow slammed into them, he felt something rake into his flesh, ripping up long shreds of skin, and a cold settled into the slices, creeping outward through his arm like a ravaging frost on a window pane.

A loud boom—much louder and nearer than any thunder they'd heard that night—shook their bedroom, and a beam of light cut through the dark, catching on the flash of ethereal grit making a turn back toward the bed. Wolf blinked when the beam hit his eyes. It was strong, blindingly so, and between the thunder and ghostly screams, he was pretty certain he'd been deafened and couldn't hear anymore.

He was wrong about that.

"Duck!" a strong male voice ordered him, and Wolf obeyed, driven more by years of responding to that growling tone than anything else.

Grabbing Tristan, Wolf rolled and shoved as much of the duvet as he could over them just in time for his eardrums to be splattered with the sharp retort of a shotgun blast echoing through the room. In that moment, the cacophony rose to a high pitch, loud enough for his mind to experience a sharp pain from the reverberations. Then an exhale later, the room was silent, with only the rain to keep their frenzied panting company. The duvet shifted, and cold air tickled Wolf's bare ass. A wide hand followed the wind, smacking him hard enough to leave a sting. Then the authoritative voice broke through the thrashing sound of rain.

"You called for me, cousin?"

Chapter 12

"HE OKAY?" Cin was larger than Wolf remembered, but then he *always* thought that when he saw his cousin. Maybe the Hellsinger wasn't large as much as the world shrank in whenever he was around. Still, as imposing and looming as Cin Kincaid was, Wolf was glad to have him there.

Even if Tristan had just spent half an hour wondering if he could quietly die of embarrassment before he saw Cin again.

A camping lantern sat on the counter, a bright burn of yellow light in the darkness. It shone enough for Wolf to spot a battery-operated teakettle and a used french press next to it. Some things never changed. Cin still ran on hot coffee and a granite will, two things Wolf was quite thankful for at that moment.

They looked alike—sort of, Wolf thought. In many ways, he'd always considered Cin his brother more than a cousin, and if the slightly older Kincaid could be believed, he felt the same way about Wolf. Now as Cin stirred cream and sugar into two mugs, Wolf grinned at their differences. His rougher, slightly grumpy cousin, with some of his hair pulled back in a topknot ponytail and a shadowy stubble over his square jaw, looked more like he was about to escape from a penal colony in a futuristic New York than make faux-espresso in a San Luis Obispo farmhouse.

Cin cast nearly as much of a shadow as the fridge. A black T-shirt stretched tight over his broad chest and firm arms, and his low-rise jeans bore deep creases, worn from a many-hour drive to reach Sey's place. He moved quietly, smoother than a man as muscled as Cin was, but there was definitely a low-simmering fatigue there, a hint of Cin's need to fall into a soft bed for at least a couple of hours. Still, Cin's beaten-gold eyes were bright and cunning, catching every detail of the room even as he puttered about on bare feet to make his cousin a cup of coffee.

And Wolf *knew* in his gut, he was one of those details Cin studied as he worked the french press.

"Yeah, he's asleep now." Wolf took the cup of caramel-hued dredge Cin offered him, waiting until his cousin sat down before attempting a sip. "He might die of embarrassment when he sees you next time, but that'll be in a few hours. He's hoping he'll get hit by a meteor or something in the meantime."

The cream Cin poured in did very little to change the oiliness of the strong brew. His stomach would regret the drink, but for right now, Wolf's brain welcomed the sharp hit of caffeine. He took a brief sniff at his armpit, wondering if he shouldn't have showered before he joined Cin in the kitchen. By the smirk on the other man's face, Wolf knew he'd been seen.

"I've smelled worse," Cin rumbled, his fingers tracing the lip of a chipped white mug. "Hell, I probably smell worse right now."

Wolf leaned across the corner of the table to playfully sniff at his cousin's armpit, only to get Cin's hand in his face and a not-so-gentle shove away.

"Asshole," Cin grunted, palming his coffee cup. "Talk to me. Let's break this down a bit. I've got a lot of questions."

"Shoot." He looked around the kitchen, or as far as the lantern beam allowed. "You put that shotgun up, right? Gildy's here."

"Yeah." Cin nodded. "It's only got rock salt rounds, so even if she got a hold of it, she really couldn't do that much damage."

"Pretty sure she knows how to make her own rounds." Wolf saluted his aunt with a soft clink of his cup against his cousin's. "You going to be here long?"

"Long enough to pull your ass out of the fire. Bridge is washed out from the canyon jump. I parked the piece of shit rental on some high ground and hoofed it the last couple of miles with my stuff." Cin scrubbed at his still-damp hair. "Think the storm washed my eardrums out. Gotta say, even if I walked in on you guys doing the nasty in my room, I at least got to see firsthand what's going on a bit."

"The first bedroom Sey put us in had some hard-core activity. We wanted to leave it to go over later. And hell, I didn't want Tristan to sleep there. This ghost is supposed to be a kid, but she plays some pretty fucking adult games." It was hard to cough up a manly thank-you after someone shotgunned salt pellets over his bare ass, but Wolf was going to give it his best try. "So, man, I wanted to say thanks for the save—"

"Yeah, let's talk about that too." The darkness around them slithered into Cin's tone. "Saw some salt down across the floor, so it looks like you at least did the basics. What the hell happened? Did you fuck it up? That's like Kincaid 101."

"I laid it down—" Wolf protested softly.

"So, then, how did that thing get in? And better yet, what *was* that thing? Partially formed manifestation? How many have you seen here? Occurrences? Or do you actually have multiples?"

"What part of your interrogation do you want me to answer first?" He eyed Cin from across the corner of the table. "Because I suck at multiple choice."

Cin eyed him right back, a searing wash of hot gold. "The salt first. Then talk about the ghost. Or do you want to start with the guy you've let hook into you? I guess it all starts there, don't it, cuz? But let's go with the salt. What the hell were you thinking?"

"As far as we know, it's a kid. A really pissed-off kid looking for something or someone who may or may not be named Simone. And she's got it in for Tris. Told you, we've already moved rooms once." He held up his hands in surrender. "I salted the sills and doors. Fuck, I even covered the mirror."

"So, then, what was that? Post-climactic spirit projection?" Cin snorted into his coffee, then took a sip. "Let me guess; he's possessed, and you were fucking the ghost out of him?"

"First off, let's talk about the salt thing. One of the window seals was blown out, probably because this place is really fucking old. Found that when I went looking for my clothes. The storm hit hard, and I guess the wind coming through cleared off some of the salt. So that's how it got through—how *she* got through." Wolf reached over and snagged his cousin's wrist, capturing his arm before Cin could bring his mug back up to his lips. "Secondly, I'm serious about Tristan. So don't—"

"You've known this guy for what? A couple of months?" Wolf had opened his mouth to protest Cin's oversimplification of the situation between him and Tristan when his cousin reached across and slapped his chin up, slamming Wolf's teeth together in a rattling chunk. "Shut up. You were going to say something stupid like it's true love or he's my soul mate. He might look like Wesley, Buttercup, but you and I both know crap like that isn't real."

"A couple of months ago, I'd have said the same thing. About ghosts. About love," Wolf conceded. Squaring his gaze to his cousin's, he peered through the kitchen's murky gloom to stare Cin down. "You've spent most of your life telling me ghosts were real, and I told *you* I needed proof—quantifiable evidence I could hold up against the harshest of critics."

"So, *now* you've drunk the Kool-Aid?" Cin extracted his hand from Wolf's fingers. "You meet *one* medium—"

"But he was the *right* medium. Well, not for the ghosts—some—shit, he can see them, and they interact with him, but none of that matters. Because when it's all said and done, I'm still a scientist. There has to be *proof*, Cin. That hasn't changed." Wolf leaned back into the chair's chrome and vinyl, grinning at the telltale squeak of its rubber-tipped legs on waxed flooring. "But I'm telling you, I believe—not just in ghosts because in my guts I know there's more out there than we know—but more that I believe in love. Something I can't see but it's there. Filling me. Touching pieces of me I could never see until Tristan got there. So now it's my turn to tell you, you're going to have to believe, Cin. No other way around it. You're just going to have to believe until you actually fall."

"Huh. Well, look who's fallen into the rabbit hole after the rabbit." Cin leaned back as well and slung an arm over the chair next to him. Picking up his coffee cup again, Cin saluted Wolf without a hint of mockery, and Wolf knew in that moment, he'd won his cousin over. "So, now tell me about what your guy upstairs can do, and why the fuck was that wraith after him?"

SO FAR, he'd been able to avoid anyone with even a drop of Kincaid blood in their veins. Although—Tristan risked a peek at the camel's foreboding face—there was a good chance the grumpy animal was actually some long-lost cousin who'd pissed off a witch and was now living out his life as a were-ungulate.

The fucker also spat with unerring accuracy, and it took three saliva missiles before Tristan found a safe spot to sit in Sey's old-fashioned barn. The cattle took up a large portion of the back end, occupying a penned-off clear space with a hay bin and trough. Nearby, in a double-wide horse stall, the camel chewed on something green and nasty, no doubt building up his arsenal for when Tristan drew into range.

Since Tristan only came to the barn armed with a sketch pad, graphites, and a thermos of hot coffee he'd made up on Sey's wood-burning stove, he wasn't all that interested in getting a face full of whatever it was the camel was brewing up for him.

He'd gotten enough of the initial design work for his next book sketched out before he'd come down to SLO, so it was easy enough to fall into working out the details of his newest monstrous main character. The villain of the piece still needed work, and as Tristan doodled, the lurker took on the distinctive sour look of a certain ungulate currently chewing a nasty cud a few yards away.

"That's nice," a soft voice said over his shoulder. "It looks out of this world, man."

He'd have thought, after so many years of hearing things go bump, rattle, and dirge in the night, he'd be used to spirits sneaking up on him, but no, Tristan's heart still jumped up and did the hokey pokey when yet another ghost slipped into his surroundings and spoke to him unexpectedly.

Slender to the point of being waifish, she was nearly solid, faint hints of color in her long wavy hair. Her bare feet were slightly grimy, and her long gauze dress looked patchy in areas where sun or bleach washed out its original color. Unlike most ghosts, she carried a scent with her, a clean powdery perfume barely strong enough to be noticed. Of course, Tristan sneered back at the camel, his foul-tempered barn companion's odor drowned out most things, including the scent of Tristan's coffee.

"Hi," he squeaked, swallowing his surprise. Coughing, Tristan tried again. "Good to see you."

"Oh, man, you are so square." Her slender hands were heavy with silver rings, and she made a pass at his hair with her long fingers. He felt the barest of ripples along his scalp, but she wasn't strong enough to do more than ruffle a strand or two.

She didn't seem to notice she had no effect on him. Instead, she squatted next to him, her legs folded in half, and she hunched over his arm, staring down at his sketches. The young woman studied the page for a moment, then looked around, her eyebrows pulling into a curious frown. She played with strings of beads dangling from her neck, wrapping them around her fingers and then releasing them as she spoke. She had a plain face—until she gave Tristan a shy, sweet smile, and then a beauty bloomed up from inside of her and spread over her freckled face.

"I'm supposed to meet someone here." Her voice wavered, and she flickered uncertainly. "I can't remember… when. Soon, I think. We were going to head up to San Francisco. Our parents—my dad's so old-fashioned. We've got to get out of here, you know? Time to start living our own kind of American Dream."

"I'm Tristan." Holding out his hand would have been useless, and she didn't look like the sort who'd welcome the courtesy. A hug or something more tribal would have suited her. His suspicions were confirmed when she flashed him a peace symbol and a smile.

"I'm Petal." Bending in closer, she whispered in a hush barely loud enough for Tristan to hear over the camel's passing gas, "That's going to be my name. We're going to cast off our old names too. Become what we're meant to be together. I wanted to be Juliet because we're like star-crossed lovers, but Ray—he's going to be Faraji—he said it was too tragic a name. We needed to celebrate our love, not mourn it. We're leaving as soon as he gets back from Ohio."

Tristan wondered if Ray ever came back from Ohio and married his pretty flower child. They'd worked out Ray'd been a part of a tragedy in SLO during the sixties, but without Ray's last name and without electricity, they had no way of finding out if he'd been one of those killed.

Staring through the young woman, Tristan began to hope she hadn't been lingering out in the barn for long, especially since he also didn't know if Ray was tied to the house or could actually come outside past the porch.

"It's exactly like Romeo and Juliet—okay, not exactly, but still," Tristan said softly, shaking his head. "They shouldn't be apart. Not when they're so close. Is that what's tying you two here? You can't reach each other?"

"Who are you talking to?" A deep masculine rumble jerked Tristan from his conversation with Petal.

This time it was a live someone who'd scared the crap out of him, and while the rough whiskey voice sounded sensually familiar, there was a dangerous edge to it—an edge Tristan'd never heard in Wolf's voice.

No, this voice belonged to a man he'd not seen before. He'd certainly heard him. As best as one could hear when one's head was buried under a mound of pillows and blankets with one's own voice chanting and praying for a swift, painless death.

That death was not forthcoming then or in that moment when he looked through Petal's wavering form and at a potently bodied pour of a man standing behind her.

He'd have known Cin Kincaid was Wolf's cousin even without an introduction—although Tristan didn't count Wolf's muttered exchange of names over Tristan's blanket-shrouded body at four in the morning as a proper introduction. Hell, he might have even thought Cin was Wolf's brother, because they shared the same strongly stamped masculine features, a glorious mix of cheekbones, wickedly sensual mouths, and a dip of a dimple in their right cheeks. The differences lay in the details, but those were strong enough to turn Wolf's aggressively male handsomeness to Cin's wild, feral beauty.

Cin's ebony hair was longer than his cousin's, a tousled, thick mane skimming his shoulders. It framed his face, falling in waves to curve around smoky gold eyes. Wolf might have laid claim to the name, but Cin certainly took it and wore it on his own skin. Dressed all in black, he appeared as a Reaper behind the ghostly sylph, lacking only a scythe to pare her from her afterlife.

The stern look on his face as he studied Tristan's sprawl on a pile of feed he'd covered with a blanket told Tristan the Kincaid probably didn't need something as plebian as a scythe to separate a head from its shoulders—even if those shoulders and head belonged to his favorite cousin's lover.

Something inside of him rebelled at the quaking tremors Cin Kincaid seemed to bring up in him, and Tristan ignored the slab of black and white granite tipped with wary gold eyes. Instead, he turned his attention back to the flower child who'd conjured herself out of the shadows to talk to him.

"Ray's inside the house," he informed her. Her face lit up briefly, then fell into a despair he could almost taste as the waves rolled off her. "What's wrong? Can't you get into the house?"

"There's something… dark in there." She nearly sobbed as she spoke. Distressed, her body danced in and out of sight, thinning in places as she stalked into a short pacing circle. "Oh God, I don't know if I can. I tried earlier, you know? To see if Missus Kincaid was around. She didn't mind me coming 'round to talk to Faraji—Ray—while he was working up here. She didn't agree with my dad about a lot of things but mostly that Ray and I shouldn't be together because—"

"Did your dad worry Ray wasn't going to be able to support you?" Tristan scowled as Cin walked through Petal's circling body. Even more annoying was the small device Cin pulled out of his pocket. A second later, an undulating, squeaky whine rode roughshod over the lowing cattle's moos.

The asshat Kincaid camel not only didn't seem to mind the noise but appeared to be encouraged by it, if Tristan could judge by the smirk in the beast's curled-lip expression.

"Some elevation in electro-magnetic activity, but not enough to be indicative of spectral interference," Cin rattled off in his strong, fierce growl. "Are you trying to fuck with me, Pryce? I'm not going to fall for your—"

"Do you think you can sublimate the asshole behavior you Kincaids seem to have in your genetic material and get the fuck out of Petal's left arm?" Tristan shooed Cin back with a wave of his hand. The pencils on his drawing pad nearly rolled off, and he snatched them up before he lost them in the folds of the horse blanket he'd found to sit on. "Maybe you can even shut the fuck up for a moment so I can finish talking to her?"

If Cin had an answer for him, Tristan didn't get a chance to hear it. One second Cin Kincaid was opening his mouth to retort something probably insanely clever, and the next, they both were being blown across the barn floor.

Tristan tasted hay, a mouthful of dank yellowness on his tongue with a hint of old bread. Then it was gone, swallowed up by a rough grit shoved through his parted lips as he struggled to stop himself from moving. His hip hit one of the beams, jarring his bones and teeth loose, and the flash of pain careened a red wash over his vision. The wall came at him fast, and Tristan barely had enough time to throw his arms up over his head before he slammed into its solid planking. Something cracked, and for a moment, he suspected it was one of his limbs, until a sharp kick to his ribs and a panicked wailing made him open his eyes and stare up at the ass end of a very scared and pissed-off male camel.

The creature's toed hoof flew out, nearly striking his head, and Tristan rolled over, ignoring the pangs of agony shooting through him in order to get out of the hole he'd just made in the stall. He was out before the camel could land another blow, but his side hurt every time he took in a short breath, and there was a now all too familiar metallic sting in his throat. His spit tasted of blood, and when he tried to clear it out, his mouth filled again, filaments of shredded cheek ticking the flat of his tongue.

The crackle of fire fought to dominate the screaming rambles of fear coming from the camel, and beyond the stall, Sey's Highland cattle shifted and spun, agitated by the growing flames. His eyes were still spinning about in their sockets, but Tristan could see Cin standing up, seeming unfazed by whatever had exploded behind them.

Or at least he seemed unperturbed until they both heard a sharp crack of something giving way, and then the world went black and thick for Tristan as Cin threw himself over Tristan's body and shoved them both up against the remains of the camel's stall.

"What the fuck is it with you Kincaids?" Tristan tried to shove Cin off, but somewhere near where he'd been sitting, there was an echoing pop. "What—"

Cin ducked down over him, tucking Tristan's head down against his chest as he tried to get loose. A half moment later, their world rushed into an eerie, odd faux silence as every noise around them hushed to a back note of sound beneath an ear-bleeding boom, and then Tristan felt nothing but the throb of percussion in his ears and the rattle of his skull slamming into the barn's hard concrete floor.

Chapter 13

THE FIREBALL lit up the morning sky. Its glow threw sunset streamers of light through the foggy drizzle, and Wolf's heart lurched to a stuttering stop. The boom preceding the blaze had drawn Wolf to the window, but the lick of flames he'd spotted through the open double doors got him running toward the barn.

"Sey! The barn!" He burst out through the back door, nearly ripping the screen from its hinges. Flying over the soaked grass, Wolf skidded when the ground gave way under him. It was too wet from the downpour, and his bare feet dug into the mud when he hydroplaned over the lawn. A second later, his panic hit the stratosphere when he remembered his lover'd fled to the barn for peace and quiet. "Shit, Tristan!"

He was through the doors closest to the house in a full run.

It was like being in the middle of a war zone. It was easy to find the fire. Oddly enough, it was a small blaze but was eating through a hay bale set against a vulnerable wooden wall. He had a slight panic at the sight of Tristan's abandoned sketchpad and pencils scattered over the floor, and Wolf was torn between fighting the fire and finding his lover. A soft moan from behind him answered his question about Tristan's whereabouts. He and his cousin were splayed out a few feet away, their bodies pinwheeled against one of the horse stall's outer walls.

More alarming was Cin's brief shock and widened eyes, then his cousin twisting about to land on Tristan's long body. Tristan groused something about Kincaid men, but Wolf was already diving for cover, driven more by Cin's instinct than anything else.

A half beat and a suck of breath was all the time Wolf had before another one of the hay bales burst in an explosion of sound and heat. Smoldering straw bit into his exposed flesh, welting and burning his skin. The backs of his hands took most of the damage, and as soon as the crackling echo of sound faded in his ringing ears, Wolf was up on his feet and running toward the flaming hay bales.

It'd been a long time since he'd last hefted bales, but Wolf figured he wasn't going to be judged on form. With one bale fully engulfed and another one on its way to being consumed by the rapidly spreading fire, he wasn't going to waste time on appearances. Wolf snagged up one of the horse blankets from a nearby stack, then tossed it to Sey as she came in.

"Soak that in a puddle or some mud," he shouted over the shushing rain. "I'll clear a way in."

Thankfully, Sey didn't argue. She was outside in a flash, leaving Wolf to work through the center of the pile, where the two bales were beginning to spread their fire.

Seizing a bale in front of him, Wolf felt his shoulders burn with the packed straw's weight until he shifted his hold to balance out the load. The flames were spreading quicker than he liked, and it took him only two more bales in to reach the growing fire. The smoke choked him, and he reached down to hook his T-shirt's collar. Dragging it up over his nose, he dove into the hay pile.

Wolf grabbed one of the newly smoking bales' bindings, hoisted the block of hay up, and threw it as hard as he could toward the door. It cleared the rest of the stack, landing with a squishy plop on the damp ground. He was reaching for another one when Sey returned, her arms full of dripping wet blankets.

"Over there!" Directing Sey toward the other end of the bale the flames were stretching to, he picked up one of the thick wool throws and began beating at the bales.

"Where's Cin and Tris?" Sey shouted through the smoke. "Shit, the livestock."

"We can get this out!" Wolf caught a bit of movement out of the corner of his eye. It was Tristan emerging from a pile of Cin and board bits from the camel's stall. "Tris! Cin? You okay?"

"I'm good, Kincaid," Tristan said loudly. Wolf's insides turned to a sweet pudding when Tristan gave him a weak smile.

The barn could have burned down around them, and Wolf wouldn't have cared—much. He nearly cried with relief at seeing Tristan rise up relatively unharmed. He was moving a bit slow, too tenderly for Wolf's liking, and he almost dropped the blanket to go check on his lover when he was pulled back to reality by Sey's alarmed screech as the fire leaped to another bale.

"Yeah, I'm good too, Wolf. Thanks for caring!" Cin extracted himself from the mess and wiped at the trail of blood coming from a cut on his forehead. "Quit making cow eyes at the kid. He can help me get the animals out. Sey needs—"

"Fuck, you're a dick." Tristan didn't wait for Cin, ducking into the camel's stall. "You go get the other guys out." Cin tried to grab at him, but Tristan growled over the remains of the wall, "Get a move on, Cin! I'll take care of the camel."

"He outweighs you by about five tons," Wolf heard Cin arguing. Satisfied Tristan was okay—and Cin appeared to have emerged with his grumpiness intact, Wolf returned to beating out the flames.

"They okay?" Sey called out.

"Yeah, they're arguing. Right as rain." The blanket he'd been using was already dry, and he threw it at the open doors, hoping it would land in some water in case they needed it again. Grabbing one of the wet covers, he started in again, shouting at Sey as he worked the fire. "Can you turn the hose onto this? Might have to lose the whole batch to save the barn. It's spreading too fast."

"If you can hold it back long enough for me to get to the spigot. The hose is on the other side, but it'll stretch."

"Go!" Wolf pounded at another section. "Because if we don't do it soon, we're not going to have a barn anymore!"

TRISTAN NEARLY lost his tongue down his throat in a choking fit. As soon as he could get the world to stop spinning, he tried to get up. Large hands were wrapped around his arms, and he shook them off. He coughed again and stood. At first he couldn't seem to find his own feet, but Wolf's shout brought him around. Wolf was beating at the growing fire with a blanket, stopping long enough to study Tristan for injuries.

"I'm good, Kincaid," Tristan called out. Next to him, Cin worked loose of the debris and reassured his cousin he was fine. There was a brief domination game from Cin about getting clear of the barn, but Tristan shoved back.

"Fuck, you're a dick. Go get the other guys out. I'll take care of him." Tristan eased into the stall through the hole he'd made with his body. His head hurt, and he was pretty sure some of his ribs were now in different places, but everything seemed to be in working order. "Can't be much different than a horse."

Or at least he hoped it wouldn't be any different.

There were Kincaids shouting behind him, but Tristan focused on the camel. His eyes were rolling, sliding white with panic. He shed his shirt and hoped to hell someone'd taken the time to desensitize the animal to blindfolds. Tristan patted at the camel's neck, trying to soothe him, then reached up to loop his T-shirt over the animal's forehead. He remembered Sey telling him the camel's name was York, more of a description of the noise he made when he spat than an actual name, but it was better than calling the animal Spitting Smelly Asshat. York stamped, narrowly missing Tristan's foot, but shifted back when Tristan snagged the leading rope around the camel's neck.

"Okay, dude, let's do this." He moved quickly, unlatching the door to the stall while keeping one eye on York.

Cin was working the far side barn doors as Tristan guided the animal out. The ground beneath their feet was slightly wet from the rain and mud they'd tracked in, and Sey nearly barreled over Tristan as she ran past with a wide-mouthed hose in her hands. It sprayed a thick spout of water, splashing everything in range, and Tristan paused, pushing York as far into the stall wall as he could manage so his legs wouldn't be tangled in the twisting hose.

"I'm going to go open the gates. They hook into the barn doors. You should be able to just lead him out," Cin yelled through the barn at Tristan. "Move him slowly. It's really wet over here. If he goes down and lands on you, Wolf will kick my ass."

"I might just kick your ass on principle," Tristan muttered under his breath. "Okay, after I club you over the head from behind. Jesus, what the fuck did they put in your corn flakes when you were kids? Steroids?"

Highland cattle were unflappable beasts. As soon as Cin got the gates connected and opened the door of their inside paddock, there seemed to be a short meeting held by the larger mounds of red fur before they paid even the slightest bit of a attention to the enormous Scottish man trying to herd them out to safety. With a bit of shuffling and head tossing, they ambled outside, the fuzzy calf kicking up his heels as he bounded out into the rain.

"Okay, they're clear!" Cin shouted at Tristan as he closed the paddock door.

With the way clear, Tristan urged York to move forward. The camel balked a second, then reared his head forward when Tristan tugged lightly on the lead. It was slow going at first. The makeshift blinder didn't seem to bother the ungulate as much as Tristan thought it would, and after a few hesitant steps, York fell into a fierce trot, habit leading him to the open doors connecting the barn to the paddocks.

As soon as they were free of the structure, Tristan tugged the lead rope free and yanked his draped shirt off the animal's head. A few of the cattle were gathered up against the fence as if to watch the spectacle, and one let out a soft low at the camel as York plodded up to the small herd.

The air outside was thick with drizzle and wisps of ash. A musty dampness clung to the breeze. The rolling storm front let loose another furious spit and Tristan found himself sluiced with icy water. The rain made the paddock gates slippery, and he fought to get them closed, hoping to pen the animals in before they decided to wander back into the smoky barn. He'd gotten one side closed and locked down when Cin shouldered up next to him, taking the gate pull from his numb, cold hands.

"Shit, you look like you're about to fall over," Cin muttered. "Where the hell is Wolf?

"Probably putting out the fire." It was funny how the embarrassment of his ass and cock being on full view was wiped off his mind with just a spritz of anger. He'd turned on his heel and taken a few steps toward the barn when Cin grabbed his arm.

"Hold up. You can't go back in there. Stay here—"

"You guys okay?" Wolf called out as he walked carefully across the damp grass. "Fire's out. Some of the hay's ruined to shit, but I got enough clear so Sey will be okay for a week. Hopefully, we'll be able to get across the bridge by then. If not, it's going to be a trek up and down that gulch."

"Swear to God, if you don't let go of me, I'm going to punch you in the balls." Tristan shook Cin off—yet again. "Wolf—"

"Help him get to the house, Wolf." Cin spoke over Tristan's shoulder to his cousin as he approached them. "He's about to fall over."

"I don't need help to get to the damned house," Tristan spat at the man. "I don't know who you think your cousin is fucking, but it's not some damned princess in an ivory tower—"

He'd planned a glorious takedown—or at the very least, a spirited, defiant rant—before he collapsed at Wolf's feet. Gearing up to further challenge the larger man, Tristan grabbed at the fence for support, since the ground seemed to be a bit wavy, and opened his mouth to continue his rant.

A crooning wail cut him off. A very familiar keen spiced with the anger of a young girl cut down before her prime.

She came out of the morning brew of fog and smoke, a figment of drapery and skin. There wasn't much of her feet. They were more sketches of light and shadow than shapes, and her skeletal hands ended in dips of long black. Her hooked talons scraped through the mists as she drew close, leaving ghostly trails in the damp air.

The ghost hadn't grown any eyes since the last time Tristan saw her. If anything, her sockets were sunken in, and the skin covering them was parched and wrinkled.

Unlike Petal, Tristan had no doubt Cin saw her. Wolf too. Hell, even the damned camel grunted and gasped behind them. York took off like a shot, disappearing into the murky rolling paddock grounds. The cattle were hot on his toed feet, shuffling after him, hovering some distance away from the humans—and the ghost—their hooves churning up the ground.

"Motherfucking hell." Cin's raspy swear echoed Tristan's own shocked thoughts. "Shit. Is that—"

"Yeah, that's her." Tristan edged closer to Wolf. The man smelled of smoke, coffee, and a hint of jam. Sadly, he could have used less jam and more rock salt. "Tell me you've got a replica of Lot's wife on you, Kincaid."

"Sorry, babe. No can do. All out of moral-lesson icons. Although I'm pretty sure I might have a quarter. But the old cherry tree thing isn't going to do us much good."

The specter came closer, wailing and bobbing through the mists. The ground smoked behind her, curls of heat sending plumes of steam up from the muddied grass. She wore an old-fashioned dress, something more Gibson girl era than the sixties attire of the other ghosts he'd spoken to, and quite unlike the other spirits, she didn't have a friendly air about her.

"Let me see if I can talk to her." Tristan took a step forward, only to find himself held back by Cin's hand on his shoulder. Looking up at the tall Kincaid, he ground out, "You put your hands on me one more time, you're going to be choking on your fingers."

"Let him go, Cin." Wolf tugged at his cousin's elbow. "Tris knows what he's doing. Mostly."

The *mostly* wasn't exactly the vote of confidence Tristan'd hoped for, but it was going to have to be good enough. It certainly was for Cin, who let him go, but not without Wolf stopping Tristan long enough to mutter into his ear.

"When she's gone, you and I are going to have a long talk." Wolf brushed a kiss over his lobe. "Keep her occupied. I'm going to see if Sey's got some salt lick stuff in the barn. We can use that against her."

"Deal," Tristan agreed. "And you don't have to whisper. I don't think she can hear you guys. Hell, Petal didn't even see Cin, I don't think."

"Who the hell is Petal?" Wolf asked as Tristan stepped closer to the apparition. "Never mind. Be careful, Thursday. I'll be right back."

Tristan didn't answer. He was focused on the wild-haired phantom floating over the ground in front of him. Her mouth dropped impossibly open, stretching her nostrils down into two stygian ovals as her chin reached the scalloped lace yoke on her dress. An ethereal wind caught the pale frizz growing over her emaciated skull, pulling it up into a corona around her head.

The inside of the ghost's mouth was as black as her fingertips. There were no teeth, no tongue that Tristan could see. Just an all-consuming inky hole reaching back into a hell only the specter knew existed.

A hell she shared with them when her screams sliced through the dank morning to cut deep, painful furrows into Tristan's mind.

"Siiiiimoooooooooooooooooone!"

It echoed and turned around until Tristan couldn't be sure if she'd started a new keen, or it was merely the stain it left on his eardrums. Gray tendrils leaked from cracks forming in the skin around her eye sockets. They bled back, caught in the same wind as her hair, and she leaned forward, screaming with all her spectral might at the blond man she'd caught in her spell.

"Who is Simone?" Tristan winced when the pitch of her moan changed. It grew higher, and beyond, in the paddock, the cattle began to howl back in discomfort. From the camel, there was no sound, but then, Tristan reasoned, York *had* taken one look at what was going on and hightailed it off to parts unknown. Another wail, and he was forced to cover his ears, muting the waves of sound assaulting his hearing. "Fucking camel is smart as shit."

"What is going on?" Daylen leaned over the porch railing and called out to the yard. Of all the times for Sey's intern to show up, now was certainly the worst as far as Tristan was concerned. The man had to be dead to any spectral activity because he tromped across the back path, heading right to the phantasm. "What's making that noise? Where'd the kid come from?"

Maybe not so dead to it, because the shriveled-up ghost spun about and reached for the Canadian, and Daylen let out a small scream of his own when he saw her face.

"You—whoever the fuck—"

A screaming rant from the ghost broke through Cin's warning, and Tristan heard Sey calling out to Wolf in the barn.

"Shit."

"Daylen! Get back!" His Converses weren't made for wet lawn. Hell, they were barely made for dry sidewalk, and Tristan slid more than he walked, but at least he was going forward toward the ghost. "Get away from her."

"You have Simoooooooooooooooone." Her hands curved up, tiny sickles looking sharp enough to cut through flesh. They ate up the light, and Daylen reared back in horror as the reality of what he was seeing sunk in.

"Oh God! What is this? What is going on?" Daylen tried to backpedal, but the ghost was too close. Her arms flung out, as elastic as her jaw, and her hands grabbed a hold of Daylen's chest, sinking her talons into his flesh.

Too many things happened at once. The man's chest began to spurt blood, gushing hot streams of red through the little girl's filmy arms, and his pained screams drowned out even her caterwauling. The cattle began to low and call from behind them, and Cin sprinted across the lawn toward the unsuspecting Daylen. Tristan took off after him, careening wildly over the wet grass. The short distance seemed to be an eternity of running; then suddenly he was on the wraith.

Tristan didn't know what he thought he was going to do. He'd hoped to talk to her like he'd done with Ray and Petal, but reasoning with the little girl seemed to be the furthest thing from possible as she raked open Daylen's chest. Cin passed through her and slammed into Daylen's twitching body, trying to loosen the ghost's grip.

She was strong, too strong for Cin to break Daylen free, but where she'd been incorporeal for Cin, Tristan was shocked to find his hands closing over her thin, cold arms.

It was like holding dry ice. Her skin burned through his, and Tristan didn't think he could hold on for much longer when Wolf came out of the barn, running with a small plastic feeding scoop filled with chunks of dull ruddy fragments. Yanking on the girl's arms seemed to work, or at least Tristan hoped she was letting go because he'd pulled on her and not because she was turning her attentions onto him.

Wolf got within a few feet of the ghost and flung the scoop's contents out, yelling at the top of his lungs, "*Fugite! Confugo!* Shit—"

"*Terga dare?*" Tristan offered up.

The fragments struck her, and the salt sparked and popped wherever it landed. Her keens broke into a furious howl, deepening in tone until the air rattled with the sound of her shrieks. She began to crack, bits of dust flying off her body, then dissipating in the mist. Tristan fell to his knees and grabbed at salt chunks on the ground and tossed them at her, lighting up her body with more crackling hot lines.

She had turned, her fingers raised to scratch at his face, when he found a large chunk of the broken-up salt lick in the wet grass. Sticky with slime, it was hard to hold onto, but he scooped it up from the ground and flung it, striking the ghost in the remains of her face. He caught a flash of rolling red fire when the skin across her eyes burst apart, and her sockets filled with a flame hotter than the burn of her flesh on his hands.

Then she exploded into a burst of sparks, burning phantom stars into his vision, as if he'd stared into a blazing sun for a moment longer than he should have.

"Fucking hell." Wolf panted to catch his breath. "Shit, babe. Your hands."

"I'm okay," Tristan replied. "Bit red, but I've done worse. We've got to take care of Daylen."

The young Canadian was passed out, limp in the cradle of Cin's arms. With the ghost extracted from his chest, his wounds didn't seem too bad, but his blood-speckled shirt was probably hiding bruised flesh. Wolf nodded thoughtfully, and the cousins seemed to share a confusingly similar look Tristan liked to call Wolf's come-to-Jesus glance.

His suspicions were confirmed when Cin hefted Daylen's unconscious body and stared down at where Tristan had fallen. "I'm going to get him settled in with Sey. Then you, me, and your ghost whisperer are going to have a few words, Wolf. Because it's too fucking dangerous to let the two of you wander around without a leash. You're going to get us all killed."

Chapter 14

ONE OF the overhead lights flashed on when Wolf reached the second landing on the stairs. It was an unexpected spark of bright in the gloom creeping through the house, barely a whisper to hold back the darkness coming in from outside. The light danced and flickered for a moment before settling down, and by the time Wolf reached the bedroom, he could make out the hum of the house's electronics coming on. A tiny red dot shone out from the camera he'd mounted to record the hallway's activity, but Wolf didn't need any video to tell him his lover would be waiting for him inside the room.

If the trail of soggy footprints on the floor wasn't warning enough, the hot, angry look Tristan gave him before he headed into the house did the trick.

He was partially right. Tristan was in the bedroom but not waiting to tear Wolf a new asshole. The sound of water from the shower made Wolf smile, and he slipped into the bathroom, hoping to catch Tristan unaware.

When Sey redid the house, she'd taken one of the long walk-in closets peppering the upper floor and divided its space out into the bathrooms on either side. The added space went mostly to include enormous travertine tile stalls surrounded by glass, a luxury Wolf was certainly now quite glad for. Especially since the stall could hold two grown men and had a bench built in near the forest of showerheads if they wanted to sit under a misting steam and relax.

From the tightness in Tristan's naked shoulders, Wolf figured Tris needed as much relaxation as he could get.

The small opaque windows set high on the bathroom's outward-facing wall gave Wolf all the light he needed. He didn't like the purpling marks on his lover's body. Not at all. There were various scrapes and digs on Tristan's pale skin, but for the most part, the man was... hot. It was really the only word Wolf ever thought of every time he caught sight of Tristan's naked form.

The man's legs did him in, long and lean with tight muscles, leading up to one of the most succulent asses Wolf ever had the pleasure of seeing, much less having his hands on. The time Tristan spent in the Grange's swimming pool showed in his chest and arms. Standing under the showerhead, Tristan was a study in sinewy grace with a face seemingly stolen from a Waterhouse painting.

"I'd be a fucking idiot to let you get away," he whispered to himself. Wolf's luck chose then to run out, and Tristan's eyes churned a gray, stormy green when he spotted Wolf through the shower's glass enclosure. "Hey, sexy."

"I'm not talking to you," Tristan snorted at him, menacingly waving a soap bottle at Wolf. "Your cousin's an asshole. You're not much better."

"I never said he wasn't." It wasn't the best defense Wolf could have come up with, but it was the best he had. "Cin's never been... he's had it rough."

"We've all had it rough. It's called life," the blond pointed out.

"You've got to admit, Thursday. You're a bit much for the average guy to take in all at once. Even for a Kincaid." Wolf shed his clothes quickly, conscious of his lover's watchful eye. "And I've apologized for my assholeishness."

"Is that even a word?" Tristan mumbled through a spray of water as he tilted his face up for a moment.

"Pretty much the Kincaid family motto." His pants fought him for a moment. They were too wet and caked with the right amount of mud to be difficult. He finally got them undone and shucked while Tristan watched him through the glass.

"You think you're coming in here with me?" Tristan drawled. "To save hot water, I suppose."

"Power's on, and this place has three water heaters. It's geared up for a lot of bodies taking baths at once." He kicked his mud-splattered clothes over to where Tristan had laid his on a towel. "And I'm not coming in there to save hot water. I'm coming in there so I can hold you and then get clean."

"Watch your step," Tristan warned. "We have company."

He almost missed it. How he could have, Wolf didn't know, but he did, and he had to step quickly to avoid the red rubber ball he'd sent rolling around on the shower's tile floor. Bending down, he picked it up and carefully placed it outside of the stall and closed the door behind him.

"Yeah, good luck with that. I've already put it out there twice." Tristan snorted loudly. "But then, he listens to you more than he does me."

"Stay outside, Jack. We'll play later." Wolf had nowhere else to focus on but the ball. He'd liked to have said it quivered in response— just for sanity's sake—but the truth was, it sat there on the bath mat and was simply—a red ball. "Maybe it's not his."

Tris crooked an eyebrow at Wolf, mocking him. "Right. Because everyone has red rubber balls suddenly appear in the shower with them."

Tristan allowed himself to be turned around, and Wolf squeezed his butt before resting his hands on Tristan's hips. Stroking the man's side, he leaned in and pressed a soft kiss onto Tristan's mouth. They were both growing hard, languidly aroused, but Wolf was more interested in comforting the slightly chilled man he'd found himself falling in love with.

"Let's get you clean so I can take care of your boo-boos." Wolf bent his head to lick at the water streaming down Tristan's neck.

"Is that what the kids these days are calling it? Their boo-boo?" The mockery continued, but there wasn't any heat in it, and Wolf wrapped his arms around Tristan's waist, grinding their bodies together. "Keep that up, and my boo-boo is going to turn into a bam-bam."

"Just a cuddle." Wolf rocked his lover gently. "Can I be honest with you? And not have you lose your shit?"

Tristan regarded him with his large gold-bled green eyes, then nodded. "Okay. Shoot."

"I know you're capable. I know you're strong," Wolf murmured as he reached up to take Tristan's face in his hands. "But there are times, like today, when I want to hide you someplace safe so nothing can ever hurt you again."

"It doesn't work that way, Kincaid." Tristan kissed the inside of Wolf's left wrist. "Even if I wasn't being attacked by some ghost your family or friends dragged up, I still have my relatives to deal with."

"Yeah, I'm thinking deep holes and a shovel for those fuckers." The water was beginning to run lukewarm despite his claims about an endless heater feed. "Come on. Let's finish scrubbing the filth off of you and let me take a look at your bruises."

"So long as that's all you look at." Tristan built up a heavy lather on the scrubby he'd been using, then began to run it over Wolf's body, slowly working over his skin. "I don't think we're going to get a moment's peace until Cin gets to interrogate me."

"Damn it. Guess you're right." Wolf lifted his arms and caught himself purring when Tristan's hands spread through the hair on his thighs. "I think Cin's the least of our worries. Sey's ghost is going to kill us long before Cin ever gets around to it."

A HEFTY dose of ibuprofen washed down with a creamy cup of hot coffee helped ease a lot of Tristan's aches and pains. The naughty suggestions Wolf whispered into his ear as he stirred sugar into his mug also helped, but it gave him a creaking ache he knew he wasn't going to get rid of until he had either Wolf's hands or lips on him.

Maybe even both.

Dressing was easier than taking his clothes off, mostly from taking a handful of meds and letting them work through his body, but also Wolf seemed to take great delight in buttoning up his jeans and shirt. It only took Wolf two times to get the buttons lined up into the right holes, and by the time he was done, they were both laughing like drunken idiots.

His cheeks hurt nearly as much as his side did, but for the most part, Tristan wasn't feeling any pain until he caught sight of Cin's scowl from across the living room. The man's fierce expression promised an endless agony for anyone who didn't bow down to his every whim.

So Tristan stuck his tongue out at Cin and went to the kitchen to get something hot to drink before heading back to the living room to face the Kincaids gathered there.

"How's Daylen?" Tristan settled down next to Wolf, drawing his legs up to keep warm. A pair of thick socks worked for his feet, but the rest of him seemed to have a chill he couldn't get rid of. Something poked him in the back, and he leaned forward, finding Jack's rubber ball wedged between him and the couch. Holding it up for Wolf to see, he smirked at his lover. "Really?"

"I did *not* put it there. Hell, I haven't even seen him," Wolf confessed. "And to answer your question, Daylen's fine." Frowning slightly, he glanced at Sey sitting in one of the wing chairs next to them. "He *is* fine, right?"

"Sleeping. It's really not that bad. Or at least it doesn't look that bad," she replied. "The cuts seem shallow, but he said he was cold. I don't know if the pain made him pass out—"

"He fainted," Cin contributed. "Don't know how much of it was the pain or the shock of having a ghost bury its hands into him."

"It burned when I touched her." Tristan held up his hand, showing the Kincaids the bright red streaks he'd earned across his palm. "They're fading fast, though. It was worse before."

"Let's see if we can't hash some of this out so Tris can get some sleep," Wolf cut in.

"Sleep?" Gildy scoffed. "I'm about five hundred years older than you, and I'd be taking that boy upstairs and give him as good as I've got. Even if he is possessed."

"I am not possessed," Tristan cut in.

"Gildy, leave him alone." Sey spoke up first. "You're not helping."

There was no doubt about it. The old woman was a bit crazy. Smiling sweetly at Sey, she nodded and murmured her consent. As soon as her niece looked away, Gildy forked her fingers in front of her eyes, then pointed them at Tristan, mouthing she was watching him. He was busy rolling his eyes when Cin spoke up.

"Okay, so you really see and talk to ghosts?" The Hellsinger leaned forward, resting his elbows on his knees as he spoke. It was such a Wolf thing to do Tristan could almost forgive him when he then asked, "How do we know you're *not* possessed? Maybe even drawing the activity to you?"

"Don't be an asshole, Cin," Wolf pushed back on his cousin. "Leap of faith, remember?"

"I just don't want to be leaping from the frying pan and into the fire," Cin shot back. "But okay, let's go with medium. Most of them get vague impressions or whispers. Your boy here pulls in full apparitions like I've never seen before."

"His boy is right here," Tristan said, waving his hand in front of Cin's face. "I'm not a dog. I have the power of speech, and if you can't talk to me directly, I might as well fucking go upstairs and crash while you all figure shit out."

He braved Cin's gaze, him staring down until Tris saw something shift in Cin's eyes. They softened, then relaxed when Cin nodded slowly.

"Fair enough," the man murmured. "Wolf told me you've been seeing ghosts since you were a little kid. When did it start happening?"

"When didn't it happen?" Tristan gave a quick rundown on the Grange, and Wolf jumped in to sketch out their encounter with Winifred. The Kincaids listened quietly for the most part with the exception of Gildy, who offered up elated advice on how Meegan should have conducted the exorcism.

"Yeah, it wasn't the best course of action, but it got the job done," Wolf agreed.

"Shit, I'm sorry I couldn't be there." Cin leaned back.

"You were in London, right? No helping it. Fact is, we're all here now with this thing. Short of burning the house down, how do we get her out of here?" Wolf reached for Tristan's hand, then tangled their fingers together. It felt good to have Wolf's heat on his skin, especially since he needed an anchor to keep his thoughts from skittering about.

"I don't think burning the house down is the answer. Although she got a good head start." Sey rubbed at her face. The shadows under her eyes were a deep purple, and fatigue pulled at the corners of her generous mouth. "She had to have caused the mess out there. There's not an outlet near the haystack, and they were too damp to rub together to catch fire. We lost some hay, but it didn't touch the structure."

"Animals seemed eager to go back in, so that's a good sign she's not there anymore," Cin commented. "Okay, let's go over what we know. She is looking for Simone."

"That's a doll or maybe someone she knew," Tristan supplied. When everyone but Wolf looked at him in surprise, he shrugged. "Ray told me, remember? He really wasn't sure. She's got him kind of rattled."

"Okay, so if she appeared a few weeks ago, I'm going to guess you got a shipment in from somewhere, Sey, and that doll is in there. What did you get in, and where did you put it?" Cin reached across to Gildy and pressed her back in her chair with a light touch of his fingers to her shoulder. "Information first. Burning and salting artifacts later."

"You don't think it was in the doll heads she put around Tristan?" Gildy asked.

"No, if she could have gotten a hold of it, she'd be done with this," Cin replied. "Chances are, she can't actually touch it for some reason, but maybe moving it from wherever it came from to here released her."

"I think if she had it, she'd lay waste to SLO and everything around it," Wolf said softly. He reached for Tristan's cup and took a small sip before handing it back. "She's angry. Angriest thing or person I've ever seen."

"Children usually are. Especially if they know they're dead," Cin pointed out. "But yeah, this is more than a life cut short. Something happened, and it pissed her off. What came in about the time she first started fucking with you, Sey?"

"A few weeks? It was slow, so it's hard to really nail down a time." Sey pulled her face into a grimace. "I bought a bunch of blind boxes from a collector's estate and a few auctions. I just haven't had time to go through the stuff yet. It's all in crates up in the storage room."

"Same place the dolls on the bed came from, but those were loose in bins."

Stretching, Wolf's spine popped a few times, and Tristan felt a small pinprick of envy at the man's contented sigh.

"Everything else up there is sealed up tight. She might not be strong enough to pop the bindings. It's one thing to have enough energy to rub straw together fast enough to spark a fire, but it's another thing to open up shipping crates banded in metal."

"Yeah, she'd have to be pretty strong if the binding wraps are iron," Cin agreed. "Okay, so we have to open all of that stuff up and see what we can find."

"Do you think she's been following the doll around?" Sey pondered. "Maybe if there was activity where she's from, it could help pin things down."

"Could be a long shot, especially if it's from an estate," Wolf said. "Don't they usually happen after a death? Anyone who was around the ghost before might be dead themselves."

"I think I can help with that." Tristan nearly pulled back into Wolf when the Kincaids swiveled their heads to look at him. "Well, I know she's here and what she looks like. I can try to do what I did with Ray. He wasn't really solid until I focused on bringing him out. I might be able to do that with her. If we find the right doll."

"We just have to do this smart." Cin flipped open a notebook lying on the table and began to sketch out a few odd symbols on the paper. "Binding circles might help while we open them, but I don't know if that'll work. Logistics would be a nightmare."

Sey wrinkled her nose. "Can't we just figure out which doll she's looking for and pitch it into a fire or something?"

"We could, but as soon as we open the crate it's in, she might be all over it. And I've got a feeling if she gets a hold of that doll before we do, shit's going to go to hell in a handbasket faster than we can throw rock salt," Cin said in his low rumble. Tristan met his hard gaze straight on when Cin looked at him from across the coffee table. "Unless Tristan here's got some mojo inside of him to stop her. And *that* is something I've gotta see."

"GOD, I am dead tired." Tristan made a small bounce when he flung himself facedown on their bed. "How the heck did Sey not know she had about thirty boxes put up in that room? Fuckers were heavy. It's going to take us forever to go through them tomorrow."

Dinner'd been a hasty gulp of sandwiches while discussing what they would work on next. The animals needed to be moved out, especially since the barn seemed inclined to burst into flames at a moment's notice, but relocating Sey's crates was on the top of their list. The Kincaids agreed they'd move the livestock over to neighbors who offered to take them in while Tristan dug into Sey's old inventory.

Wolf wasn't happy about Tristan's going at the boxes on his own, but Cin scorned his overprotectiveness.

"You're telling me he's been doing this kind of thing for years now, Wolf," Cin admonished. "He's a big boy. If things go to shit, I'm pretty sure he can take care of himself. Maybe."

It'd taken them nearly an hour to remove the furniture, finding places for the heavy pieces while fighting Daylen off from opening the smaller crates. After Cin threatened to cut off his dick and fingers if he touched one more thing, the young man crept back onto one of the chairs they'd left in the room and proceeded to flirt with Tristan.

Wolf was pretty sure he was going to kill the posh-accented young man before they could get rid of Sey's ghost. And he was also certain if he let Daylen live for maybe another day, Cin would help him.

Sitting on the edge of the mattress, Wolf stretched his arms up and shook off the aches in his shoulders. He tugged his socks off. Then with a quick twist of his fingers, he turned them into a ball and tossed them toward the chair he'd left a hoodie on. They bounced once, then arched off the seat and onto the floor. Making disappointed crowd hisses, he flopped over and buried his face into Tristan's lime-scented hair.

"I like this shampoo you use. Very citrusy. I can grab some minty one and we can try to muddle ourselves together into a mojito." He snugged up against the man's side, working his hand down Tristan's spine. Tristan didn't flinch or react when Wolf lightly skimmed the spots he'd bruised in the fight, but he still wanted to be cautious. Kissing Tristan's ear, he whispered. "You are simply the most gorgeous man I've ever seen."

"Wow, you need to get out more," Tristan laughed as he turned over to face Wolf.

"Don't do that." He shook his head, hearing a familiar deprecation in Tristan's snark. "Don't put yourself down. You deserve better."

The wariness was back on Tristan's face. It was spiced with a bit of caution and stubbornness, just as it'd been the first time Wolf saw the blond man behind the Grange's reception desk. Much like that moment, Wolf was struck with the man's haunting beauty and a small whispering need to kiss away the shadows in Tristan's changeable eyes.

Stroking Tristan's cheek, he inched himself as close as he could get to press into Tristan's body. "You are something miraculous."

"You're just saying that because I see ghosts," he scoffed. "And you're a freak that gets turned on by that."

"No, I'm saying that because you're a weird, geeky pretty man who makes me stop and think about what I'm saying or regret it immensely when I don't." Wolf stole another kiss, stretching out their contact until he was certain he'd leave Tristan without any air to draw on in his lungs. He was right. When he pulled back, Tristan was panting, and their erections fought for space between them, lunging and parrying in an attempt to break free of their sweatpants prisons. "You're the first guy I've ever wanted to avoid hurting before. I'll be the first one to admit it, Thursday. I'm an asshole, but you being around? It makes me want to be good enough to be with you. Even if I do fuck it up something royal every time I open my mouth."

"You open your mouth a lot," Tristan agreed.

Wolf recognized the faint glint in the man's eyes, and he trailed a hand down over Tristan's hip, stroking slowly to feed Tristan's flickering arousal.

"We should talk—"

"Of cabbages and kings," Wolf quoted. "I'll be the cabbage. You be the king."

"I've always felt more Jabberwocky than king," he admitted. "Especially now. Shit, Daylen could have been killed. Sey could have lost the barn."

"None of which are your fault."

"I feel like it is. Inside. Down deep."

"Do you think your parents' death was your fault?" Wolf was surprised when, a heartbeat later, Tristan still hadn't answered. "Oh fuck, babe. There's no way you were responsible for that. You were a kid."

"I wonder sometimes, you know?" He cocked his head, and a fall of gold hair partially covered his face, leaving most of it in shadow. "If I hadn't been so weird, maybe they would have stayed home more. Stayed with me more."

"I don't know why they weren't with you, Tris. I don't. I don't know them enough to judge, and fuck, I don't think anyone should judge them. You three were in a tightly wound situation, and from what it sounds like, the adults in the equation were a bit emotionally compromised." He returned his fingers to Tristan's face, rubbing at the man's lower lip with a press of his thumb. "So no, just because you're looking at it from the self-centered perspective of a kid's world doesn't mean that they were running from you. Chances are, they were running from themselves."

"Didn't say it wasn't stupid, just that it feels like that sometimes. Especially since, you know... my brother."

"That's all on your parents. They were carrying around a lot of pain and guilt. From what it sounds like, anyway. Doesn't mean you're weird because of it." Wolf tweaked the end of Tristan's nose, liking the husky laugh he got from the man. "You're just weird because you're weird. Not like I'm the poster child of normal."

"I'd have said you're the most normal one in your family. Until I met Sey, anyway."

"Gildy is definitely stranger than me." They'd taken a bucket of cleaning fluids and other household things out of Gildy's room. She'd protested their removal of her exorcism kit, but Wolf wasn't fooled. The old lady was playing them over something, but he hadn't quite figured it out yet. "She's crazy like a fox. She's up to something, or she could just really be insane. I haven't decided."

"I know what you're up to." Tristan rubbed his hips against Wolf's. "Totally easy to figure out."

"Baby, my dick is like Lassie around you." He chuckled. "It gets hard for no reason, and I'm always asking it, *What is it, boy? Do you see something you like?*"

"Way to kill the mood." Tristan pushed at Wolf's chest, but it wasn't a hard enough push to budge him. Tristan's palms lingered on Wolf's nipples, rubbing at them through his T-shirt. "Never ever call your dick Lassie or anything animal related. That's just… gross."

"How about Godzilla?" Wolf countered. "I can make rawr noises. They're pretty sexy. From what I've seen, you really like it when I sound like Godzilla."

"Do you remember the last time you were making rawr noises? We not only got a ghost, but Cin came through the door. I don't know if my heart can take that again." Tristan jerked his thumb toward the windows. "And you wouldn't believe where some of that salt ended up. I was picking it out of the paint. I should totally tell Sey. She'll kick his ass."

"No Cin this time. I locked the door and made sure the windows were sealed up tight. We're fully salted up and ready for her this time." He slid his hands down again, working his fingers past Tristan's waistband and down to the soft milky skin of his hips. "So, my rawr noises? You wanna hear them?"

Tristan cocked his head as if thinking about it, then smiled, "Yeah. Thought you'd never ask."

Chapter 15

THERE WOULD never be a time when sliding his body against Wolf's would be anything but a sensual pleasure. With Wolf pressing him down into the bed, Tristan stretched out and tried to touch as much of Wolf as he could, luxuriating in the feel of soft hair against his thighs and Wolf's balls and dick brushing over his cock.

Wolf's pulse thrummed under his skin, and it reverberated everywhere along Tristan's body. His own heartbeat echoed in his ears, and with the silence of the world closing in on them, all Tristan heard was the push and pull of their breathing, then the quiet wet of their tongues finding comfort in each other's mouths.

There lay a mingle of rain and man in Wolf's mouth, a savory hint of an after-dinner hour spent slogging through the paddock to round up very stubborn shaggy red cows and a single grumpy camel named York. His lover'd almost needed another shower when the not-so-tiny calf barreled into him, but at the last moment, the out-of-control youngster veered off and slammed into Cin, sending the man ass over teakettle into a mud puddle.

Tristan's laugh brought Wolf's head up, and they shared a moment, a simmering heat caught in the light drizzle coming down between the house and the barn. The fire they'd set then remained between them, fed by the slow touches of their hands as they met on the porch, then again when Tristan scrubbed away most of the damp on Wolf's face and hair with a warm towel.

They'd tumbled upstairs, laughing softly at stupid things, like Daylen's gaga face over Cin's naked, slightly furred chest when Wolf's cousin stripped off his muddy shirt in the middle of the kitchen and nearly followed suit with his pants before Sey stopped him. Gildy and Daylen's protests fell on deaf ears, and Cin was chased off to his room, grumbling all the way there that he'd just have to carry his filthy clothes back down.

"God, it feels good to have something we can do to get rid of her," Tristan sighed.

"Let's leave our ghost outside. I didn't salt this room up like a pretzel only for you to be dragging her back in here."

Wolf kissed him again, and Tristan opened his mouth to let Wolf take what he wanted. They drew out the connection, their lips nearly bruised from tasting one another, until Tristan needed to breathe. Wolf was panting a bit heavily, but his cocky grin promised Tristan there would be a lot more kissing as the night went on.

"Turn over," Wolf said as he sat up, reaching for the lubricant he'd tossed onto the bed. "I want to see how much I can make you squirm, baby."

The sheets were soft on Tristan's belly, and he frowned at Wolf when the man tapped his side and told him to lift his hips. Canting his rear up, Tristan felt the rougher grip of a towel being slid under him, then the soft press of Wolf's mouth on his ass before Wolf gently pushed him back down onto the bed.

"I know you hate wet spots," Wolf explained over the pop of the lubricant cap being opened. "So, there you go. Towel. Now close your eyes and hold on, love. I'm going to take my time opening you up for me."

He gripped the sheets, wrapping as much around his fingers as he could. There was going to have to be trust between them, Tristan realized. Especially for things like what Wolf was about to do to him. It was all so very new, so very bright and sharp in his mind and on his body, and Tristan wasn't sure if he ever was going to be used to Wolf's fingers and mouth on his skin.

With all of the trembling and goose bumps crawling over him, Tristan found he didn't ever want the prickle of anticipation to go away. And he found himself already aching for Wolf's thick girth to spread him apart. His cock was definitely in on the thrill, because it was already wet and stiff in its prison against his belly, so Tristan shifted, hoping to ease some of the deep-seated ache building up in his balls and shaft.

The moving did no good. His cock still throbbed worse than his thumb did when he hit it with a hammer, and all the shifting about did was earn him a stinging slap on the ass from Wolf's broad palm.

"Stay put, Thursday. I don't want to be fumbling about when I'm looking for what I want between those asscheeks," Wolf grumbled over him. "Or anything else. Just. Lay. There."

Trust was a hard thing. Not nearly as hard as his dick at the moment, but it was a close second. There'd not been many times when Tristan fell and there'd been someone to catch him. But then, he didn't remember a time when he hadn't been falling. It'd only been since he'd met Wolf that he finally felt the ground beneath his feet.

Other people spoke longingly of having the wind beneath their wings. Tristan would have killed just to have the earth between his toes or the grass tickle his heels.

Or better yet, the feel of Wolf's fingers invading him.

He could smell the oil, and he tensed when he heard Wolf's hands squishing together. His shoulders knotted up, and Tristan forced himself to relax, but there was no running from the edge of want building up inside of him, and his hole clenched and gave between his cheeks, kneading in and out in anticipation.

The shock came when Wolf's hands didn't slide down to part his ass. Instead, they slid over Tristan's shoulders, where he began to work at soothing the taut muscles along Tristan's spine.

"What the fuck are you—?" Tristan lifted his head and tried to catch Wolf's attention. "Not what I—"

"Put your head down and let me do this for you." Wolf continued to softly dig into the hard knots Tristan didn't know he had on his back. "When was the last time someone massaged your back for you?"

"Considering you're the first one to get his dick inside of me, what makes you think someone else has ever been near me while I'm naked?"

"Then definitely let me do this for you, babe," he murmured as he kissed a spot between Tristan's shoulder blades. Wolf's faint stubble feathered a tickle on his skin. Then the scrape of whiskers grew deeper when the man's mouth moved down his spine, his lips catching on every ridge of Tristan's backbone. "Try not to fall asleep too deeply. Because I fully intend to take advantage of a boneless Thursday Addams."

"It is so silly when you call me that. But okay." He was already drowsy, and Tristan swore he'd fight off the languid tendrils creeping through his bones. It was hard going, especially when Wolf did a delicate dance over his bruised ribs, and instead of the soft-sharp ache he'd come to expect, there was a rolling release of pressure, and he could hitch a breath in without his side tightening up.

"See, one of the best things about being a Kincaid is that you get dragged to places most people never see." Wolf's husky voice lapped over him, as hot and gentle as his fingers as they moved Tristan's aches and pains out of his body. "By the time I was ten, I'd already been to twenty countries. But the best part was, I sucked up as much education as I could wherever I could find it. Including how to give a very good massage."

"Can't think," Tristan mumbled. "Lost my tongue."

"Maybe I should help you find your tongue," Wolf suggested. "What do you think?"

"Good idea." He shifted, too loose-limbed to do much more than flop halfway over. Staring up into Wolf's hooded blue eyes, Tristan gave his lover a goofy grin. "Need help doing this too. Might even just lie here while you take advantage of me."

"Now where would the fun be in that?" Wolf slid him over the rest of the way. The bed dipped as he lay down on his side next to Tristan, his oil-slick fingers tracing odd shapes on Tristan's firm belly. "You awake enough for the main course?"

"Wolfgang Starfox Kincaid, I've been waiting for the main course since before we had breakfast." Tristan hooked his hand around Wolf's nape and pulled him in for a kiss. A fit of chuckles hit him, and he tried to swallow them but instead ended up choking on his own spit. Clearing his throat, Tristan wiped the silly off his face and said in as serious as a tone as he could, "I'm sorry. What was the question again? Something about food?"

"God, never ever use my full name again," Wolf laughed into his mouth. "Ruins the moment. Hell, it ruined my childhood. I'd rather not have to fight it off as an adult."

"You could change it, you know."

"Nah, that would hurt my mother's feelings, and I can suck it up for her." Wolf's hand was on the move again, and one particularly adventurous finger traced down the length of Tristan's stiffening cock. "How about if we work on making this as soft as it can go?"

"So long as it's the long way around."

"Well yeah. Kind of like through the woods and to Tristan's secret happy place with a picnic basket trip." The man's fingers were deadly, because no sooner did he find the tip of Tristan's cock than he flicked his nail over Tristan's seed-damp slit, and the ping of pain was a soft promise of what would come later. Wolf smeared some of Tristan's come onto his finger and brought it to his mouth, giving himself a taste of Tristan's spend. "God, I really like your secret happy place."

"You're getting cheesier than a plate of poutine."

"What do you know about poutine?" Wolf was rooting around the sheets for something which, from the delighted murmur he made, Tristan gathered he'd found.

"It always looked interesting. Like things you'd eat at a fair," he said with a faint hint of embarrassment. "I've never actually been to a fair. Or a carnival. Always wanted to, but—"

"I'll take you to the biggest fair I can find," Wolf promised as he coated his fingers with more lube. "And Mardi Gras. And Carnevale in Venice. But right now, I'd really just like to take *you*."

"Cheddar breath," Tristan teased. "Sooooo much cheeeeese. Like cheap greasy nachos."

He stopped laughing when Wolf's fingers pressed against his cleft, demanding more from Tristan than a chuckle and a smile. He gave Wolf the smile anyway and rolled over onto his back. Wolf rubbed up and down the heat of his parted cheeks, his mouth smoking a line of kisses down Tristan's chest. When Wolf's teeth found one of Tristan's nipples, the torturing nibbles were the right mingling of pain and pleasure to fill Tristan's cock with a hard excitement. Groaning, he lifted his knees up and out, begging Wolf to fill him with his long fingers.

"That's the plan, baby," he said between sucklings of Tristan's nubs. "And once I get you primed, it's going to be my cock."

He'd lost count of how many times he and Wolf'd made love. He shouldn't have. It was still too new—too raw of an experience to have become normal, and he'd lost that number a few weeks ago, in a rush of a long night and slow kisses. Not that Wolf touching him would ever be truly normal. Some part of Tristan's mind wanted to count, to keep that number growing and secreted away in his heart, but like the rain, he couldn't imagine trying to hold in a storm while standing in the middle of it.

But oh, he knew that burn. That delicious, aching stretch of something slick forcing his body open and then curving up to stroke his most intimate places. He couldn't stop arching his back, riding the length of Wolf's fingers as they intruded past his rim. Even with the sleek glide of oil, his skin burned at the man's touch.

"Do you like that, baby?" Wolf whispered into his ear, and Tristan could only nod. "Lie back and just… take it. Let me do you. Let me see you like this."

He wouldn't last long. Hell, even if he had an eternity with the man, Tristan didn't think his body would ever gain much control over his climaxes. It seemed like only a few seconds sometimes between when Wolf entered him to when his orgasm ripped through him, and in the times he'd buried himself into Wolf's tight heat, he couldn't say he lasted much longer.

Wolf assured him they did fine. And the porn Tristan pointed out as evidence of his defects were as much smoke and mirror as a magician sawing his assistant in half. Since he didn't have the answer on how *that* was done either, Tristan could only nod and hope for the best.

And from Wolf's pleased expression, Tristan knew his best certainly was good enough for the man who could play him with a stroke of a finger and a lick of his tongue.

There had to be at least three of Wolf's fingers in him, and Tristan strained to hold back his release, grabbing at the base of his shaft to hold himself in. Wolf's dark chuckle was enough of a clue that he was enjoying teasing Tristan, and the next time Wolf came in for a kiss, Tristan captured Wolf's lower lip in his teeth and bit down lightly, shaking the plump to get Wolf's attention.

"Now," Tristan muttered through the bite of Wolf's lip. The slide of Wolf's fingers leaving him made him whimper, but he rode out the emptiness, knowing he'd be filled soon. "Get in me now, Wolf. Before there's nothing of me left."

He let go. He had to if Wolf was going to move down between Tristan's legs and take him. Wolf moved slowly, drawing out every gliding touch until Tristan thought he'd scream in frustration. By the time Wolf's hands were under his thighs and raising Tristan's legs up over his shoulders, Tristan's cock was weeping its need.

"You are so fucking gorgeous, Tristan," Wolf whispered, drawing his fingers down over Tristan's cock for another taste of his seed. It was maddening to see the man's seed-daubed fingertips run over his tongue, especially since Wolf drew his tongue out to lap at the milky cream. Winking, he dropped his hand down and guided his thick cock to the edge of Tristan's hole. "Hold onto me, babe, and whatever you do, never ever let me go."

THERE'D NEVER been a man he'd wanted to be in so much as Tristan Pryce. Hell, if Wolf was going to be honest—blazingly unforgiving and honest—he'd admit he just wanted Tristan against him—touching him—even just near him.

Although, Wolf told himself as he bent forward to lick at the dapple of moisture built up on Tristan's sleekly defined chest, being inside of Tris was certainly his idea of heaven, and he'd like to spend as much time bringing pleasure to his aggravatingly sexy lover as he could.

He loved the first hiss of breath Tristan always made when he pushed his cock into him and then the small panting mewls when Wolf paused to let him get used to the intrusion. Those sounds were so Tristan, the few constants of his wildness in bed, and Wolf found himself listening for them amid their joining.

Even as his own toes curled when Tristan's ass closed in on him and seemed to suck the very breath out of Wolf's lungs because Tristan felt so damned fucking good on him.

Tristan's legs pushed him down and in. Hooked over Wolf's shoulders, the man's powerful limbs were lined with muscles built up from rambling the Grange's grounds with his wolfhound by his side, and he used them instinctively, drawing Wolf as close as he could when Wolf leaned over him.

Their bodies knew what to do. They *fit*. No matter how they were arranged, Wolf and Tristan fit together and found delight in pressing skin against skin or even the barest finger brush against the palm of the other's hand. Every kiss felt like sex, and each time they tumbled together to make love, it felt as if they were discovering the first kiss over and over again.

It scared him. Wolf could feel the fear welling up in him as strong as the rush of his climax boiling down in his balls. But when Tristan's eyes bled gold with desire for him, Wolf's fear whispered away, and all that remained was Tristan enclosing him.

And the unfamiliar, strange happiness Tristan spread through him.

Tristan's hole refused to let him go. The edges of his entrance held on, working around Wolf's cock in a twisting hug before Wolf could draw out all the way.

"God, you...." Tristan groaned and dug his fingers into Wolf's shoulders. He threw his hips up to meet Wolf's thrusts, folding himself up to take Wolf as far in as he could.

Tristan's long cock wove about in the space between their pressed-in bellies, rolled in tight when their bodies met, then slid around in its own spilled smear when released. Wolf reached down into that tight, fragrant space and caught up as much of Tristan's spill as he could, slathering it onto the man's chest so he could dip his head down and taste it.

It was like a burst of stars—as if he'd gone outside as the night sky fell in on him, and he'd thrown his head back to drink his fill.

For Tristan, he would gladly become Tantalus just for the taste of that star-tinseled sky.

He began to move, harder and finding the sweet spot Tristan's body hid from him. The length of his cock glided up and down on Tristan's core, and his lover shuddered with each stroke, his knuckles turning white as he held onto Wolf's upper arms.

They grunted and panted, their hips slamming hard against bone and skin until Wolf was sure they'd break apart into a million pieces. He knew he was close, and Tristan was even nearer because the clench on his cock tightened to an impossible grip, and Tristan's limbs stiffened, nearly unseating Wolf.

"Bring yourself over, babe," Wolf grunted. "Let me watch you. God…."

His lover's eyes were blown out, the black swallowing up nearly every bit of color. It was as much of a sign of Tristan's peak as his leaking cock or the death grip of his legs on Wolf's shoulders. Tristan struggled to find his cock, laughing a bit when Wolf kissed the corner of his mouth, then held Tristan's dick still until his lover's fingers covered his.

They found a rhythm there too. A stroke up, then a stuttering fall back down to the trembling base. Wolf's own balls roiled and pulled, tucking up into his hollow. The slap of their wet skin and the scent of their sweat perfumed the air, a delectable teasing brine to counter the sweetness of the rain outside.

"Love you." Tristan's whisper was faint, but Wolf caught it, and it broke him.

Letting go of Tristan's cock, he grabbed his lover's hips and plunged down into him. His strokes grew shorter, harder until he lost any sense of being apart from Tristan's hot clench. He heard Tristan gasp, then a splash of salty bittersweet slapped him in the face. Satiated, Wolf let himself fall, breaking loose into the sheath of his lover's body.

He rode the fire erupting between them, rocking into Tristan's core and drawing out every satisfied mewl and sigh left inside of his tousled lover. He wrung them out, gently taking Tristan in hand to milk him a stroke or two while Tristan shuddered out the rest of his climax.

They dove down together. The short distance of a roll onto the sheets was like wings catching up around them to soften their fall.

"God, I love you, Thursday." Wolf kept his arms around Tristan's sweaty body, not caring if they smeared the sheets with their spend. He'd do laundry if he had to. Anything he could do just to hold Tristan for a few moments more. "You make me crazy sometimes, but damn if that doesn't make me want you more."

"If you want me any more, neither one of us is going to be able to walk." Tristan was panting, and he worked the words out between heavy breaths. "I think we moved the bed. We're in the middle of the room."

"Well then, time to fuck me, Tris." Wolf let go of his lover and sat up. "Looks like we're going to have to have a round two to see if we can move it right on back."

Chapter 16

IF THERE was any proof of hell's existence, Tristan was sure he'd found it.

Or at least a circle of it.

Looking around the small room they'd cleared out, salted the baseboards, then piled up with boxes from Sey's estate purchases, Tristan counted at least thirty crates and boxes they'd need to go through. And by they, he meant him and one fluffy, foul-faced Persian named Crowley. Other than the cat, his only company appeared to be the boxes and a rapidly cooling cup way too small to hold the coffee he'd need to shore himself up as he dug through the dusty remains of other people's lives.

The morning came in bright at first, with intermittent drizzles covering the grounds. With a promise to join him shortly, the Kincaids all peeled off into different parts of the barn to help out with the livestock, but the cat followed Tristan into what he now thought of as The Hall of Doom. Daylen had taken one peek at the stacks of boxes, paled, and declared himself too weak to help dig Tristan out of the trenches.

"Okay, let's see what we can find in this one," Tristan said to the cat, who'd found the single watered-down sunbeam in the room acceptable to warm his long gray fur.

They'd already come to an understanding of sorts. Crowley would lay still for a few minutes, then meep his disapproval at the dearth of rubs along his soft belly. That barely there squeak was Tristan's cue that Crowley's belly was open for rubbing business, and he would spend a second or two to ruffle the cat's fur before going back to what he was doing.

Which was, so far, pretty much opening up crates to find himself staring at books, papers, and a Narnia wardrobe of junk drawer debris.

He couldn't *not* go through everything. For all he knew, Simone was *this* empty spool of thread or *that* book of S&H stamps from 1942. There were a few toys and even one small box of pressed tin windups he'd have loved to play with, but he had to put them aside for what turned out to be a box of old German philosophy textbooks. His brain told him it wasn't what he was looking for, but he couldn't be sure. Not until he looked at *everything*.

He was dirty and tired, but most of all, he wished someone else would come in and rub the fucking cat's belly so he could get through all of the boxes and do something else. Like tumble Wolf over the end of the bed or come up with an entire new series of zombie ducks who moonlighted as superheroes during the darkest of times.

"Hmmmmm. Zombie superhero ducks." Tristan turned the idea over in his mind. "That could work. Kids like gory stuff. Hell, I like gory stuff."

The cat mewed at him, and he scrubbed at its obviously neglected belly. Glancing down at Crowley, he said, "You know, you could help."

"Be careful with that beast. He about took my face off when I tried to pet him earlier." Daylen strode in, nattily dressed in a short-sleeved polo shirt and pressed Bermuda shorts. He carefully stepped around the cat oozing over the room's floor. He handed Tristan one of the two water bottles he brought in with him, then collapsed into the only other chair in the room. "Please accept the water as my peace offering for being an arse. It's just been... hell, I don't have a word for what it's been."

"Overwhelming?" Tristan tossed in as he opened the chilled bottle. Taking a welcome swig, he swallowed slowly. "How are you feeling?"

"Well, emotionally or physically?" Daylen shot him an incredulous look. "I... can't absorb everything that's happened in the past day. To be honest, if I could have, I'd have left this place in my rearview mirror."

"Yeah, I get that." Tristan set his bottle down. "I wish I could tell you it's going to be okay, but I think it's going to be one of those worse before better things. Last time I went through this, it went to shit and gone pretty hard and fast."

"Last time?" Daylen's voice climbed to a squeak so high-pitched Crowley mewed his displeasure with a modulated growl. "I had a creepy skull girl-thing digging her hands into me! How much more shit can that get? That thing was... God, I can't even—"

"It was a ghost," Tristan broke in gently. "And honestly? I think a lot of what happened is kind of my fault."

"From what Big, Dark, and Badass told me, you were the one who got that thing off of me." Daylen used his foot to edge the cat away from him. Crowley batted at his sock-clad toe, and Daylen gave up trying to move the cat away. "You say ghost, but I guess I'm having a hard time—

look, this is all so strange. I came here to learn about vintage toys. Not… vintage people. And especially ones that seem to want me dead."

"I don't think it's you per se," he reassured the man. "So far I've… look, what are you doing?"

Apparently Daylen took that as an opening to let his hand roam down Tristan's leg. The man looked down, as if astonished to find his fingers brushing over the seam of Tristan's jeans. It was odd to have someone other than Wolf touch him there, and Tristan's brain froze, caught on the etiquette of how to throw someone's hand off a leg in the most polite way possible.

Smiling, Daylen slid his hand up and down Tristan's thigh and said, "I just wanted to say thank you—God, for everything, really. This is scaring the hell out of me, and you seem to be the only one who wants to talk to me about it."

"Um, sure," Tristan mumbled as he carefully closed his fingers around Daylen's wrist and lifted it away. "Don't… look, Wolf and I are…."

"He's a bit angry, isn't he?" Daylen didn't seem to mind the reproach, although his mouth tightened around the edges. "Unless you go for that whole burly Scotsman thing. Some blue face paint, long hair, and a kilt, and he could be tossing cabers. And really, a parapsychologist? What kind of degree is that? Who gives that out? Did it come in a Kinder egg?"

It was a small sound but one that grew louder with every passing second. Tristan started, wondering if he was hearing thunder off in the far distance, but when the rolling shudder of sound continued, he realized it was coming from the boxes.

The same boxes he'd dreaded going through one by one were rattling, rocking back and forth in a jitter across the floor. Crowley took off at the first loud boom of a crate landing too close to his tail, weaving through the thinning paths in the room. Tristan grabbed Daylen's shirt collar and tried to hoist him out of the chair, hoping to get them both as close to the open door as possible.

They didn't make it. Daylen fought Tristan wildly, and they both stumbled over the shifting crates, crashing to the floor. The next loud boom they heard was the door slamming shut. Then the quaking began to increase, shaking the panes in the window until Tristan was sure they would crack.

He let go of Daylen to bat at the loose papers and things flying up at his face. The spools of thread he'd disparaged earlier seemed particularly pissed off at him, smacking Tristan in a rapid-fire barrage. The papers sliced and cut, drawing their edges along Tristan's skin until his arms and cheeks were spotted with thin beaded red lines. The sudden impossible wind battered him back, pushing Tristan to take cover behind one of the heavier crates. Reaching over, he tried grabbing at Daylen's ankle to pull him to cover, but the man wasn't having any of it.

Then the moaning began, and the hell Tristan *thought* he'd been in came to him in full force.

His mind knew what it was seeing. Even if the press of tiny faces coming out of a crate's wooden sides was impossible, it was definitely what Tristan's eyes were taking in. Their mouths moved, growing sooty around the edges of their cavernous maws before the black began to slowly fill in. None of it made sense. Not the boxes growing and absorbing faces only to have others take their places. Not the weird keening moans creeping out of the boxes' opening lids, and certainly not the serpentine crawl of sound coming out of Daylen's stretched-apart jaws.

Any reason was gone from the man's eyes. Instead, they were bleached out white, sucked free of any color. Even the pinpricks of his pupils were gone, replaced with a caul-like fuzziness where his bright gaze had been. Smoky blue and black veins began to thread under his skin, working outward from his nose, ears, and mouth, and Tristan could only watch in horror as they stretched out, eating away at the pale of his flesh in their burrow for his extremities.

"Simoooooooone," the crates and boxes cried around him, and Tristan scrambled back when Daylen turned his sightless gaze toward him, an intense scowl pulling down his dark eyebrows until they nearly met over his long nose.

"Daylen, don't let it—" Tristan didn't know what *it* was exactly, but it seemed like the best word to use. "Don't let it take you. Fight it."

It was stupid to talk to the thing eating away at Daylen's brain. He clearly couldn't respond to Tristan. Or at least not in the way Tristan hoped he could. Instead, the young man who'd come down from Ontario to learn about soft-bodied teddy bears and craze-cracked doll heads was now getting to his feet in a loose, broken-limbed shamble and seemed intent on heading right for Tristan.

"Tris! Open the door!"

Wolf's voice came through, but anything following his name was buried under the avalanche of noise hurtling toward him. Tristan tried to dodge into any open space he could find, hoping he could at least reach the door to unlock it, but one of the heavier crates slammed into his side, and he gasped at the sudden rush of pain.

Suddenly the faces on the crates were no longer merely apparitions. One clown head, its eyes bleeding red from the diamonds painted around its extruded sockets, snapped at Tristan's clothes and nipped at the tender skin under his arm. Yelping in as much surprise as pain, he tried to pull free, but the mouth held him fast. Another snapped over his bicep, its mouth stretching unimaginably wide to clamp over Tristan's muscle.

All of it was unimaginable, he reminded himself. These were wooden crates and cardboard boxes, caked with dust and neglect from sitting in storage after their owners passed on to wherever they'd needed to go. As material as anything else in the room, they shouldn't have been rattling and gnawing on Tristan's limbs.

Even worse—even stranger—was Daylen's elongating arms being pulled down past the ends of his sleeves by God knew what—or whom.

More terrifying than the screams was the sound of bone and skin cracking in front of him. There was only so much give flesh had before it tore, and whatever was now living in Daylen's body had little concern if its vessel survived the experience.

Daylen's joints stretched and snapped, the bones beneath his skin warping out as he tried to reach Tristan over the crates blocking his way. Small cracks began to form on his skin, and then a gush of blood spurted across the crate's lid, splashing the undulating faces growing there. The pressed-out visages mewled and screamed in response, and the black in their maws snapped out like tentacles to suckle at the splashes before the dry wood could soak it up.

Unperturbed by the forest of ebony cilia clamoring for his wounds, Daylen mounted the crate, and Tristan gulped when he realized Daylen could almost reach him. Kicking at the heavy crate, Tristan tried to get some distance between them, but the thing wearing Daylen's skin wasn't having any of it.

More pops, and this time, cracked bones exploded out of Daylen's forearms. His hands craned forward, their tips broken, and his finger bones creaked slowly out, nearly brushing Tristan's face. They were turning black, spiraling out into claws. One snagged a tangle of Tristan's blond hair, and he yanked his head to the side, breaking contact.

A confetti of old papers momentarily clouded the space between them as the gusts picked up, and the tiny pieces littered Daylen's shattered body. They stuck wherever he leaked blood, and another cracking twist of his arm separated something deep in Daylen's bones, because as he tried to snag Tristan's face again a foamy chunk of spongy red material fell out of a crevasse in Daylen's upper arm. The mouths on the crate fought a fierce battle with their lengthening cephalopod extensions, slapping at whatever was near to fend off competition.

"Simoooooone!" Daylen screeched, his fingers hooking and kneading the air. "You kiilled meeeeeeeeeeeee. You tooooook heeer and killed me!"

"I don't fucking *have* Simone!" Tristan shouted back. "I don't know where she is!"

It would be easier if one of the boxes actually screamed back that it held Simone. Shit, Tristan would have welcomed a ghostly version of Marco Polo if it would just get Daylen free. But other than screaming along with the possessed man, the faces were no help in finding what the ghost was searching for.

"Sheeee ruuuuiiinnned everythiiiiiiiiiiii—"

The man didn't even look up when the door blew in. Tristan did, and when he spotted Wolf bringing up the muzzle of a dangerous looking shotgun, he dove down among the crates as best he could and covered his head.

He would have been better hidden if he'd dressed himself in a bunny suit and sprinted in front of a pair of greyhounds named Ickle and Jim as they lazed about in a small backyard. Rolling over, Tristan wedged his back into the base of a crate as Wolf peppered Daylen with salt-filled rounds.

Daylen screamed and writhed when the coarse fragments struck him, and as one, the boxes' faces howled with him in an air raid of terror. Wolf cracked open the double-barreled shotgun to eject the rounds, then caught them before they hit the ground. Snapping apart the unfired round, Wolf filled his palm with the crystals and threw them into Daylen's stretched-open mouth.

Daylen choked, and his eyes rolled back, the color slowly bleeding back into them. The faces gave one last modulating howl, then vanished, leaving behind black pockmarks on the boxes to show Tristan hadn't hallucinated the whole thing.

Wolf caught Daylen as he fell. Blood poured from the man's wounds, but his bones were pulling back into place, submerging once more beneath his torn flesh. Welts rose on Daylen's exposed skin where he'd been hit by salt, and blood matted down his once perfect hair. A thin trickle wove down out of his nose, dropping bright red splatters on Wolf's bare arms.

"You okay, babe? Shit, that round was hot. Burned my hand a little bit." Wolf hefted Daylen up and waited for Cin to push a wider path through the boxes. After passing the unconscious man over to his cousin, Wolf helped Tristan out of his corner and hugged him tightly. "God, what the fuck happened in here?"

"I don't know," Tristan admitted. "But what we need is in here somewhere. And as soon as we find it, we need to destroy it, because this ghost is going to kill every last one of us if she can."

"DID YOU get them on their way?" Wolf looked up at Cin as he came into the kitchen. His cousin was drenched and muddy, but other than a bit of fatigue around his golden eyes, Cin didn't seem to be too worse for wear getting Sey, Gildy, and the injured Daylen across the gulch and into his car. "You came back fast. I expected you to be gone longer."

"Yeah, I didn't drive them in. Sey told me to get my ass back here. She didn't want to leave you guys alone in case the ghost came back." Cin began to strip down, then stopped to eyeball his cousin. "You don't give a shit if I do this here, right?"

"No. I don't want to mop the fucking stairs," Wolf muttered over his coffee cup. "I called the farm guys across the way and told them Sey needed some help. They came and got the livestock out of the barn. Told them she had a short, and the rain sparked up a fire. I didn't want the animals to get fucked up in this."

"We should have done that at the first sign of trouble. Sey's so stubborn. It's like a family curse." Cin peered out the window toward the barn. "So they've already come and gone?"

Wolf quirked his eyebrow. "Worried someone will see your naked body, get overwhelmed by your sexiness, and come tap your ass?"

"I was going to ask if they needed help, but sure, we'll go with my sexiness." Cin picked up his clothes and walked over to the mudroom. A bang of a metal lid and a few rustling noises; then Cin came back in, dressed in black jeans and tugging a shirt down over his head. After checking the coffeepot, he helped himself to the steaming brew, then flopped down in a chair next to Wolf. "Fuck, I am tired. How's Tristan doing?"

"Rattled a bit. He's worried about the kid," Wolf said. "You gotta admit, that was some pretty scary shit."

"Scary doesn't even begin to describe it," Cin agreed. Rubbing at his face, he mumbled through his fingers, "Where the fuck do we start? How many dolls are in those damned boxes?"

"So far, thirty. I've got them all in a couple of bins in the living room."

"Tell me you've got them in a circle." Cin growled at Wolf's eye roll. "Look, it's a valid question. You're not—"

"I'm not a Hellsinger because I was tossed out of the family," Wolf reminded him. "Doesn't mean I don't know the basics."

They'd tossed the crates quickly, pulling out as many of the dolls as they could find. Sey'd cautioned them about separating the toys from their original boxes, or she'd lose track of the toys' provenance, but after Daylen's bones were wrenched clear of his flesh, she no longer seemed to care about anything other than ridding her house of its malevolent spirit.

"Salt?"

"Sugar," Wolf said smugly. "I've found it's got a better resonance and reflective level."

"It also attracts ants," Cin shot back.

"Ants are the least of our fucking problems, Cin. Did you see what she did to that kid? You think I want that to happen to Tristan?"

"I think Tristan's the one that brings this shit out. If you ask me, he's the reason this thing manifested. There's something about him, Wolf. Something dark that makes these things come out."

Wolf was out of his seat and pushing Cin before his cousin could say another word. "Tristan is not—"

"Wolf!" Tristan's sharp voice cut through their raised voices. "Don't. Cin, let him go."

The cousins parted, each grumbling under their breath as they dusted off their clothes. Wolf lifted his chin and stared Cin down, poking at his cousin's chest. "Don't you say another fucking word about—"

"About me bringing this all down on us?" Tristan held up the red rubber ball they'd found in the shower. A few feet away, Jack bounced up and down, his stubby transparent tail moving so quickly it was a blur of light trails and shapes. "Do you see him, Cin? The dog?"

"Shit, she's got a dog now too?" Cin reached for the salt shaker on the table, but Wolf stopped him.

"Don't. That's Jack. He's… he really shouldn't be here." Wolf frowned. "I really thought you'd just brought a ball with you. You know, to fuck with me a bit, but—"

"Nope, he followed me. Or you. Depends on his attention span." Tristan bounced the ball across the kitchen floor, and the terrier lunged after it, chasing it into the next room. There was a rattle, and then a scramble of claws up the stairs was followed by Crowley's outraged howls. "Shit, the cat. I've never had a cat. He probably chases them."

"You brought a manifestation with you?" Cin's weight landed hard on one of Sey's chairs. "What the fucking hell are you sleeping with, cousin?"

"Who, not what," Wolf corrected sharply.

He wasn't going to let Cin turn Tristan into something less than human. There'd been too many times Tristan called himself a freak or flinched when he spoke to his uncle on the phone. Wolf wasn't going to have one of his own blood relatives do the same to his lover—even if Cin was as close to him as Bach or Ophelia Sunday.

"He came here on his own," Tristan replied calmly. His changeable eyes were bright but evenly balanced in color. A flash of green signaled a hint of irritation, but the storm was held at bay by the wide smile he'd given Wolf. "But Cin has a point. They *do* come to me. There's something about me that attracts ghosts. Whatever happened at the Grange—whatever your mom did back then—it pushed it down a bit, but it's growing stronger again."

"Tris, before we left, Mara… you were having problems seeing Mara," Wolf confessed. Tristan's hands were chilled when he reached for them. Rubbing his palms over Tristan's fingers, he tried warming them up.

"Yeah, I know." Tristan pulled a face. "I saw her after I spoke to you. She told me I'd walked through her a couple of times. But you've got to admit, Kincaid. This ghost started getting more… real with me here. And after what happened to Daylen, we can't really screw around with her anymore. We're going to have to do something drastic."

"Drastic like what?" Cin growled. "Another one of Meegan's séances? Because that shit will kill you. And probably level the house. I can't believe you guys did that the first time without setting off a zombie apocalypse."

"Not exactly like one of her séances but maybe something close." Tristan took a deep breath, then kissed Wolf's mouth with a tender brush of his lips. "What we need to do is draw her out, and I'm going to be your bait."

Chapter 17

"IT WAS a dark and stormy night," Tristan said softly as he heard the screen door open behind him. "Who said that?"

"Other than Snoopy, I don't know," Cin admitted as he joined Tristan in leaning against the back porch's thick railing. "I think it was the same guy who said the pen is mightier than the sword."

"So, pretty much the grandmaster of the literary go-to lines." He thought about it for a moment. "Did he do a bird in the hand, two in the bush thing too?"

"I think that's a proverb," Cin replied. "Could be even biblical. I'd have to look it up."

All kidding aside, it was a dark and stormy night. Well, dark outside but stormy inside. Leaning forward, Tristan looked up into the endless black above them and wondered when it was all going to fall down on them. The air smelled of lightning and anger, but other than the hint of rain on the wind, it looked like the night was going to pass without another deluge.

The same couldn't be said for Tristan's next conversation with his lover, but he'd hoped Cin would have some success in smoothing over Wolf's ruffled feathers. From the glowering look on the man's face, it looked like Cin had as much luck with Wolf as Tristan had.

"How pissed off is he?" Tristan ventured, sneaking a look over at Cin. "On a scale of one to ten."

"I'd say four point five nine, but I think he's more pissed off he can't think of a way out of it." Cin turned, his golden eyes shaded to a burnt amber in the light shining out from the kitchen windows. "You've got the best plan. He hates that. Not the plan but that you're… the piece of cheese in the trap."

They'd gone round and round in the kitchen. Wolf had stalked back and forth outlining every single one of his objections only to have them shot down by Tristan. Cin sat there silently until an hour into the seemingly endless argument; then he weighed in.

"He's right, Wolf." If Cin had taken a knife from the butcher block and stabbed Wolf with it, Wolf couldn't have looked more shocked. "We're going to have to use him to draw her out."

"You have no fucking idea what you're—" Struck nearly dumb by what he'd obviously thought was his cousin's betrayal, Wolf shot back, "Just wait until you fall in love, cuz, and some asshole wants to offer him up like a sacrifice to Quetzalcoatl. Then we'll see how you feel."

He and Cin sat in stunned silence for a few minutes before Tristan announced he needed some air. Fleeing to the porch seemed like his best bet. He'd been about to head to the barn to stare at Sey's hippie cows, but they were already on vacation. After twenty minutes and a small panic attack, Cin joined him, and they were now both staring out onto a shadow-shrouded back garden while the house loomed behind them in silent judgment.

"Do you have any idea how we can do this?" Tristan finally asked. "Is there something in the Hellsinger bible that covers stupid tricks you can do with your paranormally enhanced boyfriend?"

"Can't say I ever saw it," Cin commented dryly. "The bible. Not the spell where we hang you out like a gutted deer to catch a cougar."

"They really do that?" Tristan shuddered. "The poor deer."

"Sometimes they have to because the cougar's poaching on herds or is too close to houses. Depending on the place, it's usually a catch and release, but it can lead to someone killing it."

"You're not convincing me to do this," he pointed out, shifting his feet. Cin said nothing, just stood there—silent and watchful. "Just so you know. I mean, I know what I'm doing here. Well, not the actual doing. I'm going to need help with that, but it feels like it's something I should do."

"Yeah, I'm not convinced either," the Hellsinger admitted softly. "But you were right—about a lot of things, actually. She's dangerous. Probably the most dangerous phantasm I've ever encountered. Certainly the most powerful. What you've got... what you can do, it's pretty scary, Pryce. Most Hellsingers go for decades only seeing orbs and EMF readings. You've already racked up God knows how many manifestations just living at... what did you call it? The Grange?"

"Hoxne Grange," Tristan supplied. "And just so you know, it's off limits to Hellsingers. Or at least anyone looking to exorcise my guests."

"I don't force out spirits unless they're problematic." Cin eyed him. "Wolf said you've got a couple of live-ins—other than the dog."

"Yeah, mostly Mara. She's the one I couldn't always see these past couple of weeks. God, when I found that out, it was like someone ripped out my balls." Tristan sniffed, refusing to cry in front of the behemoth Wolf called a cousin. "She kind of raised me. Weird I guess, if you think about it. Oh, and there's Cook too. She comes every Tuesday. She's a repeater. Sort of."

There wasn't any way he could explain how horrified and scared he'd been when Mara told him they'd not always been in sync. She'd cried when he'd been getting ready to go, and he hadn't wanted to leave, but the spectral housekeeper insisted, telling him to come back stronger.

"And he's seen them? Wolf? Talked to them?"

"Yeah, interacted with Mara a *lot*. I think she's got a thing for him. She likes his ass." He shrugged. "There were others. Ones that Winifred brought with her. And well, Winifred."

"Damn. That's complicating things right there. Bringing along captured souls. And this was the one Meegan nearly killed you with?" Cin cocked his head, his expression growing more serious. "So now I've got to wonder what the hell this one has on her plate? We're going to run out of salt. There's only so much in the barn for the animals, and even with Sey's ice cream making fetish, there isn't enough to keep out a horde."

"Wolf's right about the sound thing, you know." It'd been a song that drove Winifred back, and Tristan wondered what music he had on his phone to send a crazed little girl on to wherever she should have been in the first place. "It disrupts them. He starts talking about spectrums and ultrasound, but it's pretty much like microwaving or using sonar on them. We've just got to find where she is on that scale. Or dial. I don't have the science for that. I make up the monsters in my books. I don't actually worry about having to fight them off."

"He's been so busy trying to prove the impossible exists he hasn't thought about a way to get rid of the damn things." Cin swore under his breath, some language Tristan couldn't parse out, but it certainly was something hot enough to blister the damp from the air. "Shit, Wolf, what the fuck have you been doing with your life?"

A flare of something rose along Tristan's spine, and he stepped in closer to Cin. Sure, he had to look up to Cin to meet his gaze, and there was about a foot of muscle on either side of him when he got close, but it wouldn't have been the first time Tristan walked through shit and didn't have the sense to scrape it off before he took another step.

Poking Cin's chest with a sharp jab of his finger, Tristan growled back, "He's been trying to show the world that what you're doing with *your* life is real. That's important to him. *You. Your* damned family that threw him out because he has different ideas about… whatever the hell it is you all do."

Again the man's burnt gold stare washed hot over Tristan, but he stood his ground—even as the ground seemed to shake beneath him. A long, hard moment passed between them, and then Cin nodded, his shoulders relaxing from their tense coil.

"You're right," Cin admitted softly as he raked his hands through his long black hair. His elbow narrowly missed Tristan's nose, but he didn't seem to notice when Tristan jerked his head back to avoid getting hit. "I guess I figured Wolf would do this kind of shit with me. Instead, it felt like he turned left when I went right. And now he's going around looking to disprove everything I believe in. It's hard to swallow."

"He doesn't disbelieve now," Tristan replied gently. "He just now… really needs to be shown it *is* real. How many times have you been someplace to get rid of a ghost to find out it's just bullshit?"

"More times than I can count," he admitted. "Usually it's kids. Sometimes it's an asshole who wants to prank someone. But there are real ones out there too. Ones like this. Although this is the first time I've actually *seen* all of a ghost. Usually it's just shapes or lights. This is… *different*."

"He does the exact same thing you do but with uncommon tools to send them on their way. Okay, maybe not along, but he could." Peeling back Cin's cynicism and distrust was like pulling teeth, but when Cin quirked a small smile his way, Tristan knew he'd at least gotten one layer off. "He doesn't know what you know. He wasn't allowed to follow you because he thinks about it in a different way, but when it's all said and done, you guys did both turn right."

"Hmmmm." Cin nodded, and his attention drifted off to the yard for a moment before returning to Tristan. "I've got to think about that."

"Well, hurry up and get over it fast. We've got to take care of what Sey bought in one of those boxes."

"Yeah, the boxes." Cin looked over his shoulder toward the room they'd ringed in yards of the sequined fabric they'd found in Sey's workroom. "I'm going to mop the floor one last time to get rid of any blood we didn't catch, then start going through those damned things.

Shit, that's another thing. He probably feels guilty about leaving you in there by yourself. We were supposed to have been in there with you."

"You were helping Sey with the animals. And fuck, I don't know—I needed to do something. Maybe I felt like I had something to prove, I guess. He treats me like I'm a fricking teacup he found in a china cabinet."

"More like a coffee mug someone left in a phantom tollbooth."

Cin's teasing hit him unexpectedly, and Tristan laughed despite the gnarl of stress sitting in his belly.

"Why don't you go see if you can go talk some sense into him while I start in on the room?"

"Might be a while," Tristan warned. "He's pretty pissed off."

"Don't forget, I've known Wolf since he was a larva. I know you're going to be a while." The man's grin was pure wickedness and Kincaid. "You're going to have five minutes of argument and then after that? An hour or more of make-up sex. And considering how sweet of an ass you've got there, Tris, I'd be disappointed in Wolf if he didn't take his time."

THE ONLY light in their bedroom was the soft glow coming from the bathroom's night sconce, and Wolf debated getting up just to turn that off too. It was hard to sulk when one's body was bathed in a soft golden murmur, and it was even harder to brood when he could hear his cousin and lover discussing him as if he were a head of cabbage they'd found in a grocery bin.

He also couldn't get up and close the window without them hearing the wooden sash hitting the sill, and it would have seriously cut down on his eavesdropping. And if there was one thing he'd carried over with him from childhood, it was stealing secrets out of the air around him.

"Curiosity will kill the Wolf." Their Nan said that so many times when he'd been a child, Wolf'd grown up thinking that was how the phrase actually went.

Of his three grandmothers, Nan'd been the constant—the one who'd stayed at the main house while her other two wives went off to con marks and sometimes exorcise a ghost or two. It'd been Nan who'd picked up Cin at the airport when he'd fled Central America after escaping his father's clutches, and it'd also been Nan who first turned her back on Wolf when he'd announced he wanted to go to school for parapsychology. It was one thing to be educated about the spirit world, she'd said, it was another thing to go around trying to prove things didn't actually go bump in the night.

No amount of explanation could dissuade her, and he hadn't been really willing to try. In true Kincaid fashion, he'd slammed doors and declared them dead to him. All except a rare few—a few that included his older and much wiser cousin, Cin.

The cousin who'd just hit on his lover in a such a roundabout way Wolf couldn't even be pissed off at him for doing it.

"That's what you get for eavesdropping. You hear shit you'd rather not hear," he told himself as Tristan told Cin he was going to head up to talk to Wolf. "And sometimes, you hear shit you really *need* to hear."

His disgruntlement was gone, burned off by half an hour of lying on the bed and staring at the ceiling. There'd been some residual anger, but it was mostly aimed at himself.

Especially at himself.

"You've got to stop acting like he's fragile, dude," he scolded himself. "He stood up to Winifred. Shit, look what he's dealt with already. Why the fuck do you treat him like he's...."

Precious.

That was it. Tristan was precious. And his—only his. Wolf sat up, suddenly wishing Tristan would take his time coming up the stairs because he needed to have a moment while his brain imploded with the knowledge that he truly, dearly loved the man he'd once been hired to destroy.

And he felt that love all the way past his fears and into his spine. Being out of control—being stupid in love with a man who saw images of dead people imprinted onto the world around him—none of that mattered because he had Tristan. Tristan was his—red rubber ball, manic ghost dogs, and howling out bad eighties songs in the shower—Tristan Pryce was his.

"Fucking shit, I'm stupid," he announced to the room, which would have been an empty witness to his private little confessional, but Tristan opened the door right as Wolf laid himself open to the universe. Their eyes met, and Tristan shot him a tentative, goofy smile—and everything went crazy in Wolf's heart. Holding his hand out to the blond, he said, "Come here."

And Tris trustingly walked across the room's wooden floor and took Wolf's hand.

Wolf didn't say anything. He didn't beg for forgiveness or revisit the argument they'd had downstairs. Instead he got up onto his knees and met Tristan halfway when he climbed onto the bed. Then he pulled Tristan down and straddled him, holding him down with his weight, and kissed him until Tristan didn't have any breath left in him.

"I'm sorry," they said at once, and Tristan's low chuckle rolled under his own hearty laugh.

"I'm not... used to having a partner," Wolf admitted. "And God, I keep fucking it up. Fucking *this* up. Guess I'm worried about how many times I'm going to end up saying I'm sorry before you walk away from me."

"Can't walk away from you." Tristan slid his fingers through Wolf's hair. "Didn't we promise we'd deal with the crap we give each other? I'm awkward and fucked up—"

"You are *not* fucked up."

"And you're bossy and domineering," Tristan finished, yanking Wolf's hair lightly. "You also don't let me finish my damned sentences sometimes."

"Yeah, I'll admit that," he conceded wryly. "I don't know how fast I can change that—the bossy part. Too used to being—in charge. Shit, it seems like every time I take a step forward, I then slide back two."

"I've just got to make sure not to let you roll me over." He shifted under Wolf, arranging their bodies so they were more comfortable. "It's not like I won't tell you to stop, but babe, you're more insecure than me sometimes. You're always expecting me to walk off, and sometimes you do it first just so you can *be* the one who lets go. I can take the bossiness because you're easy to stab with a fork, but if there's one thing I want you to work on, it's trusting me to stay next to you."

"Even as you're calling up crazy homicidal ghosts?" Wolf teased.

"If you recall, I'm not the one calling these things up. It's all on you Kincaids, and well, the last time was Matt and Gidget, but they count for your side." Tristan tugged on Wolf's ear, twisting it just enough to turn it around. "I don't mind you rescuing me, Doctor Kincaid, but I've got to need rescuing. You can't cut my steak for me just because you're sitting beside me."

"But I can stab a bull if it's heading straight for you?"

"Not one of Sey's. I like them." Tristan pulled a face. "More than I like York the camel. Fucker spits like crazy. The ghost camel didn't spit that much."

"Better manners. York's more of a bad boy biker camel." Wolf captured Tristan's mouth in a simmering kiss, sighing right before he let go. "You make me crazy, you know? Inside and out. I am absolutely crazy for you, Thursday."

"Good, because it would be awkward if I was the only one who felt like this. I think they call that stalking." Tristan worked his hand down the front of Wolf's body and rubbed at the hardening cock in Wolf's underwear. "Is this when I can make a bad pun about stalks? Because I've got one right here."

Tristan's shirt didn't survive Wolf's hands. His jeans nearly didn't make it either, but Tristan was quick to shed them before they were torn apart at the seams. The blond tasted of coffee, gold, and lightning, and Wolf dove in deep, cupping Tristan's face to ravage his mouth.

There didn't seem enough of Tristan for Wolf to consume. He tried to go slowly, but Tristan's hands kneaded and dug into Wolf's body, clenching his ass with a strong grip. His boxers were gone, probably lying in shreds on the floor with the remains of Tristan's shirt, but Wolf was more than glad to sacrifice his underwear.

"Still mad?" Tristan gasped when Wolf's teeth closed in on his nipple. "Shit... fuck."

"I'll get there," Wolf promised. "Or you in me. I'm good either way. And no, I'm not mad. Fuck, babe. I just... never want to let you go."

Tristan palmed Wolf's balls, fondling them with his fingers. Wolf spread his legs to let Tristan have room to play with them and drew out a long gasp when Tristan pressed his finger against Wolf's hole. It stung a bit, and Wolf groaned, wondering where they'd put the lube.

He didn't have to worry much longer because Tristan slid out from under his arms then reached for a small bottle of oil on the nightstand.

"Can I have you?" The question was said softly, as gently as Tristan's hand on his balls. "This time?"

"Any time you want." He didn't like hearing the shake in Tristan's voice. For his own insecurities, he'd found the mines laid down in Tristan's soul more than a few times. Usually though, when he was the most careful was when he set them off. "I just *need* you. And I kind of like that you need me back just as bad."

Tristan was gentle. For the most part. His mouth closed in on Wolf's cock tight enough that he was afraid he'd shoot off before his lover could even get inside of him. Twisting about, he returned the favor, prolonging the event with a slurp of his tongue along the firmness of Tristan's shaft. Tris smelled good down there, fresh powdery and lemon with a dash of sweat. He took care to circle around Tristan's head, amused at its lack of foreskin and how the slit crinkled up when Wolf licked at it.

"Tickles." Tristan's hips twitched, and he pulled back, stifling what Wolf was sure had been a giggle. "How the hell do you do that with your tongue? Feels like you're sticking the whole thing down there."

"Kincaid secret." He did it again, just to get another wiggle, and this time, Tristan retaliated with an insistent push of two fingers on his rim. Hissing, he huffed in his breath, taking the intrusion, then slurped down Tristan's cock once more. "God, you feel good. You taste good too."

"Don't know how long I'm going to last," Tristan warned. "Something about almost dying always makes me horny."

"You weren't going to die," he scoffed. "Aren't you the geeky sidekick? Doesn't he live?"

"I think that's the guy who heroically sacrifices himself so the lovers can survive the movie," Tristan corrected. "Wait, we're the lovers."

"Yeah, we're going to have to get Cin to sacrifice himself. For the plot, you know."

"We'll thank him in the end when we're looking off into the sunset after the apocalypse is over and we've found the hidden oasis of civilization." Tristan hummed over Wolf's dick, sending a delicious ripple through his nerves. "Maybe even name our kid after him."

"I am *not* naming my kid Cin—just no," Wolf warned, scraping his teeth around the ridge of Tristan's cock head. "And you know what, much like my mother, my cousin doesn't get space in this bed either. More sucking. Less talking."

There really wasn't much sucking left in either one of them. After a few more lollipop slurps of Tristan's mouth on his dick, Wolf was ready to spill everything he'd ever had boiling up inside of him. A quick rearranging of bodies, and he found himself on his hands and knees, legs spread apart and his back arched as Tristan's fingers stretched him open.

He hadn't had anyone other than Tristan for a long time, but really, his body didn't seem to remember anyone *but* Tristan inside of him. He could imagine how Tristan's cock looked as it slid into him, wrapped in a clear sheath, turning the ruddy clean length opalescent in the thin sconce light. He liked playing with Tristan's dick. It was so different from his own, and the sense of power beneath its silken pale skin always brought him to a delighted wonder.

Especially as Tristan worked it into the clench of Wolf's ass in a slow, agonizing crawl.

Tristan hit his nerves straight on. Wolf'd come to expect it. He did it every time they had sex and Tristan penetrated him. His lover seemed to have a dowsing rod for a cock, and Wolf knew he'd have to ride the shock wave of that hit nearly as soon as Tristan seated himself. But it hit every time, a lightning stroke blasting through him, and Wolf always lost his mind before he could even clench his passage around his lover's shaft.

Then Tristan began to ratchet his hips, and Wolf let himself be blown away.

They slapped together, inelegant and messy. Covered with a smear of lube and sweat, he couldn't get a hand down around his cock, and when Tristan leaned forward to help, it shifted the rhythm of what they were doing, enough to throw Wolf off for a beat or two. He squeezed down on his lover, finding Tristan still hard and aching inside of him, and pushed back, impaling himself on Tristan's length.

His dick was already weeping, sobbing out for its release, nearly as needy as its owner, especially when Tristan's fingers worked over its head and pinched lightly. The tremors of almost-pain were all Wolf needed, and he slammed back into Tristan, begging for more.

With each stroke he felt them building to a zenith, and he hung there, almost falling as Tristan pulled back each time, until Wolf dropped his shoulders and drove down to meet Tristan's now erratic thrusts. Their grunting grew louder, and even the far-off thunder rolling over the distant canyons couldn't drown them out. They struggled with words, turning to sounds and curses while they raced each other to the edge of their bursting nerves.

It hit Wolf fast. Not the crawl of a rippling orgasm starting at the base of his spine and working out to the ends of his fingers. No, this one hit fast and hard—much like Tristan's pounding against his ass, and he cried out, unsure if he could take much more of the man's shaft splitting him apart or if his dick would survive the breaking loose of his seed.

In the end, it didn't matter which one destroyed him, because he felt the hot shoot of Tristan's body aching to fill him, and Wolf flew out into the darkness cloaking them, carried off on the sheer glut of fire erupting out of his bones.

He came hard, filling Tristan's open palm and coursing through his parted fingers. His lover's teeth were on his back, scoring him and marking his shoulder. It was hard enough of a bite so Wolf knew he'd be sporting a bruise, but he didn't care. It would match the ache in his ass, and he'd worked so hard for both pains, especially as he clenched in on Tristan's softening cock and twisted around until he knew he'd milked Tris dry.

They fell onto the bed, too exhausted to do more than breathe, although Wolf wasn't too certain he successfully did that either. His tongue seemed to be in the way of his throat, and there was a curious upside-down feeling on the roof of his mouth as he tasted the salt of Tristan's precome still lingering along the edges of his lip.

"It's like you came hard enough so I taste you," Wolf murmured, flopping his hand over to stroke at Tristan's sweat-matted hair. "Right up to my throat."

"Yeah?" His lover's eyes were sleepy, bruised from lack of sleep and too much drama. "I'd ask you to show me what that feels like, but we're supposed to help Cin with the boxes. He said he'd expect us after an hour and a half. It's like he knew we'd end up like this."

"Cousin's stubborn, not stupid." Wolf chuckled as he glanced at the clock on the dresser. "We've got forty minutes left. How about if you catch a quick nap? And when we're done excavating the Island of Misfit Toys, I'll show you what else we can do with that mail-ordered treasure chest you brought with you. There's a couple of things in there I'm just dying to see how they look on—or in—you."

Chapter 18

THREE HOURS after he'd finally crawled out of bed, showered, and joined the Kincaid boys in the quest to bathe in dirt and debris from days gone by, Tristan was ready to admit he was sick to death of staring at toys and all of the crap people seemed to pack with them.

They couldn't really let anything slip by. Any scrap of paper tucked into a box or cavity had to be examined, discussed, and then—as they'd done countless times before—discarded so they could move onto the next insignificant shrapnel of porcelain or silk formed into a seemingly innocent face.

So many damned faces.

He used to think clown dolls were the worst, but in some ways, the shattered baby heads were the stuff of nightmares. Some cried in squeaky drones when turned, their eyes rolling about, seemingly independent of natural movement. Others were too far gone to be saved, the remnants of someone's childhood or perhaps a life spent untouched on a shelf watching the world go by without a single moment spent in play.

Rough eyelashes scraped at his hands and arms as he handled them one by one, hoping to find a glimmer of something when he touched them. Wolf and Cin pored through documentation, old newspapers and diaries, looking for a whisper of a name to lead them to the cause of Sey's troubles.

Because Murphy was a greater manipulator of lives than Fate herself, they found what they were looking for in nearly the last box left in the room.

"Hey, I might have found something, Thursday." Wolf held up an old red wraparound portfolio. "Come take a look at this."

The dark brown ribbon used to hold it closed was frayed, and at some point, it'd snapped, and someone'd knotted the two ends back together. Worn white along the folds and edges, it wore its age like a tired, frumpy housecoat, draped over its bloated body and straining at the seams.

"Keep everything together," Cin warned. "Whatever's in the box, we'll want to dig through all of it."

"You act like I haven't been doing this for the past few hours of my life," Wolf snarked back. "Dick."

"Asshole." Cin scoffed at Wolf's brandished middle finger. "How about I break that for you later? Let's deal with this shit first."

As boxes went, it was one of the smaller ones, and unlike the others, it didn't have burn marks on its exterior. If anything, the box was only slightly newer than the portfolio, and Tristan was surprised it'd even made it to Sey's house as intact as it was. Strips of peeling duct tape closed off one torn seam, and another edge seemed about ready to go when he nudged it with his foot as he sat down.

Still, everything held together as Tristan settled into a chair to peer inside.

Then he nearly sucked his tongue down his throat when he spied the face of the doll staring back up at him.

It was the little girl's face. Down to the tiny dimple in her chin and the oblong-shaped beauty mark on her right cheek Tristan didn't even realize he'd remembered until he was staring down at it.

"That's probably why she doesn't have eyes," he murmured, reaching into the box to lift the doll out. "Because the doll's eyes are closed."

The doll was old, at least by American standards. Dressed in a puff of dress and petticoats, its porcelain body showed little signs of wear, with only a few chips and lines in its fingers and face. Its wig was a riot of slightly tangled dusky blond curls, and as Tristan straightened it up to look at it, the doll's enormous glass eyes bobbed open, and it mewled out a croaking sound Tristan thought could be momma. A couple of minute teeth had been sculpted to show in its open Cupid's bow mouth, its lips worn down to a pale pink by time. Everything on the doll's body was artfully formed. From its turned-up nose to the scallops of fingernail beds on its hands, it was a perfect scaled-down version of the ghostly monster stalking the halls of Sey Kincaid's home. A tag hung from one of its wrists, and Tristan snagged it as it turned away from him. Frowning, he read off what appeared to be a name from the thick cardboard flat.

"This says Estelle." He flipped the card over, hoping for something to tie the doll to the name the ghost kept crooning and screaming at him. "This doesn't make any damned sense. If this is Estelle, then who the hell is Simone?"

"I think I've got the answer to that." Wolf's husky rumble was thoughtful as he flipped through the contents of a small thick diary he'd found in the box. "Simone was our bloodthirsty ghost's younger sister—and she'd been murdered just for touching the little bitch's doll."

"JESUS, THIS kid was insane!" Wolf couldn't believe what he was reading. If half of what Leona Sinclair of the Chicago Sinclairs wrote about her stepdaughter was true, she should have had the little girl bound to a rock in the middle of the ocean for the seagulls to eat out her liver for all eternity. "Listen to this."

Cin and Tristan both stopped digging through the box they'd dragged into the living room to hear Wolf out. So far they'd found reams of documents and recorded conversations between doctors and law enforcement, as well as family members of their ghost—Charity Sinclair, a spoiled young girl born to a man who'd made his millions investing in the expansion of the railways to every corner of North America and Europe.

If there was one truth they'd found in the stacks of papers and written accounts, it was that Charity Sinclair was probably the most incorrectly named little girl ever to be born.

"Well, we've already heard a doctor's report that she should have been bled for ill humors when she was three. How bad can it be?" Tristan blew a lock of his blond hair out of his eyes. A smudge of dirt darkened his cheek, and Wolf grinned when his lover's cheeks pinked a bit when he tried to rub a stray cobweb off his chin.

"Still can't believe they used to do that." Cin looked up from a newspaper someone thought to fold up and pack in with the doll. "Read off what's there, and I'll tell you what I found."

"It's a wedding announcement for the marriage of Clarence Sinclair to Miss Leona Markham. Mr. Sinclair has a young daughter by his first wife, who died in a tragic lamp oil accident. Miss Markham had the dubious pleasure of being Mr. Sinclair's third spouse. Here, take a look at the pictures, Tris, and tell me if this is your girl."

From what he could tell, the sullen toddler was a dead ringer for the nearly life-sized doll she clutched to her chest. The couple, a middle-aged man and a young woman barely out of her teens, stood behind her. Both were solemn faced and self-possessed, but the man's hand was placed either possessively or affectionately on her side. The woman held herself with a steeled spine and a fixed look of benevolent grace on her pretty face, staring back at the camera as if she were looking out over a vast ocean with no end of it in sight.

Wolf couldn't help but notice the way the man's coat was held tightly by the young girl, nor was it possible to miss the telltale crinkle of fabric where Mr. Clarence Sinclair gripped his daughter's frilled dress, tension beading the knuckles up on the back of his hand.

"Leona is Clarence's *third* wife?" Tristan's finger traced through the article. "Damn, it doesn't say what happened to the second one? First one? The first wife had Charity right? She probably died because the kid ate her soul or something."

"That diary say anything else?" Wolf leaned to look at his cousin behind Tristan's back. "Who wrote it? Leona?"

"It was the aunt's diary. She didn't talk about Charity, other than she'd caught pneumonia after almost drowning," Cin replied. "That's what killed her, according to the doctors."

"The pneumonia?" Normally a ghost manifested from strong emotion, and to Wolf, dying of a lung ailment didn't lend itself to a raging afterlife. "Kind of… passive, isn't it? Passive death doesn't usually lead to rage."

"Gets better." His cousin leafed through the diary. "According to this woman's very hard-to-read writing, she suspected Charity of not only drowning Leona's little girl, Simone, but also somehow killing Sinclair's second wife, who was pregnant at the time of her death. The woman apparently fell in front of a subway car while the family was on a tour of New York City."

Cin looked up from what he was reading. "So how old does that make her at her first kill? And how old are we seeing her now?"

"How old did you think she looked, Tris?" Wolf thought about how the translucent girl looked, but she'd been a flash of panic and light when he'd seen her. "Ten? Eleven? If she had a hand in the second Mrs. Sinclair's death, she was about seven when that happened."

"Isn't that kind of young for murderous thoughts?" The astonished look on Tristan's face would have been comical if they weren't in the crosshairs of one pissed-off Charity Sinclair. "Shit, I was just learning about how to draw perspective at seven."

"So obvious you were an only child." The words were out of Wolf's mouth before he could stop himself, and the small wince in Tristan's right eye was noticeable enough that he leaned over to squeeze his lover's hand. "Sorry. My fucking mouth—"

"It's okay. I mean really, for all intents and purposes, I *was* an only child." He returned Wolf's clench, then let go to pick through the papers he'd left on the couch. "Most of the kids I've ever been around are dead, and there weren't that many of them. I don't think most kids know they're dead."

"You're like a Hellsinger idiot savant," Cin said, shaking his head in amazement. "All of the knowledge but none of the training."

"Training Wolf should have had."

Wolf had to give his lover a point for loyalty.

Cin wasn't having any of it, and his cousin shook his head vigorously. "That one's not on me. I wasn't the one he had a hissy fit with. I was in Spain when all that shit went down."

"I think you were in Guatemala." Wolf tried to think back on when his life went to shit. "Or maybe it was Venice. I don't remember. No matter. We're getting sidetracked. Charity—that's what we need to focus on."

"And how to get rid of her," Tristan said as he rubbed his eyes. "God, it's late. So far we know Charity died of pneumonia, supposedly killed her younger sister named Simone, and had a doll that looked like her."

"Might have been killed by her stepmother." Wolf dug through more of the papers, looking for anything resembling another diary or book. "You know what would be good? If people put information all in one place, like study guides or something."

"They never do. At least we're not trying to walk through seventeen million cemeteries looking for family graves," Cin grumbled. "Always seems to rain or snow when I'm stuck doing that."

"Hey, ask and ye shall receive." Wolf grinned at the other men. Holding up a leather-bound book, he waved it in the air triumphantly. "Got the nanny's ledger of what happened in the family for what looks like the last few years before Charity's death."

"What? Woman just jotted down everything for shits and giggles?" His cousin reached for the book, but Wolf jerked it out of the way.

"It's how she got paid. She marked down major events and the days she worked. Then marked off when she'd gotten her money," Wolf explained. "Pretty smart of her, really."

A loud rattle came from the front door, and the three men froze in place, each alert for any other sounds. Wolf put down the diary and reached for one of the bags of rock salt they'd made as Cin reached for his shotgun. Tristan stood before the two Kincaids could and shot them a look.

"It's the fricking front door, for God's sake," he snapped. "It's not like we're in a fucking zombie apocalypse."

"We could be in a zombie apocalypse," Wolf heard Cin muttering as he put down his gun. "You never know."

Wolf headed to the front of the house. Even if they weren't being overrun by the undead, someone was still breaking in, and suddenly Cin's loaded shotgun didn't seem like a bad idea. He'd almost reached the foyer when the rattling suddenly stopped. A heavy thump, then the front door burst open, slamming into the wall. A very familiar female voice echoed through the hallway, breaking the tension in a bubbling sling of hot words.

"Motherfucking rain. This door always sticks. I've got to get it—" Sey jerked to a stop, surprise widening her eyes, and the keys in her upraised hand fell from her fingers, hitting the floor in a bright jangle. "Jesus Christ, Wolfie! What the hell is that?"

"Get out of the way," Gildy grumbled loudly and shoved her niece aside. "And that's a juju bag. Any fool can see that."

"It's actually just salt." Wolf showed Sey the inside of the bag. Taking in Gildy's bright orange scrubs and the curly green wig the old woman now sported on her head, he took a moment to gather his thoughts as Cin and Tristan came up behind him.

"What the fuck is she wearing?" Cin blurted out. "And what the hell are you two doing here?"

"We're here to help kill off that damned ghost," Gildy announced. "And since it looks like you boys haven't gotten a clue about how to do it, it's a good thing we came back."

THE KINCAIDS were insane.

There really was no other word for it, at least not in Tristan's mind. He'd never thought of Wolf as being particularly off his rocker, but oddly enough, while most people drank when they were around their family, Wolf appeared to become more bossy and dictatorial.

The others were just plain nuts.

"I still don't get why you came back," Wolf said for what must have been the fifth time since Sey and Gildy walked through the door.

"Because this is my house, and I'm as much a damned Kincaid as you are." Sey stood in the middle of the kitchen with her hands on her hips and fire in her eyes. "You think I'm just going to roll over and take it up the ass from a damned ghost?"

"You were supposed to stay safe and out of the way," Cin shot back. "And why the hell did you bring Gildy back with you?"

"Oh, like I was just supposed to go find a kitchen somewhere else so I could make sandwiches for the menfolk?" If Sey's hair wasn't already in its faux coxcomb, her spitfire sarcasm would have raised it up on her scalp. "And where the heck was I going to put Gildy? It's past midnight, so it's not like I could have swung by the zoo so she could pet the goats."

Since Sey had a fricking camel, petting goats would have been a step down for Gildy, but Tristan thought he'd live longer if he stayed out of the conversation. At some point, he'd picked up Jack's ball and begun rolling it from the kitchen chair he'd pulled over to the side and down the short hall to the mudroom. So far, the terrier remained tucked into the Veil, an unseen presence to everyone in the room, but the ball was returned like clockwork, appearing near Tristan's hand, followed by the faint scramble of doggy toenails on the floor.

"And Tristan, if you throw that ball one more time—" Sey took a breath, pausing as she shook her head. "Sorry, I shouldn't snap at you. You're the only one in this kitchen who *isn't* yelling, and I go and attack you."

"It's okay." He gave her a smile. "When my family fights, it's all brittle silence and lawsuits. Kind of nice to hear people screaming at each other."

"Your family sues each other?" Gildy snorted. "That's when you should all get into a room with boxing gloves, lock the door, and let God sort it all out."

"I was hoping for rotten eggs at twenty paces, but beating them would be good too." He rolled the ball again and turned his attention back to the fuming Kincaids. "Look, I don't know about the rest of you, but it's late, I'm tired, and they're already here. Can't we just figure out what we need to do to get rid of her and throw water balloons at each other later?"

Someone would have thought Tristan'd suggested they have relations with a dead sheep for the looks he was getting.

"Okay, so bitching each other out is part of whatever Kincaid ritual there is to get rid of her?" He cocked his head at Wolf. "We didn't do that with Winifred. Is that's why it got so fucked up?"

"That got fucked up because amateurs were screwing with something they shouldn't have been doing." Cin stabbed Wolf in the chest with a finger.

"What was I going to do? Wait for you to come back from Scotland?" Wolf gave his cousin a light shove, putting some distance between them.

"And we're back to screaming at each other." Tristan threw his hands up in disgust. "Tell you what. I'm going to go back and read through shit that really isn't going to help me figure out what the fuck to do while everyone who might have a clue can stay in here and decide who's going to be chosen for the *Mauk-to'Vor*."

He was halfway down the hall when Tristan realized he hadn't filled a cup of coffee to take with him.

"Fuck it." There was no way of slinking back in, especially not after having an exit line referencing a murderous Klingon ritual. Sighing, he flopped down onto the large sofa and picked up the ledger Wolf'd abandoned when they'd all gone to check on who was breaking into the house. Staring down at the faded crab-scrawl on the yellowing paper, Tristan tried to make sense of what day he was looking at. "There's got to be more than one of these. How long did she work for them? And what the hell do they think we're going to find in here, *To remove ghost, please read this passage while turning around three times in front of a mirror*? So far all we've found out is she was a fucking spoiled brat who maybe liked to murder people. I figured that out days ago."

Tristan'd just settled back into the couch cushions to read another few pages about the long-dead Charity Sinclair's weekly activity. From all accounts, it looked like the woman spent most of her day trying to keep people from killing the Sinclair monster child. Between her refusal to do lessons and her treatment of the house servants, Tristan was surprised Charity lived as long as she did.

"Mommaaaaaaaaaaaaaaa."

He lifted his head to look toward the foyer, not discounting Wolf's fondness of practical jokes and the very real possibility the man'd grabbed one of the dolls from the storeroom, shaking it just out of view to make it talk. In the house's echoing depths, he could make out the faint rumble of battling Kincaids: Cin's deep rumble, Gildy's querulous parrot voice, Sey's smooth, husky drawl, and most importantly, the whiskey-gravel pour of Wolf arguing a point. That only left Crowley and Ray as possible suspects, but since no one was operating a can opener, Tristan didn't think the Persian was the culprit, and Ray was certainly too old to be calling for his mother.

Then the sound came again.

"Moooooommmaaaaaaaaaaaaaaa."

It was nearby, too close for Tristan's comfort, and he slowly turned to his right to look at Charity's vintage porcelain doll. It was lying on its belly in a nearby chair, exactly where Cin'd left it. There was no way the doll could be making any noise. Especially since its voice box was old and needed a heavy pumping turn to work.

Pity no one'd told the doll that, because as Tristan stared at the inert toy, it called out again.

"Mommmmmaaaa."

This time the plea was followed by a soft sobbing, nearly too low for Tristan to catch, but the distant wail echoed in the doll's hollow head, amplifying the sound just enough to be heard. The crying rose and fell, a siren call warning anyone who heard it to flee. He almost reached for the doll, anything to make it stop, when Tristan heard another—much stranger—sound.

It was almost like rain but uneven and clumsy. He stood and took a few steps to peer out of one of the windows, wondering if somehow the weather had grown chilly enough to dump hail from a passing storm, but it was too dark to see anything outside other than the lamp glow coming from the house.

The shifting chitter was growing louder, an off-sounding chatter and roll to it. It seemed to be coming from the walls themselves. Then Tristan saw a miniscule movement at the door to the living room, and the source of the sound became clear.

The doll heads were moving, descending on the room where he stood watching in a fascinated horror at the wave coming toward him.

Anything with a full body scrambled forward by hooking fingers and toes into the cracks between the boards and dragging the rest of its weight behind. One of the larger clown dolls laughed in a maniacal melancholy whenever its body was turned, and farther down the foyer, a harlequin puppet dragged itself forward with the stumpy remains of its arms.

The hallway was filled with ambulatory toys, and the pieces missing limbs were perhaps the most terrifying.

Many were just faces, turning painted and sculpted eyes and mouths toward the ceiling while scavenged legs and arms worked in lurching strides to move their burdens to the room. Others were full doll heads, their cavities stuffed with limbs, pens, and anything else that could be used to balance their top-heavy loads. One particularly large head had commandeered several slide rules, and the wooden folds opened and closed underneath it, seesawing the old rubber toy across the hall.

The noise grew louder, a thousand scraping rubs of porcelain, rubber, and wood. The floor behind the horde was scarred and dimmed from scratches, and as the wave of jittering toys drew slowly near, the crying behind him got louder and louder.

"Mooooommmmaaaa! Nooooooo Charity! Noooooooooooooo!"

The dolls took up a cry of their own, more sound than words, but their rage was evident, a hard, raucous whine of air-forced voice boxes and high-pitched squeakers. The scrape of limbs on wood rankled the hair on the back of Tristan's neck, and then in between the sliding hack of warbling floorboards, he heard it.

"Simoooooooooooone."

There was no mistaking the evil in that childish giggle. Dripping with malice, the intent was clear. Whatever or whomever was using the doll to cry out was doomed, because Charity Sinclair was using every bit of power she'd gathered up to bring down mayhem on anyone in her path.

There was only one thing Tristan could do. Taking a few steps back into the room, he took a deep breath and cried, "Wolf! Get the hell in here! I think Charity's come out to play!"

Chapter 19

THE WALLS moved. The floor crawled. And the noise hurt deep down into Wolf's teeth.

It was a widening procession of screaming, smiling, and painted masks, carried as swiftly as space would allow. The low crackle of their ad-hoc locomotion buzzed and clicked, an undertone for the wailing of Simone's name. The heads skittered along, focused on reaching the living room until Wolf stepped into the foyer. Then their tide shifted, peeling away from their destination to head toward the warm body in front of them.

"Jesus fucking Christ." Cin slammed into him from behind. "What the fuck are those?"

Wolf didn't stop to answer him. A few of the heads were rapidly skittering around the corner and into the living room. Another step into the foyer turned up another surprise—an unpleasant one at that. It wasn't just the heads that were moving. Anything remotely toylike lumbered through the space; from rolling eyeballs to articulated hands, the floor was covered with migrating body parts.

A stud-backed eye scrambled over Wolf's foot, digging deep into his flesh. He kicked it off, but the damage was already done. His skin welted up, painfully swelling as it began to drip blood. It was too much of a reaction for such a small cut, and Wolf limped for another step before stepping on an upraised hand lurching in front of him.

"Fuck." The pain was immediate, like a snakebite along the arch of his foot. "Cin, watch your step. These damned things hurt."

"Just kick them out of—" Cin went down, his feet sliding out from under him. The dolls swarmed over the fallen Hellsinger, their gyrating limbs scraping into his eyes and forcing themselves into his mouth. Cin choked and fought to turn over, but he couldn't get leverage with the ground shifting under him.

Wolf waded through the heads, trying to reach Cin. His cousin struggled to remove a baby doll arm wiggling down his mouth, its rubber ball joint bobbing like an untied gag around his lips. Cin's teeth were clamped down over the joint to prevent it from slithering down any farther, but from what Wolf could see, the arm appeared to be winning the battle.

It was harder to get to Cin than he thought it would be. The toys were slippery underfoot, and more than once he glided across a slick, eerily moaning surface. They'd both come in and shed their shoes, walking around the house on bare feet, a decision Wolf sincerely regretted as he stepped on yet another sharp, pointy appendage.

If that wasn't bad enough, the floor was black and sticky, coated with a slime that began to burn Wolf's skin where it stuck to his feet. He fell, landing nearly on top of his cousin by a happy coincidence, and Wolf used the momentum to reach out and yank the burrowing limb from Cin's mouth.

The hand wouldn't let go. Its fingers were dug deep into the sides of Cin's tongue, and his cousin gagged, frothing up blood from the cuts along the inside of his mouth. Sey was screaming at Gildy to get back, and from the corner of his eye, Wolf could see Tristan kicking at the faces as they approached the archway to the living room.

"Shit, I've got salt." Wolf dug into his pocket while tugging at the wiggling arm. "Hold on, Cin."

Cin gagged again, seemingly more reflex than fear, especially when the appendage slipped and hit the back of his throat. His cousin was fighting off other intruders, his hands busy at clearing away the bits and pieces of toys clambering over them.

Wolf came up with a handful of salt, and with an apologetic grimace at his cousin, he warned, "I'm gonna salt you, dude."

Wolf assumed the gurgling sounds coming from his cousin's mouth were approval for his plan. He wasn't fluent in captured-tongue speech, especially since being a dentist was his idea of hell, but it was all he had. The one person who might have had a clue about how to fight the damned things off had to go and get himself throat leeched.

"Sey, can you get me water? He's going to need it when he gets this thing out," Wolf shouted at his other cousin. Dribbling a stream of rock salt into his cousin's already filled mouth, he leaned back when the rubber limb began to smoke. One good yank and the thing was free, its fingers wiggling helplessly in the air as Wolf flung it down the hall.

Cin came up spitting out chunks of salt, but he tilted his head at Sey's shout, then snatched a water bottle out of the air when it came flying at him. The cap was off the bottle before Wolf could get to his feet, and Cin was rinsing his mouth, spitting the salty water onto the doll pieces around them.

The toys smoked lightly where Cin's spit hit, and the black goo under their feet bubbled. The stinging was growing too much for Wolf to take, and he picked his way through the mass, trying to get to the living room. It was taking too long to cross the short distance, and for every step he was able to get forward, he slipped and slid what seemed like five paces back. Heads and arms were dropping down the walls, hitting tables and knickknacks.

One ceramic shepherdess seemed to wobble between answering Charity's siren call and remaining inert. A grinning clown doll holding a bunch of plastic balloons took care of her indecision, smashing her to the hard floor. Trapped in Charity's thrall, the pieces flew but not before squeaking an eerie moan demanding Simone's death.

"Wolf! The doll—it's floating in here," Tristan said over the chitter coming from the foyer. "And it's crying. I think it's… Simone. I think Simone's in there."

"Makes sense," Cin choked out through another mouthful of water.

They got another few inches when the ground behind them exploded in a spray of ceramics and wood.

The shotgun blast deafened them, and Wolf felt the splatter of shot hit his jeans. The pellets stung, but he didn't think he was hit. Cin, however, swore loudly, and the smell of spilled blood filled the air. They each dove, Wolf toward Tristan, but Cin's leap went sideways, taking Sey out of the foyer. They tumbled into the empty dining room, and from the sounds of things, they'd taken a few of the wooden chairs with them.

"Get down. I'm reloading!" Gildy screamed from the end of the hall. "Bastards don't know what's hitting them!"

"Fucking hell." Wolf scrambled to get over the crawling horde, but his hands were wet with sweat and he slipped, going down on his elbows a few inches from Tristan's feet. His toes felt like they were on fire, and the pricks in his hands and arms stung as if he'd rolled in a vat of pissed-off sea urchins.

"I've got you." Tristan grabbed at his wrists, yanking to draw him clear of the toys. They were advancing, despite Gildy's shotgun blast.

What wasn't shattered kept crawling forward, in some cases limping along on damaged bits. "Wolf, tell her to put down the damned gun."

"Gildy, drop the fucking gun! Are you trying to get us killed?" Wolf kicked at the heavy marionette tangling his feet. A two-foot-tall nutcracker snapped at Wolf's toes, its powerful jaws nearly breaking his joints.

She didn't hear him or just didn't give a shit because there was another cock of a barrel snapping together. Then the hallway went bright with another flash and boom.

The air was filled with ash, powder, and burn, with bits of flaming toys bouncing down off the walls to land around Wolf's prone body. Tristan fell back, and for a panicked second Wolf thought he'd been hit by the blast, but he rolled over onto his stomach and flashed Wolf a smile.

"I'm okay," Tristan reassured him. "But she's sure as hell pissed someone off. Charity's out for blood."

Wolf kicked free of the dolls' hold, smashing as many as he could, and got loose. Sure enough, he didn't need an EMF reader to tell him Charity Sinclair was walking on the remains of Sey's stock, and she was heading straight for him.

Her feet were bare like his, but unlike Wolf's smarting soles and toes, the little girl was untouched by the shards and goo. She appeared as she had every other time, sealed skin pulled down over her eye sockets and her mouth curved up under her cheekbones, a gaping black stretch held together with tattered strands of viscera and tendon. Shreds of her tongue slipped out between the torn pieces, licking at the air like a snake tasting a scent on the wind.

Charity's face turned toward Gildy, her neck twisting all about until her chin touched her spine. Her arms stretched outward, and her forehead tilted back, nearly severing her face in two. Her chest filled, expanding nearly to bursting. Then Charity screamed, unleashing an inferno of scorching sound—engulfing the hall in flames.

IN THE confusion that followed, Tristan only cared about one thing— getting Wolf into the living room. He grabbed a hold of Wolf's shirt and pulled, nearly yanking his own shoulders out of their sockets. It was funny how his lover never felt heavy when Wolf was lying on top of him, but now, when their bodies were about to be immolated, dragging Wolf seemed like trying to heave a VW Bug up onto a curb.

"Fuck, no more Red Vines for you," he grunted, giving Wolf one final yank. A few of the doll parts clung to them, but they were mostly smoking remains, burned pieces of melting vinyl clinging to Tristan's hands as he tried to scrape them off Wolf's back.

"They're fat free," Wolf grumbled. "Tell me the doll's still around."

Looking over his shoulder, Tristan spotted the blond-wigged toy spinning in gentle circles near a music stand in the corner. Its dress caught on the metal flat, pulling it along as it drifted through the open spaces. It continued to mewl, haunting echoes of cries buried beneath pleas for Charity's mercy.

"We need to find out what happened." Wolf began to head back to the hallway, but Tristan caught him before he threw himself back into the fray. "Let me go, Tris—"

"Stop," Tristan ordered, pointing across the break in the walls toward the dining room. "Wolf, they got Gildy."

"I'm going around to see what the damage is!" Cin shouted over the crackling remains, coughing at the plumes of sticky smoke filling the space. "Stop this bitch. Sey's got Gildy. They're going to get outside!"

"But—" Wolf growled, then turned on his heel. "Fuck this. We need to get rid of her now."

The ghost was gone from the hall, but the scent of her touch lingered, and there was no doubt she'd be back. The toys seemed to have stopped their progress for the most part, but a few stalwart pieces scrabbled on, rolling over the bodies of their defunct companions.

"There's a fire extinguisher down the hall. Cin'll find it." The sooty air burned his eyes and nose. He'd swallowed too much smoke, and it tore at his mucus membranes. Coughing, Tristan searched the living room for the salt packets Wolf'd made earlier in the evening. "It's just you and me, Kincaid."

Wolf limped into the room and tugged at one of the couches. "Help me get this across the opening. We're going to have to stop anything from getting in here. I get the feeling if one of those things out there gets a hold of this doll, things are going to go to shit on us."

Tristan had to stop and gape in astonishment at the man who shared his bed. "*This* hasn't gone to shit? What the hell—"

"Just help me, Thursday."

They left the doll to its dance and toppled over one of the heavy davenports, angling it across the opening to the hall. Wolf's feet left bloody marks on a beige carpet. Tristan's weren't much better. There was a filmy grit on his skin, and no matter how much he wiped his hands on his pants, he couldn't seem to get them clean of the fine oil clinging on the whorls of his fingers.

"Where's the doll?" Wolf looked around the room for the blonde toy. He snagged it, yanking it down, and the doll fell over, Simone's hold on its form giving way to Wolf's touch. He moved quickly, catching its head before it smashed against anything. "Damn, this thing is still crying. We're going to have to go new school on this."

"What does that mean?" The problem with being in a household of Kincaids was they had their own language, and Tristan apparently failed Frankenspeak before he even signed up for the course. "Wolf, talk to me like I'm a kid. What do you need me to do? And hopefully it's not something that's going to get me eaten by that ghost out there. Or wherever the hell she is."

"Tell me you've got your music player with you." Wolf grinned foolishly. "Remember when you cranked up the tunes and shook up Winifred? We can use sound to keep her back long enough for us to get some rune lines down."

"You want me to rock the ghost out? Are you nuts?"

"No, it's what I'm hoping will work on her, because tonal fluctuations push spectral entities back," Wolf explained. "I think the sonic thing she just did tired her out. I don't think we've got much time before she comes—"

"You've got to get out of here, mister." A tall, strong-faced black man flickered into existence not more than a few inches from Tristan's face.

He stepped back, his hands up to push the man away, but they went right through him. Stumbling forward, Tristan fell through Ray, and the ghost tried to catch him, leaning to scoop him up from the ground. Tristan hit the floor face-first, barking his arms on a hooked rug.

"Shit." There was blood in his mouth, and the ache in his ribs from the night before was back with a vengeance, reminding Tristan of the ass-kicking he'd already gotten from Charity Sinclair. "Ray, you're the one who needs to get out. We're going to try to—"

"Where the hell did he come from?" Wolf turned to grab one of the bags of salt spilling over onto a table. "Shit, she's—"

"Don't. It's Ray. Remember? I told you about him," Tristan groaned, unsteadily getting to his feet. "Shit, I hurt everywhere."

"I'm telling you, mister, you've got to leave. She's going to tear this place down." Ray's voice crackled and sparked from his wavering form, and for a moment, Tristan was afraid the young man was going to do what Charity did and set them all aflame. "She wants you all dead. Heck, she's not going to give up until every last one of you is gone and she can burn this house to the ground."

Tristan felt his panic rise. Sending Charity away should have been easier, at least in his mind. She was a little girl. Sure, she'd died more pissed off than a slug accidentally dropped by a bird onto a salt flat, but she was still a *child*.

Then he recalled a few of the encounters he'd had in school before his parents got him tutors, and Tristan *knew* Winifred's rage was probably a drop in the bucket compared to Charity's.

"She's coming here, mister.... I can't remember your name, but I know you, right?" Ray's expression grew troubled. "Why can't I remember your name? I—"

The young man flickered again, and Wolf handed Tristan one of the salt bags. "If he attacks you, use this. I don't care if you sat around a fire and sang Kumbaya, you get rid of him before he can hurt you. I'm going to see if I can get the runes down. Watch the doll."

Charity's doll lay on the chair, doing nothing as far as Tristan could see. If anything it looked more bored than possessed, even as its soft weeping continued. Its eyes were leaking the same black viscous substance they'd seen in the hall, and the dribbles eased slowly down its cheeks, welling a drop at a time and following a slender trail to the cushion's thick forest-green fabric.

"It's not doing jack shit, so stop trying to distract me," Tristan shot back. "I can help with this. Ray—"

He'd been about to tell Ray to flee to the barn and find Petal, hoping to push the stalwart man toward his young lover, but as he opened his mouth, Ray's body stiffened and his eyes milked over. Tristan reached for the man, unsure and confused, but something wiggling under Ray's chest made him pause.

His chest erupted, splattering Tristan's face and torso with a sticky gush of fluids. The cloudy fluid was almost spongy, flecked with black bits, and when Tristan wiped some of it from his face, stinging welts began to bubble up where it'd hit him.

Tiny pale fingers were forcing their way out of Ray, their nails clotted with a chunky ebony dirt. The fingers became hands, and Ray's entire being shook and trembled as full arms drove out of him, their pale skin mottled with stygian-blue lines spreading into a maze of frilled endings and crosses.

Blonde hair poked out next, followed by a shattered temple, a deep triangular gouge dug into the bruised skin above an eyeless socket. Dark blood mottled the wound, ancient dried-out flakes tumbling from Charity's shattered forehead.

"She's coming for you, mister…. I can't stop her," Ray looked terrified. Hell, his voice creaked with fear and panic. "I'm sorry, mister. I just can't—"

He exploded outward, coating the room with sticky ichors. In his place, Charity stood defiant, her dress plastered down from Ray's fluidic demise. Her fingers grew long as Tristan watched, turning to smoking talons, their tips nearly glowing red with an intense heat.

"Simone…." Charity hissed, raising her hands. "You took my daddy. You took…."

She moved quickly, far too quickly for Tristan's eyes to follow, and the talons flashed, leaving a hot white trail behind them when she struck. He couldn't get away in time, and she scored a hit, tearing through his shirt and down into the skin on his belly. The fire they left behind spread through Tristan's nerves, and he fell back, tumbling over Wolf's long body.

"Gotcha, babe," Wolf whispered in his ear. "You okay?"

"Yeah," Tristan mumbled. The unseen flames licking away at his skin were fading, and he clenched his fingers, working the numbness out of them. "Feeling's coming back. Still want me to shove my MP3 player up the doll's ass?"

"Trust me on this one. You grab the doll, and you find something loud and raucous to play over it. Hell, fit the damned headphones over its body if you can. Just find something ear-bleeding." Wolf kissed him quickly. "We'll free the sister at the same time we banish the brat."

Chapter 20

HE'D SPENT over a decade not catching a whiff of the afterlife. Then suddenly his world was filled with boo-wigglies and screaming phantoms eager to suck his life clean from his marrow. But despite the chills, thrills, and soul-threatening danger, Wolf had never felt more alive.

Especially since Tristan was by his side.

In a lot of ways, it felt right. Like chasing down the things that wouldn't let go of their mortal coil was what he was meant to do, even if the family didn't agree with his methods and kicked him to the curb. Wolf Kincaid was born into a line of ghost cleavers, and damned if he wasn't going to live up to the name and bloodline.

He just had to convince his cousin Cin to give him more instruction on how to do the job, because winging it didn't seem like the way to go.

It was an uneven battle. He'd spent his life trying to prove the afterlife existed, and Charity—well, she seemed to have dedicated her spectral time building up a lot of rage and ways to coax people over to her side of the curtain.

From the ectoplasm scattered about the room like the aftermath of an elephant sneeze, little Charity Sinclair seemed to take her *one* job very seriously.

His hands were dusty from the marks he'd made on the wood floor. The seamstress markers Sey'd stashed on her worktable were the closest thing he was going to get to blessed chalk. Somewhere behind him—hopefully—Tristan was cuing up his music player. There were definitely sounds of something going on and a few tinny taps of metal on metal. Then Freddie Mercury began screaming about fat-bottomed girls, and Wolf spared his lover a withering glance.

"Really? Queen?"

"You do your thing, and I'll do mine," Tristan sniped back. He'd connected his player to an auxiliary port in Sey's stereo, so the room was drowning in rolling beats and piano. "Do you think I should try to get a fire started? So we can throw the doll into it? Or is that going to hurt Simone?"

"Pretty sure Simone is as sick of being in that doll as we are of her sister." He tried to keep one eye on the ghost edging through the circle.

Charity suspected something was up, but it was hard to tell what the spirit was going to do. Her skin-curtained eyes were edged in black again, and Wolf wondered if that was any indication of her building up power. Beyond them, the sofa blocking the doorway rattled, and Wolf spotted a spray of segmented fingers digging into the cushions. A mess of tangled brown hair popped up over the edge of the couch for a brief moment. Then the doll head tumbled back down, unable to gain a purchase on the furniture.

There was a rumble of cursing coming from the foyer, and Cin appeared in the hall, framed by the blocked doorway. He made eye contact with his cousin, then held up what looked like a garden sprayer. Pumping the handle hard, Cin worked up some pressure in the canister. Holding down the trigger, he let loose with a strong flat spray, coating the seemingly immortal toys with whatever he had in the tank.

"You okay in there, cousin?" Cin shouted over the hissing and screaming coming from down the hall. He sounded rough, his words blurring. Then Wolf remembered the damage the toy'd done to his tongue. "What's the plan? And what the hell is with the music?"

"Loud music disrupts EMI. Okay, I've got salt and blood." Wolf dodged Charity's swipe, but a tip caught his cheek, and he hissed at the sharp pain. "Okay, now I've got more blood. Bone. I need bone."

"The doll's buttons. Those are bone." Tristan grabbed at the large doll, snapping the spheres lining the back of her dress. "Sey told me they made buttons out of bone or shell. Shell's a kind of bone."

"Any port in a storm," Wolf grunted and dove, avoiding Charity again. This time she missed, but Tristan's movement caught her attention, and she turned, obviously sniffing out her quarry. "Shit, she's found the damned thing. Hand them over, Tris."

Charity flew at Tristan as he flung the buttons toward Wolf. They crossed into one another, and the ghost twisted as if the tiny spheres were knives slicing through her. Nearly the size of Wolf's pinkie nail, a few hit the ground and rattled about, but he'd caught most of them in his cupped palms.

Pouring them into one hand, he then smeared his fingers through the blood on his face, coating as much of his skin as he could. Satisfied he got good coverage, he closed his hands together, trapping the buttons between them, and shook, covering the buttons in his own blood.

"I can't see your sigils," Cin shouted. "What did you use?"

"Fucking everything." Wolf piled the buttons into the center of his circle, then stood facing Tristan, who was holding Charity off with a handful of ivory umbrella supports. "You might want to duck, Thursday. This might get messy."

His lover'd gotten a small fire going. It was weak, but the flames licked and spat out sparks as it tried to eat through the kindling. Tristan crouched on the hearth with the doll between his legs to prevent Charity from getting her hands on it. In between swats at the ghost, he fed handfuls of something orange into the embers.

"What the heck is that, Tris?"

"Doritos. They make really great kindling. I had a bag in my backpack." Tristan yelped, and Wolf saw Charity had a handful of his hair. He stabbed at her with the ivory stays again, and she screamed in response, holes appearing along her ribs where Tristan made contact.

"Only you would know that, Thursday." He needed to move quickly, but it was difficult. Wolf's feet were stinging from the damage done to them earlier, and he needed to find accelerant. A bottle of old brandy was going to have to do. Grabbing a few things off Sey's desk and tables, he hopped back into the circle to finish the exorcism. He worked quickly, trying to keep the buttons coated while he organized the final few items. "Okay, nearly ready."

"Music is changing up." His lover batted at the ghost again, then tried to shove a hank of his damp blond hair from his glittering eyes. "Since Queen didn't do it for you."

The opening bars of some guitar lick wasn't one Wolf recognized, but at the moment, he didn't care if Tristan was playing "Itsy Bitsy Spider," so long as it was loud and threw Charity off her game. The music resonating from the speakers shifted, breaking into something harder, and the words pouring into the room were defiant and angry.

Don't talk to me about your God
I don't need your broken bread
Not for my soul
Not for my heart
Not for my countless sins

You want to give me something?
Something to save my wicked soul?
Give me the same as you've got
Loving who I want, and leaving me alone.

It was definitely loud and pulsing with emotion. The singer's raw blues voice rasped and growled around the tune, daring someone to challenge him. Charity was pushed back by the antagonistic sound wave, and she floundered, her swaddled eyes crawling with black dots as she tried to hold onto her power.

Wolf took the emotional ride of the song and embraced it, using the thundering beat under its words to fuel his own rolling chant. It was a nursery rhyme they'd all been taught, a simple cadence of blackbirds and falling down, but the words were strong, steeped with decades of ruin and failure. The intent was more important than the actual spell; he'd remembered that much.

With one final round of crackling words, he threw the bloodied bone orbs down on the pile of brandy-soaked rags he'd tossed into a metal bowl, then set the whole mess on fire, flinging the fireplace match into the fray for good measure.

Charity's scream shattered the windows into thousands of speckled shards, and Wolf's ears crackled in pain. He was sure he was bleeding out of his nose at the very least. Wolf heard Cin cry out, but his focus was solely on Tristan. Wincing from the cacophony hammering at their senses, Tristan squared his shoulders and murmured something Wolf couldn't hear. Gripping the doll by her ankles, he heaved her into the fireplace.

If Charity's scream was of pain and anger, the doll's caterwauling was one of release. Tristan's powerful swing smashed its porcelain body up against the fireplace's brick back wall, and it broke, falling in an avalanche of fabric and shattered ceramics into the hungry flames.

There was one final cry, and then the room went white as Charity's body unraveled before their eyes. Bit by bit, the noise of the advancing dolls in the hallway fell off, but Wolf couldn't take his eyes off the ghost as she disintegrated before them. A cold wind poured into the living room through the broken windows, and Charity's ashen remains were caught up in a gust. Before either man could say or do anything, she was gone—carried off on the midnight breeze.

THE CAMEL was back. So was the small frolicking red calf, who seemed more interested in pissing off the camel than eating any of the sweet alfalfa Sey'd laid down for them in the paddock's trough. Tristan was still moving slowly, but it wasn't anything he couldn't extinguish with a good dose of aspirin.

Wolf's kisses seemed to work just as well—and those'd come fast and furious since they'd tossed Charity out on her ass.

The cousins were saying their final good-byes. Cin was heading back to Las Vegas to clean up a few things. Then he'd join them at Hoxne Grange so Wolf and Tristan could begin official Hellsinger lessons.

Or at least as official as they were going to get. Gildy'd left them the day after they'd evicted Charity from Sey's house and somehow ended up at the Kincaid main compound, carrying tales about what the cousins had been up to. A stern phone call followed. Then Cin chewed someone apart through the lines, his deep voice ripping past arguments and pleas alike. Tristan hadn't stuck around to see what the outcome was. From what he could hear, someone was in trouble, and knowing what he did of Wolf's family, it seemed like they were looking for someone to blame.

Cin wasn't having any of it, and neither was Sey or Wolf.

"They can have the crazy old woman," Sey grumbled. "She tried to kill us!"

"I want to know where she kept getting guns from." Wolf poked Cin in the stomach. "How many of those damned things did you bring with you?"

"That one wasn't mine," he refuted. "I only do sawed-offs. I'm shooting salt, anyway. Might as well make as wide a splatter as I can. Long barrels get too clogged up. She probably stole it back from Sey."

"Sure, blame the hauntee," the woman said. "See if I cook you another chocolate chip cookie for the rest of your life."

"Sey, I love you," Cin drawled softly. "But if ever I run out of ammunition, I could use your cookies to take down a grizzly bear."

That'd been nearly a week ago. Tristan'd spent the time communing with the camel, throwing the rubber ball into the pasture for Jack to chase, and sketching out a whole community of crimson monsters who looked remarkably like Highland cattle, right down to the square-bodied baby poking its head where it would be caught on a stile.

"Well, at least the bridge is up." Cin hefted the last of his bags into his rented Jeep. "You sure you don't need anything else, Sey?"

"Nah. The guys I've got working here will help with anything else. You all go on with your lives." She stretched, then ruffled her hair until it stood up nearly straight off her head. "The holes in the hall are boarded up, and well, you all certainly cleaned up a bunch of my old junk stock."

"Yeah, next time, just ask for help to get rid of it," Wolf grumbled, crossing his arms over his chest as he leaned against his SUV. "You don't need to call up a poltergeist just to get us down here."

"Hey, better than dinner and a movie," Sey laughed, kissing Cin on the cheek as he bent down to hug her. "Bye, kiddo. You come visit more often."

"Promise," he said with a nod. He and Wolf had a quick hug that could barely pass for a manly second. Then they broke away, shoving at each other's shoulders. Cin craned his neck and called out, "Tris!"

"Yeah?" He was ambling slowly over, more from a reluctance to leave than anything else.

"You did good, kid." Cin cuffed him on the shoulder when Tristan drew in close. "Looking forward to what you can do up at that place of yours."

"Just remember, the ones that live there are off-limits," he cautioned.

"Hey, just the fact I might see them is exciting," Wolf's cousin drawled. "It'll be nice to come into contact with a ghost that isn't trying to either kill or scare the shit out of me."

"Can't promise Mara won't try to kill you," Wolf warned. "Track mud on her floors, and you're going to go the way of the dodo."

"Oh, Sey. I forgot to give you this." Tristan opened the SUV's door and dug around in his backpack until he found the nanny's ledger. "Didn't mean to walk off with it."

"Hell, you might was well keep it. Who knows what that woman saw?" She shivered. "Can you imagine raising that kid? That nanny deserved a medal."

"Or a huge retirement package," Wolf interjected. "Never did find out what pissed Charity off. Was it just another kid stepping on her place? And really, how many wives and kids did the man end up having?"

"Her father had two wives after Charity's mother," Tristan said. He'd spent a good amount of time reading through the unnamed nanny's notes, and he'd been shocked by the pervasive callousness the Sinclair family seemed to possess. "Leona had two sons after Charity died, but she was his final wife. The nanny wrote Leona suffered from melancholy on the anniversary of her daughter's death, and she wouldn't let her sons near a body of water larger than a bathtub."

"All because Simone drowned, and Charity caught pneumonia trying to save her—maybe." Sey sighed. "That family sounds cursed."

"Charity didn't die of pneumonia," Tristan corrected, and the Kincaids turned to stare at him, their piercing eyes stripping his defenses. "Well, at least the nanny said she didn't. That's what they told Mr. Sinclair. She believed Leona smothered the girl with a pillow. Charity wasn't even sick. Sinclair was away when this all happened. By the time he got home, both the girls were dead and his wife was in shock."

"Fucking hell," Cin exhaled. "That is one sick screwed up family."

"Yep, good to know there's one more fucked than ours," Wolf said. "Okay, Thursday. Time to head back to the Addams mansion and see what Cousin Itt is up to."

THE TRIP back to Hoxne Grange went by in a blur. Tristan played nearly all of the music he'd loaded onto a couple of CDs and then teased Wolf about the massive library of seventies rock living in his glove compartment.

Hoxne Grange appeared through the fog, a smatter of turrets, weathered brick, and green lawn, and Tristan felt a small flutter of happiness course through him. As much as Sey'd been welcoming and warm, he'd missed the Grange and its quirkiness. Rolling Jack's red rubber ball on his leg, Tristan sighed as they circled up into the driveway.

"Good to be home?" Wolf asked as he threw the car into park.

"You have no idea," he replied softly. "You?"

"I've never really had a home, babe. We moved around too much."

The sadness in Wolf's eyes made Tristan want to kiss away the shadows. Leaning over the SUV's cab, he pressed his mouth to Wolf's cheek, his lips tickled by Wolf's stubble.

"You've got a home here, Kincaid," he whispered.

"Thanks, Pryce," Wolf whispered as he squeezed Tristan's hand. "Okay, let's get unpacked and hope Ophelia Sunday's got dinner planned. I don't think I could choke down another slice of pizza."

"If you guys hadn't damaged the stove when we were trying to get the kitchen floor clean, that wouldn't have happened." Tristan took the steps two at a time, then threw the front door open when he reached the top.

The lobby was exactly as he'd left it, with the exception of new fresh flowers decorating the space. The reception desk was unmanned, a troubling state considering two filmy shapes were standing in front of it. A broad-shouldered man hit the desk bell once, its jingling chime echoing up into the high ceiling. Beside him, a long-haired young woman with flowers in her hair adjusted her tiered gypsy skirt around her legs, her bare toes tipped with orange nail polish. His smile was bright against his creamy brown skin, and the love in his eyes was thick enough to be poured into a champagne glass.

"Ray?" Tristan gaped at the man as he walked down the lobby to greet the ghosts. "Petal?"

"Hello," Ray replied, but the confused, polite look on his face told Tristan the young man didn't remember him.

"Someone called ahead to let me know you were coming," Tristan lied. "Let me check you in."

He went through the motions, old familiar chatter, then handing over the keys to the honeymoon suite to the enamored couple. Wolf stood at the end of the desk, listening to him and smiling. He didn't know if Wolf saw Ray and Petal or if the conversation was one-sided, but it no longer mattered. Wolf didn't think he was insane and was willing to go toe-to-toe with him against his uncle.

That was all for tomorrow. Today, he was going to enjoy having ghosts who didn't want to kill him and a good helping of lasagna after a nap.

With Ray and Petal checked in and gone, he leaned on the reception counter and wiggled his eyebrows at Wolf. The whole gay thing was getting easier, but then he'd had some practice. If he was lucky, he'd get in even more practice before Cin arrived, and Tristan said as much to Wolf when he walked around the desk to hug him.

"You think Cin's going to kick our asses?" Wolf murmured into Tristan's hair.

"Yeah, but we'll need it. Wonder where Ophelia Sunday—"

"Tristan! Good, you're home." Mara announced herself with a long squeak of her crepe-soled shoes. "You need to go to the downstairs study. Your uncle is here, and I think the young lady you left here is about to clobber him across the head with that brass monkey your Aunt Margaret got from Borneo."

"I think that monkey came from the swap meet. The Borneo story was so no one would throw the thing out. It's beyond ugly," Tristan grumbled to Wolf. He extracted himself from Wolf's embrace and straightened his shirt. "What's Uncle Walt doing here? How many times can he sue me? Shit, I'm going to owe your sister big time for having to deal with his crap."

"Not that uncle. The other one. From your mother's side—Will," the housekeeper hissed. "And they're going at each other. She reminds me of how I was at her age. We might have to dig a hole for his body when she's done."

"Uncle Will?" Tristan drew up short and stared at the gray-uniformed woman. "Here? What the hell?"

"You've got more than one uncle who's an asshole?" Wolf ate up the distance between them with his long strides. "And my sister is in there with him?"

"Did you miss the part where I said she's going to kill him? Don't know what he said to piss her off, but it's a gale in a coffee cup in there."

"Tempest, and it's a teapot," Tristan corrected absently. "And I don't think that means what you think it means."

The hallway to the downstairs study was bright and cheery. If it hadn't been for the shouts coming from one of the open doors, Tristan wouldn't have thought anything was up at all. But there was definitely an argument, and from what he could make out, it sounded like Ophelia Sunday and his uncle knew each other.

"What's up with this uncle of yours?" Wolf snagged his arm to stop Tristan before they went in. "What are we walking into?"

"I don't know. I haven't seen Uncle Will in forever. He's my mom's baby brother. He was eight when I was born." Tristan glanced worriedly at the study. If anything, the shouting was escalating, and he wanted to get in there as quick as he could. "I don't know that side of the family. My mom wasn't exactly fond of them. But then again, she wasn't very fond of me either."

"Great. Okay, well, just remember, Thursday," Wolf said, pinching Tristan's ass. "I've got your back."

"That is *not* my back."

"Close enough. Back. Rear end. Either works." Wolf winked, then swept his arm toward the door for Tristan to enter. "It's a nice one, by the way. Just in case you were wondering."

Ophelia Sunday's cheeks were a bright red, and she'd been in midrant when they came into the room. Like most of the Grange's spaces, the downstairs study was heavily furnished with antiques used by no one but ghostly guests and methodically dusted by the daily staff. It'd been the one room Ophelia Sunday'd taken over—with Tristan's blessing—and he felt odd walking in without knocking.

"It's a good thing you're here, Wolf." Ophelia Sunday planted her hands on her hips and scowled at her brother. "Look what was hiding in the woodshed."

Even after not seeing his uncle for years, Tristan would have guessed the long-limbed blond man sprawled on a velvet love seat was his relative. He looked a bit like the pictures Tristan had of his mother. They shared the same chameleon green eyes, and while Tristan's face was leaner, their bone structure was similar. The man's blond hair was cut short, with a few silver strands glinting at his temples, and other than some laugh lines near his eyes, there was little to show the eight-year difference between him and his uncle.

"I'll be damned." Wolf stared at the man lounging indolently on the couch. "Will fucking Harker."

"Hello, Kincaid." His Uncle Will stood, and Tristan nearly took a step back at the darkening fury in his relative's hard gaze. "Guess the rumors are true. There *is* a Kincaid trying to pull a con at the Grange."

"Wait, you two know each other?" Tristan shot his uncle a fierce look. "And what do you mean, pull a con? No one's pulling anything over on me."

"He's your nephew?" Wolf cocked his head at the older man, his chin rising up in challenge when Harker nodded slowly. "Well, fucking hell. I *would* fall for the one guy whose family has been trying to kill us all off for the last one hundred years. Isn't that just my luck? My boyfriend is a goddamned Harker."

RHYS FORD is an award-winning author with several long-running LGBT+ mystery, thriller, paranormal, and urban fantasy series and was a 2016 LAMBDA finalist with her novel, *Murder and Mayhem*. She is published by Dreamspinner Press and DSP Publications.

She's also quite skeptical about bios without a dash of something personal, and really, who doesn't mention their cats, dog, and cars in a bio? She shares the house with Yoshi, a grumpy tuxedo cat, and Tam, a diabetic black pygmy panther, as well as a ginger cairn terrorist named Gus. Rhys is also enslaved to the upkeep a 1979 Pontiac Firebird and enjoys murdering make-believe people.

Rhys can be found at the following locations:
Blog: www.rhysford.com
Facebook: www.facebook.com/rhys.ford.author
Twitter: @Rhys_Ford

FISH AND GHOSTS

RHYS FORD

Hellsinger: Book One

When his Uncle Mortimer died and left him Hoxne Grange, the family's Gilded Age mansion, Tristan Pryce became the second generation of Pryces to serve as a caretaker for the estate, a way station for spirits on their final steps to the afterlife. Tristan is prepared for challenges, though not necessarily from the ghosts he's seen since childhood. Determined to establish Tristan's insanity and gain access to his trust fund, his loving relatives hire Dr. Wolf Kincaid and his paranormal researchers, Hellsinger Investigations, to prove the Grange is not haunted.

Skeptic Wolf Kincaid has made it his life's work to debunk the supernatural. After years of cons and fakes, he can't wait to reveal the Grange's ghostly activity is just badly leveled floorboards and a drafty old house. More than a few surprises await him at the Grange, including its prickly, reclusive owner. Tristan Pryce is much less insane and much more attractive than Wolf wants to admit, and when his team releases a ghostly serial killer on the Grange, Wolf is torn between his skepticism and protecting the man he's been sent to discredit.

www.dreamspinnerpress.com

DIM SUM ASYLUM

RHYS FORD

Welcome to Dim Sum Asylum: a San Francisco where it's a ho-hum kind of case when a cop has to chase down an enchanted two-foot-tall shrine god statue with an impressive Fu Manchu mustache that's running around Chinatown, trolling sex magic and chaos in its wake.

Senior Inspector Roku MacCormick of the Chinatown Arcane Crimes Division faces a pile of challenges far beyond his human-faerie heritage, snarling dragons guarding C-Town's multiple gates, and exploding noodle factories. After a case goes sideways, Roku is saddled with Trent Leonard, a new partner he can't trust, to add to the crime syndicate family he doesn't want and a spell-casting serial killer he desperately needs to find.

While Roku would rather stay home with Bob the Cat and whiskey himself to sleep, he puts on his badge and gun every day, determined to serve and protect the city he loves. When Chinatown's dark mystical underworld makes his life hell and the case turns deadly, Trent guards Roku's back and, if Trent can be believed, his heart... even if from what Roku can see, Trent is as dangerous as the monsters and criminals they're sworn to bring down.

www.dreamspinnerpress.com

THERE'S THIS GUY

Sometimes all a broken man needs is a bit of light and love.

RHYS FORD

How do you save a drowning man when that drowning man is you?

Jake Moore's world fits too tightly around him. Every penny he makes as a welder goes to care for his dying father, an abusive, controlling man who's the only family Jake has left. Because of a promise to his dead mother, Jake resists his desire for other men, but it leaves him consumed by darkness.

It takes all of Dallas Yates's imagination to see the possibilities in the fatigued art deco building on WeHo's outskirts, but what seals the deal is a shy smile from the handsome metal worker across the street. Their friendship deepens while Dallas peels back the hardened layers strangling Jake's soul. It's easy to love the sweet, artistic man hidden behind Jake's shattered exterior, but Dallas knows Jake needs to first learn to love himself.

When Jake's world crumbles, he reaches for Dallas, the man he's learned to lean on. It's only a matter of time before he's left to drift in a life he never wanted to lead and while he wants more, Jake's past haunts him, making him doubt he's worth the love Dallas is so desperate to give him.

www.dreamspinnerpress.com

FISH STICK FRIDAYS

RHYS FORD

Half Moon Bay: Book One

Deacon Reid was born bad to the bone with no intention of changing. A lifetime of law-bending and living on the edge suits him just fine—until his baby sister dies and he finds himself raising her little girl.

Staring down a family history of bad decisions and reaped consequences, Deacon cashes in everything he owns, purchases an auto shop in Half Moon Bay, and takes his niece, Zig, far away from the drug dens and murderous streets they grew up on. Zig deserves a better life than what he had, and Deacon is determined to give it to her.

Lang Harris is stunned when Zig, a little girl in combat boots and a purple tutu, blows into his bookstore, and then he's left speechless when her uncle, Deacon Reid, walks in hot on her heels. Lang always played it safe, but Deacon tempts him to step over the line… just a little bit.

More than a little bit. And Lang is willing to be tempted.

Unfortunately, Zig isn't the only bit of chaos dropped into Half Moon Bay. Violence and death strike, leaving Deacon scrambling to fight off a killer before he loses not only Zig but Lang too.

www.dreamspinnerpress.com